Something's *Going On* Here

Ruth Cherry, Ph.D.

EXPLORA BOOKS
700 - 838 West Hastings St. Vancouver, BC V6C 0A6
www.explorabooks.com
Phone: (604) 330 6795

ISBN: 978-1-998394-16-6 (Paperback)
978-1-990695-68-1 (E-book)

SOMETHING'S Going On HERE

RUTH CHERRY, Ph.D.

Book 1

Table of Contents

1 Echoes of Uncertainty

Another grey misty Friday night in this small coastal town. The few street lights fuzz in the dark. Even fewer cars crawl through the clouds sitting on the deserted roads. A Friday night like every Friday night here in Los Osos. I walk alone past the closed diner, the closed used bookstore, and the closed barbershop/tackle and bait supply store. All 7,864 citizens are somewhere else. I don't know where. I moved here two months ago and I don't get this place.

I retired from the English Department at Penn State after 30 years teaching nineteen-year-olds to observe the world around them and describe it precisely in terms of sight, smell, touch, and sound. I've always been a precise kind of guy — my closets were organized before there were companies telling me I needed it. I roll my socks and stack them seven deep in the second drawer on the left side of my chiffonier. The newspaper rests to the right of my spoon at the breakfast table until I read it when I move it to the left and from there to the recycling bin. I maintain routines which work for me. Even now I rise at dawn though no classes await.

Rosemary, my wife, had tried to fit into my structured days but in her heart, she was an artist, more comfortable with chaos and spontaneity than predictability. Adapting to my lifestyle must have harmed something in her soul because, in the end, she left me. A year before my retirement she walked out of my life, wishing that I may be happy with the straight lines in my appointment book filled in neatly with black ink. Her parting words were, "Now you can do everything according to plan, not disrupted by life's inconsistencies." During my explanation that life wasn't the problem, she slammed the door and disappeared. I miss her.

In my eagerness to leave Pennsylvania winters and, secondarily, Pennsylvania summers, I allowed my cousin, Ellie, to talk me into moving to Los Osos on the central California coast. Who has ever heard of Los Osos? No one in College Station, Pennsylvania. I wanted a change — a change of scenery, a change of lifestyle, and a change in me. Something eludes me and I thought I might find it here in the mist and the clouds.

I drove my tan 1998 Honda Civic cross-country with my black lab, Hildy, snoring in the back seat. She's been with me the last ten years of my Penn State tenure and isn't going much farther in this lifetime. I wanted her to see the Pacific Ocean before she leaps or stumbles to the Other Side but she's seldom awake long enough to notice the waves. She has acclimated to this sleepy town better than I have.

Tonight I am acutely aware of my otherness. I walk through the unpaved streets and realize that my life is similarly unpaved and going who-knows-where. The fog describes my thinking, my plans, and my awareness of my wants. I have had everything I've asked for and hoped for in my early years. My carefully laid out life was pressed as finely as my button-down blue work shirts. Trouble is — that just doesn't suit me any longer and I have no idea what will. So, I walk slowly and I wait.

I don't wait more than a minute before I hear a gunshot cleanly piercing the still night. At first I don't believe it could be a gun but I know that sound. The chills shake me the way they had the first time. You don't disregard a sound that signals death.

2 Whispers of Suspicion

Three minutes later and sirens shriek past me. Two police cars and an ambulance barrel into the night. I glimpse the house lights three blocks away. A few other houses light up as I walk past. Sirens are unusual here. Something amiss has occurred. As I approach the old house, two men carry a stretcher to the ambulance. I hesitate in the shadows and watch, unobserved, as two policemen enter the small structure. Twenty minutes later they drive away, yellow tape crisscrossing the front door instructing the curious to Keep Out — Investigation Site.

The darkness closes around me and the house like steam filling a kitchen. Even though the burst of activity has subsided, something is not normal. I know enough about this place to sense the disruption in the tenor of the night. I can't see what is not right but I can feel it as surely as I feel the pebble in my shoe.

I wander back to my rented house, across seven streets and around two corners. I feel oddly discomfited as though this were my tragedy which it surely is not. I'm not even a bystander. Not technically a passerby. But something has snared my curiosity. Something other than the gunshot which I doubt this community has heard before. Something more than the death of a neighbor in the middle of the night. Something I can't put into words right now.

That fact alone intrigues me for I am never at a loss for words. Always I see what goes on, I analyze it effortlessly, and I describe it, as I said, precisely. Not this evening. I'm thrown into a twilight zone in the inky shadows and the fog and I can't understand what's happening. I fall into bed and wrestle with the blankets, sleep eluding me just as clarity has.

Daylight encourages me to forget the middle-of-the-night drama but the buzz at Cad's coffee shop would subdue 100 bees. Apparently, the victim was an elderly codger, loved, but increasingly eccentric and isolated. Henrietta, sitting at her usual stool at the counter, repeats "I just can't believe it. Al wasn't the kind to kill himself. He was touched-in-the-head, but he wasn't violent. I just can't believe it." The other bees' drone in and on and the consensus holds that he must have been distraught. That's why he withdrew from his friends and quit the smoking corner at Perry's on Wednesday nights and kept his shades drawn. No one had seen Al in three weeks, not even his cronies from the Flush the Sewer project. Everyone assumed he was "in a funk" and that he would emerge "in his own time" as he had so often before.

I stand to leave with my middle-of-the-night unease amplified. What bothers me about this case? What am I saying? I'm not an amateur detective. This is not my "case." This is none of my business. I have other things to do and to plan. I have a lot to think about. I don't need this kind of soap opera. An old man dies. So what? Happens every day. My impatience with this unfocused reverie pushes me out the door of Cad's. I practically trip across Ellie's extended foot as she rushes in.

"Nick, Nick, wait. Do you have a minute? You don't have to go, do you? No, I'm so glad. Let's sit a minute, OK?" She and her compadre, Deb, push me back into the coffee shop. "Let's take that table in the back. We need to talk to you, Nick." Ellie lowers her voice as she directs me to the farthest table.

I dearly love Ellie. Our fathers were brothers, immigrants from Malta. Ellie and I shared the family scourge of being accused of Mafia ties by our grade school classmates. Within the family we had overheard stories of acquaintances disappearing after a blowup with Uncle Sammy. His pockets bulged with peppermints and he always smelled of peppermint. We thought he was covering up a cigar habit or his homemade wine addiction or some other vice. Aunt Lanie would turn into a banshee if she suspected that he had been drinking or smoking. We wondered if he had habits much worse but we were afraid to ask.

Ellie, Deb, and I sit at the back table, close to the screen door, across from the kitchen. It is warm from the ovens, aromatic with the smell of fresh bread, and semi-private.

Ellie peers into my eyes as she leans over the table, keeping her voice low. "Something's going on here." Deb nods as Ellie speaks. The drama in their shared demeanor draws a chuckle from my throat.

Since Ellie has been in the real estate business for 18 years, she trades in the daily local news as a matter of course in her dealings with potential buyers, anxious sellers, stressed finance officers, and over-committed Rotarians. In her scant free time, she hangs out with Deb, a retired emergency room nurse, who misses the excitement of work and gladly sees potential for disaster everywhere. They are lovely ladies with well-exercised imaginations. I enjoy running into them but seldom share my concerns with them. Usually, we banter pleasantly and I excuse myself early. Today they have successfully trapped me.

"I only have a minute. I've got to…" I stammer but Ellie smiles.

"Relax, Nick. You've nowhere to go and nothing to do. Remember, you're retired? That's why you're here — to relax."

I sigh. There goes my morning. She's right, though. My minute-by-minute scheduling doesn't apply here. Folks hang. In my day we would hang out but now it's just hang. When did that term change? I wanted to stop working but I don't want to "be retired." I… and I realize that Ellie has been talking.

Her black curls fall across her forehead as she punctuates her words with nods. She looks at her hands folded on the table and at me, assessing the effectiveness of her communication. "We know, I tell you we're sure," nod, nod, "that something wicked has taken place." Nod, nod, and now Deb nods, also.

Deb's short dark blonde hair spikes rigidly. How do women do that? My thinning brown hair doesn't cover my increasingly shiny scalp. I wear an old Phillies baseball cap but that's not really my style. I found it on the floor of a closet when I packed and threw it in the front seat of my car. There it lives. I grab it for protection from the sun (of which there is little in Los Osos). Now I wish it would protect me from these intent, driven women.

"The last person to see Al was Elizabeth, the barber down the street. She said she cut his hair five days ago." Have these two been interviewing locals for an incident (we don't know that it's a crime) that happened less than twelve hours ago? Ellie continues, "She said he had been quiet. You know, he's always quiet, but Elizabeth said that he was quiet in a different way."

Deb speaks for the first time. "His brother came to visit a few weeks ago and since then Al's been preoccupied and moody and unresponsive and… just… not friendly at all." They want me to take this seriously but, really, I can't. Or, rather, I won't. It embarrasses me to realize that I was thinking in the same vein that these two are. I don't want to be like them in any way except living here.

The truth is I don't have to be embarrassed here; no one knows me. I am anonymous all the time. I find comfort in that fact. Psychically, I'm in transition from respected professor to something else and for the present I walk through the earthbound clouds here without commitment. For these few weeks, nothing counts. I don't report to work, I don't have relationships, not even friends. No one expects anything from me. I feel shadowy, like an unfocused movie screen. I'm enjoying my invisibility. I fear that Ellie wants me to commit to something and lose my comfortable non-person status.

Ellie senses my withdrawal and redoubles her efforts and the volume of her voice. "So, if you could just, you know, subtly, without anyone guessing, you're the exact right person to do this, you know, being new here, and no one recognizes you…" Ellie's speech when she's excited replicates the cadence of our childhood households. It was the reason I chose English as the focus of my studies. I wanted to leave everything about being a poor illiterate immigrant behind. I wanted to be an American — nothing unusual, strictly vanilla, mow the lawn on Saturday afternoons, watch televised sports on Sundays, paycheck automatically deposited in the bank, guaranteed retirement. I wanted to fade into the wallpaper. I didn't want to be noticed or to be different in any way. I teach English so my students will know how to be like everyone else. That is, I taught English. What do I do now? I don't know the answer but I'm pretty sure it isn't Super Sleuth in Los Osos.

"Great to see you fine ladies once again. It's always a pleasure," and I stand up.

"Wait a minute!" Ellie pulls the sleeve of my jacket so hard that my knees buckle and I collapse into the white plastic chair. I was her first babysitting client when I was five and she was twelve. She exerted her pre-teen authority over me then. My childhood fear of her still hides in my bones, emerging at times like this when she raises her voice.

Ellie is serious now and she wants something from me. It's no use arguing when she's in this mood. I acquiesce and I notice the clock ticking. Minutes of my life escape that I will never reclaim.

Slowly and deliberately she speaks. "Nick, you're the only person who can investigate this case without arousing suspicion. No one knows you yet." Something about her last statement leaves me unsettled. I want to repeat my argument that "this" is not a "case" and at this point there is nothing to investigate, but I know that this conversation will pass faster if I'm quiet so I purse my lips.

"So, Elizabeth is expecting to hear from you. She'll be at the barbershop all day. A hair cut wouldn't be a bad idea," and she touches the top of my head. Ellie is the only person alive who can talk to me and touch me as though I'm still five and have no boundaries, as these wispy Californians say. I want to go home and take a nap to make up for last night's lost sleep so I say, "Good idea, Cuz. I'm on it."

She knows I'm faking though, so without a pause she says, "Elizabeth is waiting now. I made an appointment for you. You'll be late if you don't hurry."

At least I can walk away. I head in the general direction of the barbershop with the intent to duck into an alley. Ellie, however, watches my every step. I feel her eyes pierce the back of my jacket.

So, dutifully, I enter the barbershop and without a word Elizabeth drapes me. Post-60, she moves with the ease and speed of a teenager. She doesn't ask what I like or want or prefer. She clips and trims as fast as she can. This kind of concentration should be bottled and sold. In less than ten minutes she silently hands me the mirror and I check the sides and back. I open my mouth to comment but she starts in like a train that won't be stopped. Apparently, she has anticipated this conversation.

"Al was my friend. I know lots of folks will tell you that, but he and I shared many quiet moments over his favorite Muscatel. When he was down, he'd call me and I'd go over to his place and we'd drink a couple bottles." Elizabeth speaks without making eye contact. She sweeps hair off the floor with a short broom and wipes four pairs of scissors. "We didn't talk much but I knew when he felt better and then I'd leave. He'd go to bed and sleep through the next day and then he'd be his old not-so-chipper self. Sometimes I wondered if he remembered my visits."

Still not looking at me, she folds towels. Continuing more slowly, she says, "Al knew everything going on around here. He'd met everyone. He kept his opinions to himself but he didn't miss a thing. I told him he should write a book. He just harrumphed in that peculiar way he had. He didn't like to talk about his business; his thoughts were for himself alone." She stands, silent for a moment.

I sense a caring that Elizabeth is not addressing. Clearly, she loves this old man, but just as clearly their love isn't acknowledged in public. Why the mystery? This death means much more to her than the loss of a neighbor. Her grief is solitary, though. Does Ellie grasp the intricacies of their relationship?

Elizabeth continues softly as she looks out the window at something I can't see. "Lately, he'd been especially sad. He was thinking about something but he didn't let on what it was. He cleaned out his garage and threw away 30 years-worth of magazines. When I discovered what he'd done, I asked him if he was fixin' to off himself. He just grumbled and dismissed me, said he had things to do. We didn't spend time together the last few weeks. I don't know what happened to him. He changed so much…" She lowers her eyes. Her taut, angular frame relaxes. She drifts, lost in her thoughts.

I consider Elizabeth's words as I amble home. The screen door slams behind me as I bee-line for the bedroom, unbuttoning my flannel shirt and tossing my cap across the chair onto the floor. As I slide under the covers, sleep welcomes me. I don't know how long I had dozed when the pounding on my front screen door awakens me. The only visitor I receive is Ellie and she doesn't knock.

Rubbing my eyes, I stumble into the living room to meet a gorilla-sized male with black hair I could envy. Too disoriented to be scared, I simply look at him. I guess that he's about 30. He looks healthy but he seems awkward, standing in my house. It doesn't occur to me to speak; I just stare, curious but not alert enough to be alarmed.

A full minute passes before he speaks. Gently, he says, "I'm not here to cause problems. I overheard you and your lady friends this morning at Cad's and, well, I…"

"What shall I call you?" As I awaken, I realize the absurdity of this situation and this conversation. Perhaps it is a sign that I have relaxed my expectations of reality that I am willing to participate in this bizarre scene.

"Donny, my name is Donny Slate. I'm Al's grandson." He looks uncomfortable.

"Yes, Donny. My cousin and her friend wanted to give me an assignment this morning to investigate a case that doesn't exist. But don't worry. I'm not going to do anything. I'll wait a few days and they'll be on to something else. All will be forgotten." I want to reassure him, sensing somehow that it is important that he not feel threatened.

Donny looks so sad. I continue, "I'm sorry for your loss, son. Is there anything you need?" Why did I say that? Because that's what one is supposed to say. I hope he will reply, "No, thank you for offering, though." But he doesn't.

Immediately, he looks up, meets my gaze directly and with a touch of urgency says, "I do need your help. Your friends are right, there is funny stuff goin' on, but they are wrong about what it is. It wasn't my grandfather that was carried out last night. No, he's alright." Donny stands up straighter, adding a couple inches to his already imposing size.

He continues, "But everyone in the town must think he's dead." Not a stupid insurance scam, I hope. Donny adds, his eyes darker, "I can't tell you any more right now." He hesitates and looks me up and down which I find a bit intimidating. His dark eyes widen and dart to the corners of the room and back to me. "I can count on you, can't I?" He examines the ceiling. "You'll keep my secret, won't you? Won't you?" His words come faster and his breath is shallow.

Quickly, I assure him that I am with him all the way. We are a team, nothing will upset that. I tell him we need to watch the others but that he and I are tight. He hugs me in his gratitude and desperation. I suggest that he not come here when anyone can see him and that he makes notes on all the folks he knows in town.

He seems grateful for the structure and direction. I tell him it is imperative that he leave now and not let anyone see him go. And I reassure him that we are allies. I don't want him edgy, questioning my loyalty to him.

I sigh and tremble as he leaves. A certifiably loony Los Osos dweller. We have entered another realm of nutty with the introduction of this fellow.

I lock the screen door, close the front door, and check the back door and the gate to the yard. I am spooked. I sit at my desk to think. I need to hold a pen in order to think and I can't find my favorite dark green Cross fine point. This frustration pushes me over the edge. I could hold it together while I heard a gunshot on a foggy night, saw a stretcher being carried to an ambulance, suffered through Ellie's ramblings, endured Elizabeth's anxious concerns, and received an unannounced lunatic in my own house. But not finding my favorite pen is intolerable. I stand up, throw the phone book and some newspapers on the floor, and screech like an old parrot for three seconds.

I feel relieved when I sit down. I am very glad Donny is not in my house any longer. I know very well the vibes of a paranoid psychotic young man. It was eerie how it all came back so quickly being in Donny's presence. I had not met him previously but I felt like I knew him. Clearly, he is willing to let our "connection" assume immense importance. I understand intuitively that I am not allowed to disappoint him. Another pressure in the mix of the crazy goings-on here.

My brother, Jake, two years my junior, was and is my only sibling. Being with him when he articulated his thoughts felt a lot like what I had just experienced with Donny. I had left home by the time his symptoms exacerbated to the point that my mother couldn't control him. In response to her frantic letters, I counseled her on the phone. I made suggestions, sent books, recommended professionals. But I didn't return home as she had hoped. "But we're family," she would cry plaintively. I hated that tone in her voice. Impatiently, I told her to be strong, to think this through, and to use her best judgment. "Don't be a nutcase like Jake." She bristled at my derogation.

I couldn't stand the overwhelming control that Jake's illness exerted on what was left of our small family. We had to proceed with our lives tightly and cautiously while he went off on frenzied tangents. Sometimes he was cited for being disorderly in public. Sometimes he would rant around the neighborhood and scare little children. Mostly he medicated himself with any weed he could score, lying in the back bedroom of our mother's home with the shades pulled. It made me crazy. Remembering those days, my anxiety escalates.

When I need to get back in control, I organize something. Now, I organize all the data I had collected this weekend. What do I really know? Donny said Al is alive and safe. Everyone in town is convinced he is dead, maybe by his own hand. Of course, Donny (if that is his name) was standing in my living room uninvited. Can I believe him? Why should I trust anything he says? Donny is odd, maybe dangerous, with several very loose screws. I'll ask Ellie and Deb about him. He asked me to promise to keep his secret. Do I want to honor that request? How much of myself am I willing to invest in Donny?

With that thought I hear the sound of water circling the drain. I am caught up in this Los Osos enigma and I am voluntarily taking my place in the strangest cast of characters I can imagine.

Heaven, help me.

3 Intrigue Unleashed

On Mondays I resume my routine, although, honestly, I never stray far from it on the weekends. So, at dawn on Monday I leave for my two-mile walk. I started walking when Hildy was a pup. Her explosive energy was dissipated by a long walk and my thoughts were settled. These days Hildy no longer accompanies me but I still walk. I need the time to focus my attention. When I sit at my desk, pen in hand, I pursue logical objective thought.

When I walk, another mind takes the lead and creates its own patterns. I become an observer. I observe the houses I pass and I observe the workings of my second mind which plays. It seems like play to me because it is effortless and undirected and immensely satisfying. When I've returned from my walk and showered, I know things I didn't know when I started on the walk. I always feel calmer.

Today's light spills gently over the horizon. Birds twitter. My first mind wants to solve this problem of Al and Donny and the others but my second mind wants to enjoy the freshness of the day. Since there is no manufacturing here, no big business at all really, the sky is not clouded with man-made chemicals and the air is exceedingly clean — except for the pollen. Oaks are plentiful and something about oaks irritates my nasal passages. I didn't know this before I moved here and it isn't really a problem, just another unexpected verity.

I turn the corner down the street from my old rented cottage and spy Deb, walking with another woman. She sees me, also, and waves her whole arm, walking faster directly toward me. Uh-oh, I think. I'm not prepared for an encounter at this hour. I value my privacy and was looking forward to some time alone in the new day.

"Nick, Nick." Deb is breathless, having half-run a block. I suspect that she is not 60 but her 50th birthday wasn't recent. That makes her younger than I am. Her freckled skin is moist with perspiration and her short hair is mussed, rather attractively so, I think. If she weren't Ellie's pal I might consider pursuing a friendship with her, but as it stands, she's strictly off-limits. I told myself that I would leave Ellie's friends alone when I moved here, trying to maintain some kind of independence. I've been pretty lonely at times but I won't let anyone in. I need my space. Especially now.

Deb is standing in front of me. "Nick, good morning! I'm so glad we ran into you. Lindy and I walk at this hour some days and I was telling her about the intrigue. I wanted to tell you — Elizabeth may not have shared everything. Not quite everything. I love Elizabeth, but…" I sense her conflict, "but sometimes Elizabeth just forgets. She doesn't mean to, she's… anyway… Al and Elizabeth have been lovers for a couple years but they've tried to keep it a secret. They've actually done pretty well, just a few of us know. Last year they were thinking about marrying but then Al's brother came to town. Apparently, his brother told Al to cut it off with Elizabeth, just to end it, no explanation, nothing, finis. Complicated reasons having to do with finances and a trust.

"Well, of course, Elizabeth was hurt with the break-up of their relationship but after she learned about Al's brother's interference, she exploded. Now, you don't want to see Elizabeth angry. Most of the time she's pretty calm, but I know her and I know that she has used those scissors of hers for cutting more than hair. With her temper… I just don't know. As I say, I love Elizabeth but… I wanted you to know what you're getting into."

No one, especially me, can know what I'm getting into. The deeper I delve, the more convoluted this whole predicament becomes. I feel like I'm caught in seaweed that encircles me as it grows. I remind myself to maintain my clarity and my objectivity. I live in Los Osos but I am not a Los Osos crazy. Not yet. Hopefully, not ever.

Deb and Lindy disappear down the street, walking at a

heart-pumping pace, chattering like finches. Deb unloads this info on me and then walks off in an apparently light-hearted manner and I'm supposed to sort this out?

Does this town think I've come here to save them? Do they think they need saving? Do they think I'm available to participate in their drama? I suspect that the answer for them and for me is yes, I'm available and I am participating. My first mind does not condone this decision but my second mind runs with it. Well, I had said I want a change.

I spend some time drinking coffee at the Baywood Navy coffee shop. A dozen creaky rowboats used infrequently by anyone in the mood constitute "The Navy." They are tied near a pier, 20 feet long and six feet wide, weather-beaten two-by- fours. The ocean flows through the ten-foot gap in the levee to create a tiny bay. Most of the time one can walk across the bay but this morning the tide is in. Several old-timers slouch over their coffee and rolls and reminisce.

The sun is higher in the sky and a few clouds drift overhead. It will be a mild day with a cool breeze. Why can't I just relax and enjoy this beautiful place? But that is not me. I focus, I pursue, I forge ahead. I don't unwind, lay back, trust or wait. I clean up messes and I make things happen. I'm a doer. I act.

I return home an hour and a half later to find that my place has been ransacked. Papers and books cover the floors, the chairs, and the table. Dresser drawers droop and all the lights are on. The back door bangs. I know I left it locked. This is clearly a threat to me personally, not just some local shenanigans. My heart pounds, my hands tremble and sweat beads on my scalp. Rationality evaporates and fear overwhelms me.

Of all the weirdos I've met here, only one is capable of such violence. I pick up the phone but the line is dead. Is the crackpot still near? I grab my keys and dash to my car. At Ellie's real estate office, I turn off the ignition and sit under the eucalyptus for a moment and think. Suddenly, this game has become much more serious. I wasn't expecting this turn of events and I don't know what to do. I breathe the sweet spicy eucalyptus scent as anxiety percolates in every cell of my body.

4 Solace in Unlikely Places

Sandy, Ellie's partner, makes coffee and straightens piles of papers. When I describe my morning, she calls the sheriff and assures me, "They are the best. Les is the finest guy in the world, and Arthur, honest as they come. You can trust those two, yes sir, no need to fret." As though "fretting" describes my panic.

When the sheriff's assistant tells Sandy I can return home, I jot a message for Ellie, who has not shown yet, and I slowly head back. In my front yard a tall slim older gent in worn jeans and boots makes notes in a small black spiral notebook. He barely glances up as I approach and doesn't speak. I wait for him to complete his entries.

"How long you lived here?" he demands and glares at me.

"Almost three months."

"Well, this kind of thing just don't happen here. No, not since I can recall. I lived here all my life and I been sheriff more than a few years now. Looks pretty mean to me. You have any idea what this is all about? You have an enemy, maybe?"

"No. I don't know anyone here except my cousin and a couple of her friends. I'm still settling in."

"Well, be careful. Someone picked out this place to go through. Who knows why? Maybe it's not because of you. I hope for your sake it ain't." He looks at me over the top of his glasses.

My heart sinks. I feel more alone than I have since I arrived in this town. I'm frantic to connect with Ellie. Where is she? I enter my house and, curiously unfocused, I wander from room to room, looking for… what? I don't know. This unforeseen occurrence has effectively destroyed my home base. I have no home and I have no base. And I can't find Ellie, who suddenly becomes very important to me. Now she is not someone to be avoided, she is my only friend, the only person I trust in this county, maybe in the world.

I'm alone and I'm alarmed. I sit at my desk and rearrange the notes I had written to myself about tasks I had thought were significant. What's important now? My plans to organize my office are secondary to insuring that I'm physically safe. I also want to feel connected to someone. I need to re-establish myself as a civilized inhabitant of this planet and this town. An uncomfortable feeling akin to paranoia replaces the fear I have felt for the last hour. Now I am afraid but also I wonder if someone hates me as Les has suggested, if someone distrusts me, and if someone knows me whom I don't know. Any dream of the world as a safe place has been shattered. I wouldn't have thought my security could so quickly dissipate.

This anxiety propels me to act. I drive to the phone company to order repair work and on the way back I buy a cell phone. I had resisted this 20th century device for years. When I was employed, I didn't answer my phone, not encouraging students or teachers or administrators to call me at home. They could find me in my office on campus if they needed me. Now I urgently want someone to find me and to care about how I'm doing. With an unpleasant jolt, I realize that no one at this moment is concerned about my wellbeing. Is this the natural result of all the "independence" I have so assiduously pursued? Total aloneness? I leave another message for Ellie with my new cell phone number.

I don't want to return to my house and face the mess that my life has suddenly become. Besides, my stomach reminds me that I missed breakfast. I buy a paper and slip into Cad's. Doing something routine like reading the paper while I eat my eggs over easy and drink three cups of coffee restores me somewhat. As I fold the paper, Deb rushes in. Uncharacteristically, I am happy to see her and don't try to escape.

"Hey, Nick, long time no see!" And she laughs at her own cuteness, throwing her head back. "Anything new?"

"Not much, Deborah. An ordinary breaking and entering, some destruction of property, a cut phone line. Nothing much really. Whazzup wid you?" I try to imitate her but I can't pull it off. I can't pretend to be jovial and I feel stupid for trying. Her eyes narrow and she leans forward in her chair, the other chair at my table.

"What're you talking about?" Somehow I had thought Deb omnisciently prevails over every Los Osos incident but maybe she's only human. "Did something happen? You need to tell me about it. I need to know." Gratitude for a kind ear warms my heart and a tear wells in my eye. Another human looks at me and wants to know me. I have never been so grateful for a dollop of compassion.

And, so, she gets the whole story. When I sit back in my chair, she declares, "We need to call in the troops! This is dead serious, pardon the dead, just an expression, don't you worry, Nick, we're on it. And don't stew about this town. We're good people here, a little strange perhaps, but we have good hearts." She throws her arms open and I hope she doesn't "want a hug."

She doesn't but insists, "OK, now, Nick, what you must do and it really is a must, I can't explain it, I'm off to meet my tennis group, but you've got to go to the library!" My quizzical expression launches another barrage from her full red lips. "Carolyn, the librarian, knows everyone and everything. She's the president of Rotary. She has contacts in this town that even I don't know about. You've got to tell Carolyn. I'm calling her right now." She pulls a tiny cell phone from her pocket. Usually, I would resist this interference but the morning's events have worn me down and I'm passive, both shell-shocked and confused.

"She's there. You know where the library is, don't you? Around the corner and down two blocks, Carolyn will know what to do. Gotta run. I'll call you later."

I don't give her my new cell phone number and consider that maybe I won't get the phone line in my home repaired after all. How quickly I revert. My heart was thawing. Her taking over this situation leaves me both grateful and baffled. I appreciate her being "in it" with me though, so with one minute's consideration I decide to let go of my stupid adolescent rebellion and pseudo-self-reliance. I really don't want to be independent right now. I want a friend.

Ruth Cherry, Ph.D.

adolescent rebellion and pseudo-self-reliance. I really don't want to be independent right now. I want a friend.

5   Lost in Los Osos

Carolyn wears glasses on a chain around her neck. Is that a requirement for all librarians? And a full, flower-print dress. A woman interested in comfort. Her short grey-brown hair curls in every direction. She eyes me when I enter the library and without a word she motions me behind the desk. We walk into her glass-walled office and she speaks, all business, no introductions, no small talk.

"I just talked to Les. I called him when Deb said he was already involved because I want to hear his take on this situation. He won't tell me anything, says he's not sure what's going on. That's OK. He has his moments. When his lumbago pains him, no one in the world has a chance... He'll be OK in a day or two. But I don't know how much help we can expect from him and his department — Arthur, that is.

"You see, the office of sheriff in our little town is mostly honorary. Les is a popular guy, retired a few years ago from the Chamber of Commerce, but he's 74 and not interested in too much besides his garden and his ducks. Deb woke him with her call this morning. Crime on Monday morning is such an inconvenience."

Carolyn's mouth crinkles in one corner, apparently her impression of a smile. I appreciate her straightforward approach and the fact that I can follow her line of thought. Carolyn is the most normal person I've met thus far. We talk or, rather, she talks for another ten minutes and I leave feeling somehow reassured.

Pulling into my driveway, I tell myself to be calm and to take this one minute at a time. Cleaning up is my first chore. Busy work is easy and organization is my forté. I'll just move through my little place and all my papers slowly and deliberately. I'll focus on the details of what is in front of me and, thereby, subdue my anxiety. Even hearing this thought tells me how much I've changed.

Going slow was never a value before, in my real life, the one in which I did what I wanted and worked toward a goal. Now that I have reached my goal — professional success and retirement — I need a strategy by which to live. There are no more ambitions and no meaningful future and no reason to delay. Being confronted with the present when the present is all there is unnerves me.

Before I'm in the front door, my new cell phone vibrates in my pocket. I know it's Ellie for I've told no one else my number. "Howdy, Cuz," I answer.

"Nick, are you alright?" Ellie's voice is concerned more than worried which, for the first time, I appreciate. We speak for a minute before she is interrupted by another call and begs off. Reconnecting for that minute comforts me.

I spend the next two hours sitting on the living room floor, examining every scrap of paper that lies there. I read notes to myself on three-by-five index cards I had written before departing Pennsylvania suggesting topics for scholarly papers which I had always hoped to publish. I couldn't find time to write between teaching and chairing the English Department magazine.

The truth is, scholarly papers bore me and that isn't what I want to write. I had been taunted by my colleagues, not only in the English Department, to create something noteworthy. The pressure to publish at any academic site is unimaginable but the quality of what is published is strictly intellectual, intentionally detached and cold. I produced the minimum number of articles to satisfy the chair of our department.

I, however, was not satisfied. I knew my writing lacked color. While that was acceptable to Dr. Michelbaum and, actually, preferred by the faculty, I was impatient with disembodied discourse. It seemed that the writers hid behind their verbal acuity as they sparred with concepts. Some part of me has always envied those, like Rosemary, who dive into life.

I had wondered if teaching were my way of avoiding the exigencies of dealing with ambiguity. I was precise when I could be and when I couldn't be, I didn't participate. I looked for answers and, usually, I could find them. Unless I allowed Rosemary to begin her questioning about moral relativity or expression as a means of experiencing one's creative core. Then, I withdrew to my darkened study and perused a recent reconsideration of Milton.

Now I want to produce work that is passionate and inspiring. Sitting here, I'm embarrassed to acknowledge that thought. No one who has ever known me would use the words "passionate" and "inspiring" in any description of me, especially not Rosemary. Certainly, I will never verbalize that thought to anyone.

Now I have the time. No more excuses. Now I'll see if I really can write something compelling. Teaching writing and actually writing are two very different skills. Now it is time for me to make the transition. I certainly have been handed enough material. I have the time, the training, and the inclination. Now is the season for me to prove to myself that I have what it takes, that I am more than merely a grammarian.

A pressure to live differently sits on my chest while my old ways of thinking are pushed out my ears. Sitting in the midst of my disarranged belongings, I realize that I don't want to reconstruct my old life. What a shame that Rosemary isn't here now. She would really appreciate my new outlook. I'm afraid I ridiculed her when she expressed as much to me. I was an insufferable jerk.

Never again, I commit to myself. I am a new person or, rather, I am my true old self. I am ready to display my real spirit minus the accumulated overlay of stifling respectability. No more "appropriate" choices. No more doing things as they have always been done. No more honor for tradition simply because it is the past.

I feel both exhilarated and totally lost. The perfect place to be. Lost in Los Osos.

6 Fragments of Time

I work my way to the den in the afternoon and find my photos scattered everywhere. I lift them carefully and consider the memories. I see me during a college break with my three roommates rafting down the Pocono River. I'm 30 pounds lighter with four times as much hair and a smile wider than you'd think possible, judging from my then-narrow face. We lived on beer and hot dogs for five days and emerged sunburned and joyous. We floated in inner tubes and didn't worry about a thing. We laughed all day and all night. We had no families, no relationships, no responsibilities, no burdens. The world was ours. We were blessed and we knew it.

As I place that yellowed photo on a chair, I realize that I haven't felt such freedom since then. The world hasn't seemed so open or life so easy. And I haven't felt that confidence, based not on achievement, but on the satisfaction of living every day without ambivalence. I have accomplished so much — a doctorate and a post at a major university — and, yet, I don't feel the thrill I did when I was floating down that river with a beer in hand and my best friends around me. What simple pleasure! I miss life being uncomplicated.

Then I pick up a grade school photo of Jake and me, both of us in short pants, and our mother's arms around us. She beams as we stare. I don't remember that day in particular, but I recall lots of times my Dad urged, "Get the boys, Marnie, let's take a group shot." Of course, his group shots never included him. Mom always posed but Jake and I never grasped the concept of smiling at no one. From perusing our childhood photos, one might guess that this super-enthusiastic mother fueled the family without the help of a father.

Dad's invisibility in the photos replicated his invisibility in the family. He loved us by working. His offer of relationship was providing a house and paying the bills.

Unlike Mom, whom we sought when we were young to answer questions about bugs, night, water, God, stars, Captain Hook, and why we had to take a bath, Dad was always in the wings. We knew he was around but he wasn't available for interaction. That was OK. That was his job. So, I never knew Dad, but somehow I turned out to be a lot like him. I wish I could be proud of that statement.

I recognize another photo from my honeymoon with Rosemary. She insisted that we not go to Niagara Falls as most of our friends were doing, but that we explore the back roads in upper New York state and Canada. We drove my brown Pontiac and stopped every mile or two to kiss and take pictures of the landscape and kiss some more. We traveled less than fifty miles a day and had very few pictures to display when we returned but we were immensely happy. I was seven years older than she was and I wanted to take care of her and protect her and teach her about life. How we both changed over three decades.

The next picture is Rosemary holding Isabelle two days after her birth. Clenching my jaw, I put it down and walk to the kitchen to clean up the mess there.

7 Unexpected Turns: Laughter in the Midnight Fog

Ellie bounds in the door late in the afternoon, talking to a client on her cell phone about an imminent escrow closing. There is so much excitement and hurry in her work that I wonder why she loves it but that is my answer. Ellie could not tolerate the tedium which I cherish. If it is routine, give it to me. If it requires late hours and endless phone conversations, Ellie's your man, so to speak. She is competent, considerate, professional, and diligent. But she works all the time. I have never heard her say no to a potential client. When she goes to parties, she works. When she walks down the street, she works. A living adult equals a potential client and, so, deserves Ellie's respect and attention. It doesn't bother me. That's how she is. And she's good at her job.

She says good-bye and looks around. "Whoa, what is going on? This is spooky. Are you scared? I'd be scared. Deb told me she ran into you. This is unbelievable!" Ellie always draws a smile from me. I love her dithering and don't feel a need to respond. She's expressing her care and the particular words are irrelevant. I walk over to her and put my arm around her shoulder without thinking. It's good to have her here and to have her ear for a few seconds before her phone will, inevitably, ring again.

"Thanks for stopping by. I've had the strangest week of my life and I pray it's over but let's enjoy this evening, OK? I'll take you to dinner. I owe you something for getting me into all this!" I smile and laugh for I know she's feeling twinges of guilt. She had spoken so highly of her town, a regular Chamber of Commerce sell, and I bit and swallowed without even seeing the place. With no wife and no job, I was simply glad to have somewhere to go.

Over dinner at the Hong Kong restaurant, she tells me about her latest escrow with the whiny husband and the wife who can't make a decision and I feel grateful for her company. I just want to be normal for an hour. Sitting here listening to her, I can forget about my house, no longer my home. I hadn't considered that it might not be wise to sleep there tonight but I really don't want to spend the night on her couch.

As I pay, she takes her fourth call of the evening and we walk to my car. I am relaxed, yawning and looking forward to lying in my bed. We part at my front door with her phone ringing yet again. I let myself in, hoping that when I flip the light switch I won't encounter another surprise but everything is as I had left it. Maybe all the excitement has passed. Maybe I'm safe.

I turn on the TV and let it lull me to sleep. It doesn't take long until I snore and dream. Hildy's come-save-me whimpering awakens me after midnight. I pad in my socks to the back door where the largest raccoon I have ever seen stares at us through the screen. Hildy must think he's a threatening monster and, I admit, I feel more scared than I suspect the raccoon does. How pathetic have I become?

I close the back door and move back to the den, sitting on the floor among the photos. I pull Hildy along with me, reassuring her that even with the monster at the back door, we are safe together in here. I don't know that I completely believe that, but I watch her sleep and feel glad that I can comfort her. Her breathing is coarse and I wonder if she's in pain. How will I know when it's her time? That's a decision I don't want to make so I focus on my snapshots. I find a picture of my graduation day in 1976 with my new fellow PhDs, all of us smoking cigars. Instead of being relieved to be entering the world, we disclosed that we'd miss our classes together and the campus and the long afternoons in the library. The day was bittersweet as we packed our trunks and bade each other farewell. Several of my pals had post-doctoral positions in

Other universities or jobs in community colleges. I was

staying, assisting the professors who had taught me with their freshman English classes. I was grateful for the opportunity and only slightly restless. I wondered why I was in the same place if I had achieved so much. But job security spoke loudly to me and, in the end, silenced any wanderlust. I sigh as I place that picture, now 30 years old, in a pile to my right.

Life is surely strange. I had planned so carefully and everything had gone so well and, here I am, sitting on the floor in the middle of the night in a mysterious foggy town with a giant raccoon at the backdoor and the pictures of my life strewn around. And, suddenly, I laugh out loud at how perfect everything is.

8 Paranoia's Grip: Memoirs and Mysterious Intrigue

After four uneventful days I am seduced into thinking that calm has returned and that life will proceed normally. But I would never describe Los Osos as normal and any semblance of normality, I'm beginning to believe, is simply a setup to convince me that I can relax my guard. Which would then beckon another other-worldly mishap. Which would lead me into a twisted and coiling adventure in which I would experience ever deeper layers of being out of control.

These days paranoia is not a problem but a state of being. If I'm not feeling appropriately paranoid, I remind myself that I should. This is Los Osos, the home of the unbidden, the unpredictable, and the just plain weird. It is also, for the moment, my point of alighting. I'm not rooted here; I'm just hanging out. We'll see what the next year brings. For now, I am free but caught up in something I don't understand. I promise myself that I will stay vigilant, I won't lose my anchor in what I remember as reality, and I won't trust anything that seems normal. I think that is a reasonable conclusion to draw from my experiences here.

I consider the folks I've met. If I were to trust anyone, it would be Carolyn — reasonable, focused, deliberate, orderly. She was right about Les. He has been no help. In fact, he hasn't shown himself since the day I met him. I can't count on him for help but at least he isn't a source of danger or irritation. I can't say that about Donny. He could appear any second. I am very clear that he will do whatever his loco brain leads him to do in the moment and then rationalize it. I fear him and, self protectively, I want to help him. Mostly, I want to stay in control with him.

Elizabeth is a grey memory but I don't want to let her fade

away. Intrigue shadows her. So much more happens inside her than she verbalizes. She has a secret or two. I want to understand how she thinks and concludes. Some part of that process is unclear to me. I'll create an excuse to enter her barbershop later in the week.

And where is Al's body? I had called the local hospital but he had not been taken there. There was no record of a death or burial. Is Donny right? If so, who was on the stretcher? And how does Donny know?

I walk to the library and notice Carolyn standing outside smoking. She smiles her crooked smile as I approach and she puts out her cigarette. "How've you been? I just got back in town last night and I haven't heard any news yet." Does gossip fuel this place?

No paper is necessary to spread news here.

"Nothin' too much." Am I morphing into a local?

"Well, it's funny that you should appear. I was thinking about you this morning. Each year the library sponsors some kind of writing contest. Last year we did poetry and had 120 entries. This year it's going to be memoir-writing — anything anyone wants to write about memories or the past, as long as it has a personal slant. And it came to me while I brushed my teeth, you'd be the perfect person to judge the submissions! All the prizes will be books. I don't have them yet but I'll get them. I'm making the flyer to advertise it now. May I include your name as our professional writer/judge? That would be a thrill for us!"

Imitating Ellie, I cheerfully acquiesce, recognizing that I must pretend affability so that no one suspects my doubts. Why not, a voice in my head challenges. You've got nothing to lose.

Then I hear Jake's wild laugh when he was perversely amused by his private world. A string in my heart quivers.

9 Unspoken Warnings

Ellie hasn't really told me anything about Donny and I want to know more in order to be prepared for my next engagement with him, should there be one. We had parted on a cordial note and I had encouraged him to trust me. I didn't have evidence that he had rearranged my house but he is the most likely suspect. The way things are going I don't presume I will be lucky enough to avoid him forever. In fact, I think it likely that he will find me if I don't find him first. I sincerely hope that our next encounter, if it must be, will take place somewhere other than my living room. The thought occurs that I will be more in control if I manage the meeting. But I don't know where he lives.

As if to answer my unspoken question, Deb rounds the corner. Always cheerful, she simultaneously smiles, waves, and calls, "Honey, how you be? I haven't seen you in the longest and I want to know you're just peachy!" I know she has a grown daughter. How did her daughter react to this ebullience when she was a kid?

In order to give her something without giving her anything significant, I tell her that I've just agreed to judge the memoir- writing contest for the library. She gushes with joy and appreciation. "Oh, honey, you'll love it! We have such interesting, talented geezers here." She laughs explosively. "They will be so pleased to know you are Da Judge!"

Carolyn had assured me that the entries will be delivered to me without identifying info and I can write comments or critiques or, really, anything I want. Just as long as I give her a first, second, and third prize winner. I am the prize, I realize. Anything that happens from here on is minor. Oh, well. This is not a problem. I know how to finesse big projects. I'll make this enterprise work for me.

"Hey, Deb. You know Donny Slate? I met him but I don't know how to find him." Suddenly her face clouds and she looks flustered, distinctly uncomfortable. I'm afraid she'll run away and I want to reassure her that there is no danger, but, apparently, the mention of Donny's name heralds more than I know.

"Really, there's no problem. He and I had a friendly conversation a few days ago and I just want to see him again to chat."

Seriously, she says, "Nick, listen to me. You don't know all the facts and you never will. Stay away from Donny. Just let him be. I'm glad your conversation was friendly. Let it go at that. You can't win this one, Nick. You're smart, so just walk away. I'm warning you. Let this one go." And she hurries back the way she came with her head tucked down and an arm across her waist. Watching her, I am afraid and determined at the same time.

10 Beneath Surface Shadows

There are facts I need to know. I can't reach Ellie by phone so I walk and I think. I meander around and through Sweet Springs, a Nature Preserve, as the sign says. I would have called this area a swamp. The bay gently merges with solid ground here and the roots of the eucalyptus trees reach through the soggy soil to the air in the intermediate region, neither bay nor terra firma. The scent of eucalyptus wafts through the clean air and large pebbles roll under my feet. I watch my step. I always wear socks here in deference to the plentiful poison oak. The sun's rays pierce the leafy canvas intermittently. The air is cool and the ground mossy. Little lizards sprint and freeze. If Los Osos is another world, Sweet Springs is the capital.

Eucalyptus is not native here. The trees were planted in the mid-1800s to provide wood for paper or railroad ties, depending upon which resident tells the story. The ending either way is the same. The wood was not usable and now the trees have overtaken the area, spreading over miles, interfering with the growth of what was indigenous vegetation.

Leaving Sweet Springs, I walk downtown. I compare Donny with Jake. Jake was physically smaller and less threatening. When he was suffering in the depths of his illness, he kept to himself, perhaps making a bystander who happened to glance his way uncomfortable but not engaging anyone. Donny, apparently, functions adequately in the world. Jake never could.

Can I? I don't trust that anyone, including Ellie, is telling me everything. And there is something which I don't know but which I very much need to know. I trust no one to give me the missing piece. I'm not sure what it is but some word or fact will throw all this information into a meaningful picture. I'm doing a jigsaw puzzle and I can't even finish the edges.

What is Donny's story? Was there a time when he was indistinguishable from any other grade school kid? From Deb's reaction, I surmise that others shy away from contact with him. What is Al's story? Why didn't Elizabeth tell me all the details that Deb offered? What is Les' story? Is he simply a befuddled old man? Or is he involved in some nefarious plot? Suddenly this beautiful little town seems like a backdrop for some dastardly dynamics.

I enter the barbershop and, again, Elizabeth awaits me. How does she know when I'm coming? And by her firm-footed stance, frown, and crossed arms I guess she also knows about what and whom I want to talk.

Before we exchange greetings, she says, "Nick, you're playing with fire." I hate clichés but I envision my house, my pictures, my papers, my books and my life enveloped in tall golden-orange flames. Am I being threatened that if I'm not satisfied with surface appearances, if I dig too deeply, there will be damaging consequences? Am I being told to accept the two- dimensional self-evident picture book situation? Elizabeth doesn't scare me and I push back, suddenly, surprisingly mobilized.

"I happen to like fire. Where there's fire, there's almost always a good story. What is it that burns to be told here?"

Her eyes shoot darts. But my house has been ransacked, I have witnessed some very odd events and people, and I can't get a straight story from anyone in this town. Hell, no, I'm not backing off! I want some answers!

"Why weren't you honest with me about your relationship with Al? You made it sound like you were good friends but you didn't mention that he had been your lover and that your plans to marry had been dashed by the intrusion of his brother. So, why not? Why are you lying to me?"

This is the most direct I have been with anyone here, much

more direct than I had planned to be with Elizabeth, but I'm tense and I feel brittle. She looks aghast. Clearly, I have crossed a line and she isn't overlooking that fact.

"Listen, you. Get out of my shop right now and don't come back. You're not welcome here." And she slams the door behind me.

This is interesting, I think, suddenly calm. There is something going on here.

11 Seeking Solace in Shadows

I trust no one. Not even myself. Surprisingly, that isn't an unpleasant admission. I'm here on the edge of the continent, far from an urban center, and it's up to me to discern the rules of engagement. There are some givens. They're just not the ones I was expecting. That's OK.

What I know for sure: things aren't what they seem. People aren't who they present themselves to be, at least not at first, second, and third glance. A tightly woven community shares a history but doesn't advertise it. A kind of substratum loyalty exists which closes the borders of this town to outsiders. There is a ferocity in maintaining the local privacy.

All in all, it isn't much. I'll go about my daily life and watch and listen. I spend more time working in the front yard, subtly proclaiming my availability for informal conversation. Once in a while a neighbor greets me or a walker waves. While I wait for some clues, my yard looks better. I recognize the traffic patterns, who walks when and where and in what groupings.

Jimmy, the seven-year-old from the corner house, rides his little bike over and stops for a visit. He has time; he likes to avoid his two younger sibs, twin girls recently born who demand his mother's full attention. He shows me his frog, Elmer, which he pulls from his pocket after he parks his bike.

"Hey, Mr. Sanders. Whatchoo doin'? Me and Elmer, we're jus' ridin' around. Want to see him?"

Of course, I do, and Jimmy points out his distinctive markings, his "ears," and shows me how he has trained Elmer to jump. We squat in the dust until my knees complain and I offer Jimmy some lemonade.

"What do you like best about living here?" I ask him.

"Oh, I dunno. I like ridin' my bike and I like sitting in my tree house. And, I guess, I jus' like bein' here. I have lots of friends. My Mom lets me go anywhere I want. Almost. Only place that's a no-no is behind the dump. Sometimes my Dad takes me there when he cleans out the garage. He has a beer and he lets me have red soda. My mom don't never let me have red soda. But we don't tell her. My Dad says she'll be happier if she don't know." And Jimmy jumps on his bike and pedals off.

I wander past Al's house and notice that the yellow tape has been torn down. The darkened windows betray no sign of life. I wish I knew what secret that house hides. Even if I break in, I don't know what I'm looking for. I can make an enemy of Les and a fool of myself if I'm not careful.

After dark, I listen to the TV and reorganize my photo albums. As I peruse the family photos I can't help wishing that Rosemary were here. Her perspective on this place would be so different from mine. I close my eyes and imagine Rosemary sitting on the other side of the room.

"Nicholas," she'd offer, "You're thinking like a university professor, not like a human being." She often said that to me the last couple years of our marriage. I didn't know if I should be offended or not. So, I let it pass. But now that she isn't here, I answer her.

"What do you mean? What should I see that I don't?" Talking this way to no one is surprisingly easy. Much better, in fact, than actually having her in the room.

"You're looking with your eyes, trying, trying, trying. Sit down and just notice. These people live real lives here. What's that like? Be one of them. Don't look at them from the outside. And, for heaven's sake, remember that, unlike you, most folks want relationships. They like to be liked. They need companionship. They want to be known. You could exist alone forever if someone supplied you with food and books, but real humans aren't like that."

Even when she's not here, she's cheeky. I open my eyes and think that I will pretend I'm human. Hildy walks over and nuzzles my hand. She knows I'm human. How come Rosemary never could believe it?

The first two or three years of our marriage were idyllic. We played at being married and keeping house and looking grown up. At least she did. She enjoyed cooking, even when she served eggplant almost every day for six months because it was cheap. She'd tidy the house all day, cook something with an enticing aroma in the afternoon, and freshen herself up before I arrived home, usually just before five o'clock. She did everything she could to keep the honeymoon going. And she did very well. We played games in the evenings, tennis in the summer and canasta in the winter. I tried to teach her bridge but after a few weeks, she wasn't interested. And then she lost interest in all other activities, too. The house was clean enough, but not as neat. Rosemary was often distracted and restless.

We had said we wanted children and now, when our life was unraveling, I thought it would be a good time to try. Rosemary was wildly enthusiastic and, briefly, the magic returned. It wasn't four months before we were pregnant. Our daily activities carried new meaning for each of us. I took my teaching more seriously and thought in terms of decades with the lessons. I found comfort in that long-term vision. Rosemary tried new recipes but soon quit when she felt nauseous almost continually. She survived on oatmeal for weeks and couldn't tolerate the smell of anything spicy. I stopped at the tavern near campus on my way home every night for a burger and a pint. We spent our evenings reading in separate rooms. I hoped that with the birth of our child a semi-normal life would return.

Isabelle's birth was the greatest miracle I have ever beheld. I cradled Rosemary's head as long as she would allow and I recited prayers of thanksgiving when I couldn't participate otherwise. Isabelle was stunningly beautiful because she was ours. We adored her and grew closer to each other in the following days and weeks. I liked going to work with my briefcase and my family picture on my desk. I returned home to find two women waiting for me. Family meals resumed, differently, of course, with Isabelle's irritations and Rosemary's exhaustion. The house was a lived-in mess. I was satisfied.

One morning in her third month, Isabelle didn't awaken. Rosemary was frantic in her grief and I didn't know how to comfort her. She visited her mother for a month but was never the same. I had hoped that time was all that was required to fully restore her so I backed off and waited. I read and read. I knew she was crying in the bedroom but I didn't know what to say.

Over the years, Rosemary enacted her wifely role but never with the innocent joy of our first years. She pursued her own creative interests — quilting and crocheting and, once in a while, she performed with the Little Theater. We did all the things faculty couples were expected to do but there never again was a real sense of togetherness. We lived parallel lives which intersected amiably at points.

I actually could have continued that way but eventually Rosemary announced her resignation from what she called "our pretend game." I hadn't thought I was pretending. I read and worked and I thought that's what life is. I thought I was being responsible. But when Rosemary walked out, I felt a real loss. I can feel it now, imagining a conversation with her. I need her insight and her heart.

When we lost Isabelle, I reverted to my brain. Everything I attempted filtered through my mind. I approached students, other faculty, administrators, work, play, and diversions rationally. I was safer that way. I told myself that I could handle unpredictable occurrences if I weren't too vulnerable. Rosemary's vulnerability scared me as well as enticed me. When she lost that tender part of herself, we lost "us."

Now there's no more need for my intellect. But I sorely need some gentleness. I am truly lonely.

12 Unraveling the Enigma

Outside at dawn a couple days later, I look in the oaks for a mourning dove whose winsome call beckons an unseen partner. Hildy noses the ground. Still sniffing, she pulls me along. What must that be like — knowing the world through your nose? I can't imagine. First, I don't want to get that close to anything that gets walked on. Second, what would my mind do? So I wait while Hildy smells everything. I daydream about something which is forgotten as soon as she tugs on the leash. She lopes through flower beds and lawns dragging me behind. She hasn't moved this fast in years and I fear she's detected a skunk, but she stops at a high fence, winces, and turns back toward the road. I don't understand but then I don't understand much lately. And, actually, that doesn't bother me. There was a time it would have, but now I'm learning to focus on the tiniest detail and be glad if anything positive happens.

Once in a while something unexpectedly fine does occur. Like yesterday, when I was shopping for apples and coffee at the Market. I can't find the strong dark coffee I like here and I was pushing around cans and bottles on the narrow shelf, scanning the limited selection. A slender woman carrying a miniature dog asked if I needed help. Her straight brown hair smelled like coconut. Of course, I said, yes, thank you, and she directed me to a natural organic coffee-flavored barley drink which I never would have tried on my own, but my heart was touched. I carried it and my apples home and remembered feelings I hadn't known for a long time.

I sit at my kitchen table peeling apples and inhaling the earthy "coffee" when Ellie walks in. Now I'll insist on some answers. But before I can speak, words tumble out of her mouth like apples falling off a grocery store shelf.

"You're making some friends I hear, Nick. What's going on?" She stops and puts her hands on her hips, looking directly at me. "Carolyn has big projects planned for you. Lauren called me this morning and asked about a balding stranger in town." In response to my quizzical look, Ellie continues. "She saw you in the grocery store, and, I don't know how you shop, but you made an impression on her!" Ah, yes, the barley coffee lady. Apparently, my face betrayed my interest.

"Careful, Nick, she's married. Or essentially so. She and Greg have lived together for more than 20 years, two kids, a houseful of pets." That's OK, better really. I know myself well enough to know that I don't need an involvement right now. But something floats around the edges of my mind saying wouldn't it be loverly?

"I'm more concerned about Elizabeth," Ellie goes on. Which gives me an entrée.

"And I'm more concerned about Donny," I interject. "You've never mentioned him. I want to know where he lives. Where he hangs out. How he spends his time. And is he as dangerous as I suspect he might be?" I'm forceful in my questioning and she understands that I will not be dissuaded.

Ellie stiffens. I've never seen her face so pale. "How do you know Donny?"

I don't feel the need to be too forthcoming or too precise. "He stopped by my place a couple weeks ago. We had a friendly chat. I'd like to catch up with him, have him over again."

I can see by Ellie's expression that she doesn't believe a word I speak. "Donny doesn't chat." I recognize Deb's sentiments. Ellie continues, "He doesn't stop by. He's not a friendly neighbor. Give it up, Nick. What's going on? You don't have any idea what you're getting into. You stroll in here and things happen. You'd better be careful. I'm protecting you as much as I can but if you're not a little more cautious, I won't be able to save you." And she glances out the corner of her eye as if to say, "I'm serious and you'd better be serious, too."

I feel cocky so I push on. "You, and it seems everyone else in town, know Donny and know something about him that I don't. Why don't you just tell me and save us all some trouble?" And I sit back, cross my arms on my chest and wait for her to speak. When we were kids we used to dare and double-dare each other. That's what this feels like. I had double-dared her and you don't back down from a double-dare.

Ellie inhales audibly and sits at the kitchen table without looking at me. Even before she speaks I know she has decided to tell me the truth. "Donny has had some hard times. He was born a little slow and there was the bicycle accident when he was in junior high. Teachers here tried to help him along, but as he got bigger and angrier he was impossible to handle."

I interrupt, "So, is it true that he's Al's grandson?"

"Oh, yes, but his mother died more than ten years ago and he's been lost without her. He got in some trouble shortly after her death when he was so upset and spent some time in jail. He was out in a year or two and has kept a pretty low profile since then." She pauses and looks at me. "Until he gets excited. And then who knows what he will do." She sighs and clenches her hands like she wants to wring the blood out of them. There's something she's not telling me. I watch her silently and I wait. Is she debating with herself?

Very deliberately and quietly she continues, "A few people around here smoke some local weed. They grow it in different patches and have cross-pollinated it so that it's unusually strong. A couple of the young guys sell some out of town once in a while when they need a fast buck, but we try to discourage them because we don't want law enforcement sniffing around."

This explains Les. He looks easy to dupe so he won't cause problems for committed lawbreakers. I'm surprised to hear Ellie speak about this so matter-of-factly, though. I hadn't suspected drugs. Maybe I'm naive, but I still don't think drugs are the big story here.

"Al's son, Chase, is Donny's father. He lives in New York, doing some important job in the stock market. He seldom comes here but he deposits money in the bank for Donny's needs. Occasionally, Al knows 'just what Donny needs' and withdraws funds 'for him.' Of course, Donny doesn't see that money and, for a while, we don't see Al, and then life reverts to usual." I notice she didn't say normal.

She fidgets and I know she has more to say. She looks up abruptly and continues speaking. "Donny's mother was in an accident on Los Osos Valley Road. Her car skidded off the road and she died immediately. A horrible incident."

"Had she and Chase been divorced long?"

Immediately Ellie responds, "They were still married. Chase was inconsolable after the accident and moved to New York within six months." Something tickles my brain.

13 Shattered Reflections

After Ellie leaves, I sit at the table a long time and think. I twirl a pencil in my fingers but don't write anything. I have 100 more questions. Rosemary had said people want to be liked and to be together. Did this family? Chase isn't with his son or his father and, apparently, doesn't want to be. Why not? What had his marriage been like? I think of more questions to ask Ellie. I appreciate her candor today. I need candor. But I don't really trust anyone else.

At precisely that second a rock flies through the living room window. Reflexively, I duck even though I don't really think I'm in danger. As I sit under the table, I ask myself why I think I am not in danger. Elizabeth has told me to stay away, Deb and Ellie have each warned me, Les is unforthcoming, Donny is a nutcase, and now I know that some local kids smoke enhanced cannabis regularly. All the ingredients for a conflagration and I, unknowingly, have supplied the match.

14 Unveiling the Hidden Menace

My cell phone is in my pocket. Do I want to call Les and report this incident? No, but I want a public record of it. I'm getting angry. Stupid local games are one thing but threatening my physical safety is completely unacceptable. I call Deb and ask her to call the police. Of course, she assents. This gets her involved and neutralizes the tension between Les and me. Or so I hope.

Predictably, she's at my door within five minutes. I crawl out from under the table and try to regain some composure. She walks in before I'm in the living room and she finds a six-inch grey rock.

"Listen to this," she squeals, peeling a paper out of a rubber band around the rock. 'Be at the graveyard by 4:00 p.m. alive or dead — your choice.' She looks at me. "Ooooooo, such intrigue, such danger, such..." and I interject, "drama." I'm not intimidated but I am intensely annoyed. I cannot be treated this way and I must let this small time predator know.

"OK, Deb, let's head to the cemetery. I'm ready."

She lives for this excitement and flings the door open before I reach it. In my car, I'm glad to have some time to talk with her alone before Ellie has told her about our conversation this morning.

"So, Deb, does this kind of thing happen regularly around here?"

"No, Nick. Never. Well, almost never. We have a clean, quiet little community with no violence and no mayhem." Does she think I'm buying this? I look at her and smirk. "Well, since I've been here, I've heard a gunshot in the middle of the night, seen a stretcher being carried out with what I thought was a body which I can't place now, have had my home desecrated, have been told by three women — you, Ellie, and Elizabeth — to back off, been approached by the local loon, and now I've had a rock lobbed through my window with a note about a cemetery. No, Deb, this is not my idea of Pleasant Town, USA. Sorry. Your Welcome Wagon has a lot of work to do to convince me that all's well here in Los Osos."

She falls silent for a moment, the longest she is ever quiet.

"Granted, that's a lot, but I'm sure there's an explanation."

I interrupt her. "What I really want to know about is Chase's wife. You know, Al's son, Chase," I add in response to her quizzical look. "What was her name?"

"Julie."

"And when did Julie die?"

Deb hesitates and looks out the window. I can't see her face but when she turns back she's wearing her usual hail-fellow-well met expression.

"In '08 or '09, right around Halloween, you know when the days are shorter and the nights are nippy. But it was early, very early in the morning."

"Why was she driving at that hour? Coming back from a party?" "No, nothing like that. Julie was a third-grade teacher. She

didn't party. I don't know why she was out at that time. But there was this fluke oil spill on the road and she must not have seen it. She didn't have a chance when her car spun out."

An oil spill? On Los Osos Valley Road? I must check the old newspapers in the library.

We pull in to the cemetery and drive slowly on the dirt road. I don't know why but I'm determined to be here. If anything happens, I'm present. I park, we get out and walk in different directions. It's sunny and cool with a strong breeze. I notice the headstones, mostly from1950 through 1990. Many families have several members buried here. The grave markers are simple, weathered stone. A few have inscriptions after the deceased's name — Loved by Family and Friends or His Memory is Cherished. Nothing elaborate. A simple, small-town graveyard.

I saunter toward the back, passing dozens of graves and the farther back I walk the older the dates are. Now I am in the 1920s section. I can't read most of the names. The plots are overrun with crab grass and here and there a crushed paper cup nestles against a headstone. Apparently, this isn't an area frequented by visitors. I see plastic flowers on two graves but other than that, no adornment, no sign that any living soul is interested in this place.

And then I notice a freshly dug hole near the back hedge, not large enough for a coffin but too large to be dug by an animal. I walk over to it and look in.

My Phillies cap lies in it.

I don't want to alert Deb so I walk back quickly, find her, take her arm and direct her to the car. "Well, there certainly isn't anything going on here today. We followed directions but I don't see a thing." I want to distract her.

On the way home she prattles about relatives who are buried there but I am not listening. When I pull into my driveway, Les sits on my porch, writing in his black notebook. He doesn't look up when we approach. I hope our meetings don't become a habit.

Deb speaks first, "Hey, Les, we've just returned from the cemetery. Did you see the rock and the note?"

Les looks bored. "No rock, no note here," he grumbles, still writing. I look around. Did we leave the rock and the paper on the living room floor? I search the sofa, under the sofa, on the table, under the table, in the kitchen, on the porch, in the front yard. Did we take it in the car? I examine the car, front seat and back, but find nothing.

"You say a rock flew through your glass window? I don't find no rock and I don't see no note. Your story doesn't make sense to me."

Deb and I stare at each other. She breaks our silence. "Les, I saw it, too. It was about yaay large," she holds her hands six inches apart "with a rubber band around a letter size piece of paper. It told us to go to the cemetery. The exact words were: 'Be at the graveyard, dead or alive, your choice.' How creepy is that? But we didn't hesitate. No sir. We headed right there and we walked around and, well, we saw nothing and no one. So, Les, you have Nick's word and you have my word. And, for heaven's sake, you can see the hole in the window! Something's going on here!"

Les is unimpressed and I am unwilling to share my discovery. I won't tell anyone the cap detail. But I trust that Deb will fulfill her position as town crier and let everyone know every other detail. Only the perp and I know about the cap.

15 Unearthing Shadows

The next morning, Saturday, I walk in the library as soon as the doors open. I want to read the old newspapers, now on microfilm, from late 2008. I want to get a feel for this town at that time. And I want to know the specifics of Julie's car crash. Third grade teachers don't usually die before dawn on a school day because of an oil spill.

Carolyn greets me groggily. She's not a morning person, I gather, but she shows me how to search the old papers. Lots of news about children's events, pumpkin races, a town council discussion of a motion to forbid the sale of alcohol in the city limits, a question about possibly installing a sewer, and new restrictions for building permits. Yawn and yawn.

On page 14, I find a short article about Julie's accident. "In the early hours of October 31, the car of Mrs. Chase Slate skidded off Los Osos Valley Road at Stenner Creek Lane. The coroner pronounced her death to have occurred at 3:00 am. The car was found shortly after dawn, about 6:45, when a delivery truck reported a suspicious sighting. She is survived by her husband, her son, and her parents. Funeral arrangements…"

Her death was placed at 3:00 am? Nothing is going on at 3:00 a.m. Nothing is open at 3:00 a.m. Nothing about this makes sense. And what doesn't make sense most of all is how blasé everyone in town is about it. Something reeks so badly I'm having trouble breathing but no one else here is concerned. Except maybe the person who dug the grave for my cap. And perhaps the one who invaded my apartment. And then the stone-thrower. Was I dealing with three crazies or one busy, organized crazy?

I continue reading but the stories from that time are of no interest now. Except to note that nothing much changes here.

What about her parents? I jot down their names. Nothing was written about Donny. Time for some "in person" investigation.

I find Carolyn and thank her profusely for her help and ask if I may take her to lunch. She accepts — for tomorrow, though, not today. She can't possibly get away today, not on a Saturday, the busiest day of the week. Fine, I agree. See you at Cad's at 1:00 tomorrow? She nods as she turns her attention to a young reader.

At Cad's the next day, lively conversation dances in the air like fireflies on a summer evening. The after-church crowd is dressed up, the sports crowd is suitably decked out, and a few loungers like me relax in their back-of-the closet duds. I wait almost 20 minutes for Carolyn and drink three cups of coffee. I appreciate the caffeine after the barley drink and realize how much I've missed it.

Carolyn rushes in carrying a briefcase and an oversized purse. She tries to remove her sunglasses but she's a hand short and they fall on the floor near my feet. I retrieve them for her and place them on the table. She sits quickly and leans toward me. Her curly hair is thinning in spots.

"Rotary is sponsoring its annual spaghetti feed next month and I must round up some responsible volunteers to man our tables. It's not a difficult job, just tedious with a thousand details. I've done it before but this year I have four other projects going and..."

Before she can say more, with my nose shining brown, I jump in as gallantly as a modern man can and tell her I'm available whenever and wherever she needs. "Don't hesitate to ask for anything. You've done so much for me already. I'd like the opportunity to reciprocate."

Carolyn is not as easily swayed as Deb or Ellie. She hesitates, peers over the top of her glasses and says, "Yeah? Well, that's very generous of you." I know she's trying to understand my offer and I know she senses my duplicity. I must be more circumspect. I tell her, "I want something from you — information — and I also want your silence. I will do nothing illegal or even questionable but I also do not accept the appearance that everyone here seems to be selling."

I wait while the waitress pours coffee for each of us. I

hadn't planned on telling Carolyn everything but now I realize I must. This woman is educated, focused, and competent, the only person I've met here who fits that description. She gives me her full attention. That, in itself, I find slightly uncomfortable. This is a powerful woman, more powerful than I had guessed initially. She is not someone I should try to manipulate. I will only embarrass myself. Catching my breath and realizing I must immediately develop a Plan B, I ask her about herself. While she speaks I can regroup my forces. But she's too good even for that.

Brusquely she suggests, "Why don't you just tell me what you want? Let's not waste time we don't have." She offers these words reasonably with direct eye contact while leaning forward in her chair. I gulp, realizing I cannot get out of this one and, really, I don't want to. But I'm moving into an arena I cannot control or even direct. So why not jump in?

"You know, I moved here with no expectations. I retired and let Ellie sell me on this place. But since I've been here, almost four months, I've had my apartment ransacked and a rock thrown through my window." I hesitate and drink some more coffee. I don't want to reveal the secret details.

"Actually, I like it here but I get the feeling that someone here doesn't like me. Yesterday when you helped me read the old newspapers, I was researching the death of Julie Slate in 2008. That seems to be connected somehow but I don't know how."

I fear I have said too much with the last statement. I don't want to talk about Donny's appearance at my house or the stretcher in the middle of the night and definitely not the baseball cap. I speak faster. "Ellie told me about Chase moving to New York after Julie's death. Did you know Chase?" I don't want to mention Al before she does.

Carolyn is suddenly suspicious. Of course, she knew Chase. Everyone knew Chase.

"No," I interrupt. "Did you know him well?"

Carolyn sits back in her chair. Immediately, the waitress appears but we both say "the special" and she leaves. Carolyn crosses her arms high across her chest. "Chase Slate grew up here. Not many folks who live here now did. The ones born here left and retirees moved in from northern California or southern California or, like you, from other places."

I want to keep her talking about Chase but she seems guarded and distrustful. Why shouldn't she be? I need to give her something about me which I hope will soften her reticence. "I certainly am glad to be here. I lived in Pennsylvania all

my life, teaching at Penn State. This little town is…" and I can't find an adjective which is believably descriptive and still soothing to Carolyn's distrust. Quirky? Not complimentary. Strange? Too judgmental. Quaint? Unbelievable. I look around the room as though I might find a word floating among the tables.

"Curious?" she offers. "Unique? Unusual? Original?"

"Yes, but with a bit of mystery." There I had said it. I am relieved to see Carolyn's shoulders sink.

"There is that," she admits. "The old-timers say it's from all the ghosts of the men who died here. When the cattle ranches were established in the 1800s there was competition, rustling, gunfights. When the railroads were built north and south, Chinese laborers laid most of the rails. They were treated miserably and died from cholera and mosquito bites which spread malaria. This little area has a brutal past though it looks pleasant enough now." There's that word again. I will never use the word "pleasant" to describe this town. Carolyn notices my grimace.

"OK, the pristine landscape is only surface. Most newcomers don't get the underlying layers of controversy going on here." Kaching. I have struck pay dirt. Or so I hope.

Our omelets have arrived and we are silent. I don't want to foster any doubts that she can trust me by pursuing too aggressively the issues of Julie's death or Chase's move. I want to cement an alliance with her today but she is so sensitive.

She speaks first. "Our town isn't perfect but it's home to a few thousand families and retired seniors. We like what we have here. We're living our simple lives and, for the most part, enjoying ourselves." She hesitates and looks away. I feel a wall rise. When she doesn't speak, I ask her about drugs here. I won't break Ellie's confidence. I wonder if Carolyn will mention the pot fields. She hasn't mentioned Donny or Al.

"Drugs are everywhere these days and, yes, they're here in Los Osos, too. In Rotary that's one of our projects, to wipe out drug abuse in this county. Having the state prison so close doesn't help that."

"Why would a prison influence drug sales here in a town, twelve miles away?"

"Please don't be naive. If addicts are near, drug sales occur. That's true anywhere on the planet. We're not exempt from the lure of fast money." She sighs but she doesn't mention the potent weed. Carolyn is sharp. I want her to trust me but I don't trust her. She knows much more than she says. It's tortoise tempo with her.

The waitress removes our empty plates and we both decline more coffee. This meeting hasn't gone as well as I had hoped. I tell Carolyn I'm looking forward to reading the memoir-writing contest entries. She glances at me over the corner of her glasses and says flatly, "Great."

Walking home I realize she hasn't told me anything at all. The historical folklore is a matter of record. The platitudes about drugs are not specific to this area. She doesn't want me to know too much. Or is that my paranoia? I can't count her on my side yet. I thought I could orchestrate a mini-investigation using her insights but she absolutely will not be used. That I have discovered for certain.

Walking home I encounter Jimmy on his bike. "Howdy," I greet him. "Where are you off to today?"

"I dunno. Jus' goin' 'round. I go 'round and 'round." He seems satisfied. Small town life. Doing the same thing every day and finding contentment. When will I discover contentment?

My project is not proceeding smoothly. It's more than not having the facts. A countervailing force opposes me, pushing hard to maintain the status quo. It's not the individuals, it's not a group effort, it's the local culture. This town doesn't want its secret discovered. This place has its own mythology and the folks who have lived here and breathed the air for years don't seem to recognize it, don't seem to find anything unusual or even noteworthy. Carolyn is right. This place is haunted. Not by the ghosts of the past but with its own indomitable spirit. Now I'm sounding nuts.

I turn the corner and see Donny sitting on my front porch. The meeting I have dreaded.

"Hello, Donny! It's such a beautiful day, let's go for a walk, OK?" I want to keep him out of my house.

"But you said we should never be seen together. I been thinking. I got some things to tell you." I am trapped by my own words. I usher him in the front door but leave it standing open. I hope Jimmy will come in even though he has not come to my door before. How lame is that — to hope to be rescued by a seven-year-old?

Donny explains a convoluted theory about a plot to subvert the social order involving aliens and ladybugs. He is much more stressed than he'd seemed at our first meeting. Thinking without feedback from anyone else has sent him spiraling downward in a closed self-defeating loop. Apparently, in his mind, he and I are teammates and he is just checking in, bringing me up to date.

Our friendship is his strongest asset in my estimation. His comfort with me and his need to speak with me make me dismiss him as a suspect in either of the two violent incidents in my home. He trusts as innocently as a child. Has he not spoken with anyone else?

"Donny, you've been doing some creative thinking and it's admirable that you tell me. But, listen, I haven't seen your grandfather for a while. I remember you told me he's OK, but where is he? I don't notice him around. The lights aren't on in his house. Where did he go?" Surely, he will believe me even if Carolyn won't.

"Oh, Gramps is OK. Don't worry 'bout him. He's at the farm. He'll be back in a week or two. He needs some time to himself." What is this information? The farm? Time to himself? Be back in a week or two? Nothing makes sense.

"Have you ever been to the farm?"

"No, I can't go, but it's a good place for him. He comes back and he feels better. A week or two. He's OK." Donny is not concerned as far as I can tell.

"Does someone take your grandfather to the farm? Or does he drive himself?"

"No, no, Gramps don't drive. The guys, they pick him up and take him out there and then they bring him back."

"Who are 'the guys'?" But Donny isn't concentrating on our conversation any longer. He has noticed the hole in the window with cardboard taped over it. He touches the cardboard. "What's this?"

"Seems like someone made a mistake and threw a rock through my window."

"It weren't no mistake," Donny offers immediately. "I heard 'em talkin' 'bout it. The guys, ya know."

"No, I don't know. What guys, Donny? The same guys who took your grandfather away?"

"Well, some may be the same. The young guys. The ones who hang around the old train station. The ones who cut the weed. They always cuttin' or smokin'."

I know the abandoned train station. It is more than a mile out of town. It was busy in the mid to late 1800s but not since the first years of the 20th century when the new railroad tracks were laid closer to town. I didn't know there was any activity there now and, apparently, any activity there is intended to be unknown.

"What do you say we take a ride out there, Donny? Are you up for that?" I'm not sure what I am suggesting but, there, I had said it.

Donny looks around, distracted. "I'd like to have you join me but if you don't want to go, I can drop you off at your house.

What will it be?"

"I guess I'll come. I got nothin' else to do." I may greatly regret this. But Donny's size and friendship appeal to me at the moment.

16 Fire in the Greens

The shack that served as the old train station barely stands upright. The sun sneaks through the roof and the walls. The two-by-four planks are grey, any paint having long ago vanished. The wood is warped and very dry. A strong wind could level it. The old rusted rails peek through the grass extending both north and south a quarter mile.

Vehicles driven without benefit of a road have left trails in the tall grass. They crisscross and stretch far back into the field which ends in foothills about one and a half miles out. So, these are the famed growing grounds.

I don't want to drive my car through the field so Donny and I walk. In the spring these fields and the hills are a vibrant emerald green, so I've been told. Now they are a dried tan. It really is beautiful here, open and unspoiled. If we weren't on a mission, I would enjoy a leisurely walk. I want to investigate the fields farther back, those not visible from the shack. Donny and I walk in silence. He doesn't lead but clearly, he has been here before and knows where we are going. We walk more than 20 minutes through assorted vegetation, up a small hill and down again. We face a twelve-foot grassy embankment which we climb over slowly.

Suddenly, acres of marijuana plants sway in the breeze as far as I can see. Donny just looks around like he has been here 100 times before, no surprises, nothing of special interest. I am amazed to witness the vastness of this enterprise. The plants look healthy and large, sprinklers intermittently spouting water. I have never indulged nor been tempted but I can imagine some entrepreneur proudly making millions off this field. I respect what is done well, even if it is illegal.

And with that thought an explosion rocks us. We look back in the direction of the station to see flames dancing in the air.

17 Fields of Deception

Ellie gives me her I-told-you-so expression when I tell her about it the next day. "You don't understand what you're doing, Nick. Please be more careful."

"How can I be more careful if my car explodes when I'm not in it?" Now I am flummoxed. I had spoken with the insurance adjuster yesterday evening and he had asked what I was doing in the field. Just walking, I had replied. Silence on his end of the line. I hoped he was not local and didn't know about the produce grown there.

Ellie insists that I do something differently, but I don't know what that could be, unless it entails staying inside my home and reading although my home isn't all that safe, either. Someone watches me. I don't see him. I don't know him, nor do I want to know him. But he is someone I need to know, nonetheless. My safety depends upon it and maybe my life. Suddenly, this mystery is not only about these people in this strange town. Now I am intimately involved, also. I thought I could investigate from the vantage point of outsider but now I am entangled.

I need Ellie to be completely frank with me, but I doubt that she is withholding information. I would bet $1,000. that she truly doesn't know what is going on and, probably, really doesn't want to. Her life can proceed smoothly without understanding all the details but my life certainly cannot. Someone has upped the stakes. It's quickly approaching life or death and I suspect it may be mine. "You don't need to be out there wandering through pot fields," she continues impatiently. She's pacing back and forth across my living room while I slouch on the old soaulooking at the ceiling. It's the old popcorn design and gently falls like the finest snow onto the furniture. If this were my house, I would renovate extensively but the landlord repairs only what absolutely requires repair. That's OK. I'm not here long. In this house, I mean.

Our conversation must be important to Ellie because she

sets her cell phone on vibrate and leaves it in her purse by the door. "Les has had it. He told me he wants you to move away, but I reminded him that you haven't done anything wrong. You just happen to be there whenever anything wrong happens. He finds that suspicious."

"You know, I do, too. I'm just a reasonably nice guy, starting his retirement, ready to enjoy some low-key days. I just want to settle down, have an easy time of it in this beautiful place and nothing's worked well since I drove in. Beats me." Insincerely, I shrug my shoulders but she doesn't fall for my folksy drawl and stands up straighter, her fists clenched on her hips.

"Be serious, Nick, you can get us both killed!" That thought hadn't occurred to me. As far as I am concerned she is not involved but, of course, she is. People here call her and ask her about me and give her messages for me. I've made her vulnerable. I feel stupid and naive with this realization. I see why she's angry. I've behaved recklessly in regards to her. I assumed that since she was so wellentrenched here she was safe, but no, of course she's not.

"I am so sorry. I didn't think this would affect you at all but I promise you, you will never be in danger because of me." I raise my right hand in a Boy Scout salute.

"What does it take for you to wise up? You cannot guarantee anything at this point. Can you promise that my car won't be blown up? Can you promise that another rock won't fly through your window? You don't know anything about anything that's happened and what's happening now is getting much more serious! And you don't get it!"

"What do you want me to do? I will do anything and everything to keep you safe. If you want me to, I will move away. I don't want you to be uncomfortable and I definitely don't want you harmed."

"Thank you. Please keep me in mind when you wander around and talk to strangers. Remember, you are not alone. Trust that everything you do is noticed. Act like you're constantly being filmed, OK? Forget spontaneity. Keep your wits about you and think about every move you make."

After she leaves, I lie on the couch and think about what

she's said. It confirms my belief, no longer a suspicion, that this place is haunted, with evil wafting in the breeze. I know everyone here is not malevolent. Or do I? Is everyone here participating in this drama? Does everyone know something I don't?

I'm sounding like Jake. He had an especially bad "episode" while I was home the Christmas after our father died. I was in college and Jake was trying to finish his senior year in high school. Since Dad's death, Jake had lost his anchor. He fell in with the kids who took risks, lived on the edge, ditched school, and, yes, smoked weed. As far as I knew, he didn't do any drugs heavier than marijuana but our relationship deteriorated at that time. Mom was desperate to insure that he graduate, thinking that at least a high school diploma would open some doors for him. He wouldn't cooperate and withdrew from all of us. That Christmas was joyless; we all missed Dad so much. Jake insisted on wrapping presents with Dad's name on them and putting them near our miniature tree.

On Christmas morning when Mom emerged from her bedroom, she found all the boxes wrapped for Dad torn apart, paper and cardboard scattered over the living room. The tree was knocked over, the tiny lights burning the carpet. On the wall Jake had scribbled, 'Nothing is as it appears.' I feel like that now.

18 Igniting the Flame

I stay close to home the next few days, walking in the morning and at night but busying myself indoors most of the time. Hildy appreciates the company and I am glad to be with her. We don't have much more time together. She moves slowly and stiffly and doesn't raise her head often. She eats and sleeps and once in a while asks to go outside.

I think a long time about my talk with Ellie. While her reaction to these "incidents" is fear and withdrawal, mine is the opposite. An anger I haven't known before races through me and I appreciate its strength. I fantasize situations in which I tell an undetermined bad guy that his threatening destructive behavior is unacceptable. Of course, my words are met with respect and deference. I dominate the situation and effect an outcome of my choosing.

These fantasies are satisfying because nothing like this has ever happened in real life. My writing can be convincing and I certainly appreciate the poetry of language but power and passion are only theoretical constructs, not applicable to the reality of my relationships or my conversations. However, this anger draws me passionately and powerfully to act. I will not be intimidated. I will not back off. And I will not compromise.

My concern about Ellie's safety slows me. I will protect her in the face of any threat but this threat is so elusive and so unpredictable that I don't know how to defend against it. I'm assuming it's an "it" and not a "them" although Donny mentioned "the young guys." Are these unrelated acts of violence? No, they couldn't possibly be. This destruction could not be random. It's pointedly, viciously, malevolently directed against me. The fact that it may harm Ellie infuriates me. I will absolutely not tolerate any victimization of my family. My Maltese blood won't allow it. I invoke Uncle Sammy's spirit to guide me.

19 Ink and Resilience

Carolyn delivers the first batch of memoir writings to me, handing me two bags at my doorstep. No, she won't come in. No, there's no hurry about returning the papers. No, she doesn't need any critiques except a few words about the best three. And, yes, there will be more. These are just the early entries, who knows how many there will be? And she shrugs her shoulders. Gotta run. Enjoy reading.

Thanks. Thanks.

My house is pretty well organized these days, my having spent a week "nesting" as Rosemary would say. I needed to re-establish my home and I have. My pictures and certificates hang, though they pull me back to past times, so I add meaningless bright abstract pieces designed to induce a light mood and a cheerful heart. The new me.

I place the brown bulging bags on the floor by the dining room table and make a pitcher of iced vanilla chai tea. I had run into Lauren again and couldn't resist her recommendation. I settle in to read, expecting to be amused.

As a writing teacher, I understand the sensitivity of the creative process. Initially, I encourage my students to simply open to their imaginations and let any words, images, or story line come to them without effort. I tell them that making up tales is play that humans have enjoyed since the beginning of time. I want them to trust their own well-spring of ingenuity and dip into it plentifully. I tell them that the more they use their creativity, the stronger it will grow, and the more they can trust it.

I believe what I say. For them. For me, the creative process has always seemed forced, my results being prosaic, indifferent, and uninteresting, that is, not creative. This fact is a source of great embarrassment which I try to hide. I cannot do what I teach. Somehow I cannot tap that well-spring. I cannot relax and surrender to the writing spirit. I've wondered if it exists in me. Has my need for predictability choked any Muse who may want to visit?

Today I don't have to be concerned with my ability. I can focus on the work of others. I enjoy that. In my classes I inspired others in ways I can't seem to inspire myself. I was good about not offering too much feedback so that my students lost touch with their own voice. I encouraged and supported but never directed. And in the process of evaluating their writing, I always found enough to champion so that the student writer would continue confidently.

In these papers transparency is not lacking. Good grammar sometimes is, metaphor often, imagery frequently, but always I grasp what the writer feels and wants to express. Most of the writers are retired Baby Boomers. The writing isn't always technically correct but the message is always heartfelt. I appreciate these folks sharing their lives and their most intimate experiences. There are a few from very young writers, apparently an eighth-grade class assignment to describe a young person making a moral choice. And one from an aspiring Hemingway, a Los Osos interpretation of the running of the bulls at Pamplona with sixth graders on bikes substituting for the beasts. I chuckle with that one.

But the one that grabs my attention relates the story of a retired English professor from Penn. State who moves west to retire and meets with a gruesome death. Details of his ghastly end were spellbindingly elucidated. The tale was told in the first person with the professor concluding, "I shouldn't have done it. I've hurt too many."

After a second reading I place that paper on the stack of papers and lie on the couch to think. The writer described my car, Hildy, my rented house, and me. I want to call the writer "he" because of the daring aggression in sending the piece to me this way. He's taunting me.

He wants to play psychological games. I won't respond. I won't change my habits or anything I do or anywhere I go. I had placated Ellie by promising never to visit the pot fields again. That's OK, I've seen them. But other than that, my life will look exactly the same. I may even take more risks — going out at night, perhaps. Why do I think that the writer will more likely act in darkness? All the violent incidents have happened during the day.

Is only one individual, the writer, responsible? The writer is one person whom someone has seen. He had deposited his paper in the box at the library which means that he is someone who is known or at least blends in. The paper was printed on a standard computer printer, no telltale marks.

What would Mickey Spillane do at this point? He was a writer; he would write. So I begin writing. Everything I've experienced, thought about, done, decided not to do, imagined, feared, remembered. I write all afternoon and through the evening and into the night, stopping long enough to attend to Hildy but compelled to record my life for the last six months. I write until dawn, purging my soul, expressing every here-to-fore unrecognized reflection. My fingers slow only when light fills the house. I fall into bed and sleep peacefully.

By writing my experience I have underlined it and said, "Yes, this is who I am. This is my story and it deserves to be told. I have a point of view that counts. Acknowledge me. Listen to me and take me seriously. I am here and I won't disappear."

20 In the Depths of Deception

After the phone awakens me at 2:00 pm, I pull on my plaid fleece pants and walk to the coffeehouse at the bay for some real coffee. I carry it back to my house, sipping the hot liquid while steam tickles my cheeks. I pass Al's house, still dark, and I think about Donny, Julie, and Chase. And Elizabeth. So many loose threads. I grimace when I hear myself using clichés. I've always said that a well-educated person can express himself directly from his experience, not by hoisting another's words, used over and over, until there is nothing individual communicated by them.

I enjoyed last night's writing session because it was completely personal, my story as only I can tell it. And I did tell it. I gave voice to every impression, concern, and opinion I've carried these last months. I summarized my experience as poignantly as the contest entrants. I presented myself forcefully and convincingly and ardently.

The urgency about living my life and telling my story increases daily. The stress from the recent incidents has pushed me beyond my anxiety and fear about not being appropriate, eliminating any self-imposed limitations. I don't care what anyone thinks. I'm getting threats almost weekly now and I have a pretty strong sense that I'm hated, at least by one fellow. Interestingly, that doesn't bother me. In the past it would have and I would have done anything to prevent it. Now it energizes me. My chest expands as I breathe determination.

Sitting at the dining room table with my coffee and my pen in hand, I think. What about Donny? He disappeared after our last outing. Elizabeth has some information I need but she has made her feelings towards me very clear. I wonder what Deb would say. I surmise that Ellie would say, "Stay away." I'll wait. But I need someone to give me precise information about Chase, his marriage, and his family. Deb is the obvious choice. I'm so glad to know someone who knows so much, likes to talk, and has very few inhibitions. She's also a walker so I know if I'm out I will eventually run into her.

Sure enough, two days later I see her early in the morning. It's getting light later so she carries a large black flashlight, an impromptu weapon, if need be. I ask if I may join her and, as always, she's delighted. I listen to her for ten minutes before I bring up Chase and family. I try to be indirect, waiting until we pass Al's house as though that reminded me.

"So, Deb, I notice Al's house is still closed up. Looks like no one's been in there for weeks." "Hmmm. Yeah, I guess so."

"Did Chase grow up there? You and he went to school together, right?"

"We both went to Los Osos Middle School but he was four years ahead of me. I didn't know him or his family." Why is Deb suddenly quiet?

"I've been thinking about what you told me about Julie dying on Los Osos Valley Road early in the morning. I read about it on microfilm in the library but something still bothers me." She doesn't ask what or offer any more information. She stares straight ahead and keeps walking. Instantly, her vibes are cold and uninviting.

Feeling unwelcome, I have trouble forming words. "You see, I..." I glance sideways at Deb but she stares straight ahead, her jaw set. "Can you tell me anything?"

"Not really. That was a long time ago," she utters sharply. We wait for a slow car to drive in front of us as we cross the street.

Trying a direct approach, I ask, "Have I offended you? You don't seem to want to talk."

"Some things are better left unsaid. Why don't you concern yourself with what you can do something about?"

"Good thought. You know my car was burned a couple weeks ago when I was with Donny. I think that is connected to Julie's car accident. And maybe to the rock thrown through my window. Do you think those things deserve my attention? Because I'd sure like to know more about them.

Do you think Chase might know anything about those two incidents? I would dearly love to ask him. That would be OK with you, wouldn't it?" I am steamed and she feels it. Whom is she protecting and how dare she stonewall me?

Very slowly she says, "No, don't think about contacting Chase. He's a dangerous man. We're fortunate he's not here anymore. New York is a good place for him. Let him be. OK, I know you're frustrated and I suspect no one has been straight with you. Don't say I said this, don't tell anyone it was me, but that family is bad news. Chase hasn't been convicted of anything but he's constantly under investigation. The Feds want him for conspiracy to commit fraud, interstate trafficking, and a couple drug selling charges. He hasn't spent a night in jail because he can afford the most expensive lawyers in the country. Chase is a man so powerful that presidents ask his advice."

I laugh at that statement, it sounds so dramatic, but Deb looks at me insistently. Apparently, she's not kidding. "Julie was a sweet, innocent young woman with no worldly experience. She was simple in the best possible sense. She hadn't traveled and didn't want much from life, just a home and family.

"Well, she had Donny after they were married a year and he became her lifelong project and preoccupation. Donny's needs came first — physically, mentally, emotionally. He was more than a full time job but Julie was up to it and gave him everything she could, including all of herself.

"Rumor had it that the marriage was rocky and definitely unsatisfying — to Chase, that is. Julie would never ask for much but Chase spent more and more time away on business. He was gone more than he was in town. Clearly, he had a life Julie didn't share. She never complained. She was committed to Donny. She was the best mother he could have had."

I interrupt. "Why would Chase marry Julie? Sounds like they had nothing in common."

"Chase was wild in high school and wilder when he went away to college, so they say. Al gave him a thriving import business on the condition that he marry a local girl and live here. For a twenty-two year-old with no direction and some expensive habits, that was a good deal."

"Al provided a business?"

"At that time Al was doing well. In his prime he was a big success, bigger than anyone in this town today." Deb becomes quiet. "I shouldn't be saying all this. Please don't repeat any of it."

"Deb, you have my word. I will safeguard this information and protect you. I'm very grateful that you've been honest with me. Things are fitting together a little better." And I truly am grateful. There is a meaningful pattern here even if I don't fully grasp it.

It isn't until the next morning that I learn that Deb has met with "an accident" and is in the local hospital with a broken leg and two broken ribs. I know that somehow I am responsible.

21 The Sinister Game?

Ellie calls me, furious. "You did this, didn't you? You wouldn't leave Deb alone. She's a generous loving soul and you took advantage of her good nature for your own selfish purposes. Well, are you satisfied now? She's in pain, she won't be able to move around on her own for weeks, and she's scared to death. Tell me, Mr. Bigshot, was it really worth all that?"

I feel terribly guilty. It's true. I had intentionally used her as I knew I could. I was only thinking about myself. I hadn't suspected that a conversation, which I'm sure no one heard, could have resulted in this. But I will vindicate myself. I will uncover the nefarious goings on here. Ellie doesn't care about that, however.

"So, what, you'll save the day? My best friend is lying on her back in the hospital because I introduced her to you. Have you no shame? No matter what you uncover it won't erase the trauma she's already endured. You're a lousy, selfish bastard and I'm ashamed to be related to you." She slams the receiver down.

She's right, she's completely right. I won't say I'm doing all this for my amusement. It's beyond that, but I'm not thinking about the consequences to others from my contacts with them. Even after my promise to Ellie.

Of course, how could I predict this? Deb and I were simply two friendly neighbors taking a walk and she ends up in the hospital. I am obviously a dangerous person. Anyone I speak to risks her health simply by the fact of knowing me.

I hear Carolyn leaving more papers on the front porch. To protect her, I suggested that she drop them off, that we not meet or talk. The most I can do for people is to keep them away from me. After her car pulls away, I open the door and haul in three more bags.

I'm irritable, frustrated, sad and hurt for Deb and Ellie, angry, confused, and worried for myself. I am determined not to let this or him or them defeat me. But I don't know what

I'm up against — just what Ellie and Deb have told me all along. I can't trust my own judgment. Others suffer.

Being without a car now, I walk or stay home. I want to buy some sandwich makings and settle in for a long read. As I leave the little grocery, Elizabeth walks in. I smile and say, "Good morning." You'd think I'd thrown tar the way she responds.

"How dare you show your face around here? The longer you stay, the more damage we suffer. What's next?"

I realize that her question doesn't require a response but I take the opportunity to engage her. "I truly am sorry for the events that have happened but I didn't perform any of them."

"Nothing would have happened if you weren't here! I don't know what kind of devil you are but be gone, Satan!" A couple shoppers look up but don't return my smile. I conclude that she probably won't be available for conversation soon.

I make a triple decker ham and Swiss and turkey sandwich on rye with caraway seeds and mustard, tomatoes, and romaine. This isn't my favorite sandwich but it is a reliable standby. When I was in school I loved the Philly cheese steaks on thick buns. You can't make those, you have to buy them. And by the time you're over 40 with some blood pressure concerns, well, those sandwiches are a wonderful memory.

I pull the pitcher of iced tea from the fridge and sit down at the dining room table, hoping for a low-key few hours. I'm not used to the kind of excitement I've suffered here and I'd like a return to my boring existence.

The first four papers I read fulfill my hopes. These later entrants aren't the super-motivated first-to-respond author wannabes. Today's writers are hum-drum, looking for a project, but not committed to creating anything of excellence. Their papers are dull, I would guess even to them, for they didn't seem to take the time to rewrite or polish or edit adequately. Exactly what I want. No problem. Throw the bunch of them away. This job is easy.

It is the fifth paper that catches my attention. Written in pencil it contains a blood smeared thumb print at the lower edge. The one-page text reads, "I stroll the streets but I know not where they lead. I wander in the dark, hidden by the shadows. What awaits me?" As a piece of creative writing, I find it intriguing though rough. If I take it as a message to me, I am infuriated. How dare he threaten me?

I have personified my adversary — male, six feet tall, 40s, muscular, intellectual, and well-organized. He's good at waiting and then striking when it serves him. He may work with one or two others but definitely he's the leader. Did he attack Deb? I can't believe that. He wouldn't throw a rock through my window, either. That's too unsophisticated for him.

He's probably college-educated but folksy so he can fit in here without arousing suspicion. Does he live here? Does someone know him but not suspect his hidden life? There aren't that many residents in Los Osos but there are a dozen small communities near. However, a stranger is noticed.

I even give him a name — Edward, a noble worldly name. It makes it easier to address him. "You're getting bolder, Edward. This game we've got going is picking up speed. What are you trying to do?"

"Just wait. I'm running the plays. You can't anticipate my
moves, just watch out," I imagine I hear. "Are you trying to scare me?"

"Why, whatever would make you think that? I'm simply your worst nightmare come to life. Remember when you were a kid and the Jensen boys stole your lunch every day for a month and you were too scared to tell? And when that Montgomery bitch backed out of going to the prom the day before because she had had another date all along and was just toying with you?

"Can you remember all those times you didn't stand up for yourself? And how sick you felt inside because you knew you were not a man? You're just a brittle shell of an intellect. You've been faking your way through life and you're pathetic. You disgust me. You think I'm the adversary? I'm a better man than you'll ever be. Quit whining and play the game. It will be the best thing you've ever done."

He's right. He knows me and he knows what I need.

Nevertheless, I will defeat him.

22 Vulnerability

Thankfully, the next three days are quiet. I read and reread all the writing contest papers and choose my tentative first, second, and third. At least I have a basis for comparison with the new work Carolyn will bring.

The days are surprisingly cool. I huddle inside on the longer nights, writing and thinking about all that has happened and about myself. Edward's words reverberate in my skull. Not only is this craziness about me-in-the-world, it's about me- inside-my-own-world and how undeveloped that world has always been.

Edward is right, I've used my head to power through life and I've used it to try to decipher the intrigue here but it's not working. Real human beings are hurt and I can't extricate myself from them even though I didn't choose to be linked to them. I wanted a solitary, focused, maybe self-indulgent retirement in a new locale but I'm realizing I can't be so self-contained. The small but real external world impinges on me and is affected by me. It's a closed system, no energy escaping or unused or unnoticed. A bit eerie.

Definitely more than my mind is required to play this game. I don't know what that is, however. The scared parts of me to which Edward referred I don't want to know. I had thought the best way to deal with that vulnerability was to push it away and get on with life. That's reasonable, isn't it? And I hear Rosemary's voice, "Reason is irrelevant. It's time to move into your heart."

I answer her even though I don't see her. "How is that going to help?"

"What's your choice? You've done everything your way and you've ended up alone, except for a dying dog. One friend has been brutalized and is lying in the hospital and you're afraid to visit her. Your cousin fears that you might damage her life. Another lady hates you. You want to continue doing things your way? Is considering an alternative such a bad idea?"

"What alternative, Rosemary?"

"I've told you before. Pretend you are human and that you need relationships."

So, if I need relationships, and this will be a big pretend, I have to imagine needing something I can't make happen. I've always resisted depending upon something I couldn't control. Why do that? I saw Jake and I saw my mother and I saw how their lives tumbled and jerked. And without even trying, I see my father. His consistently placid surface appealed to me. I only remember one time that he and I shared alone. I must have been eight and he was polishing his shoes on a Sunday evening. The wind was howling through the almost bare tree branches but he seemed unaware of the weather — the dark, the falling temperature, the changing season.

"Nicholas," he said which alerted me because he never used my full name. "Don't ever be stupid. Some things you can't predict and some things will wrap themselves up in front of your eyes and some things other people decide. But most of your life, you can create as you choose." I remember that he sighed then as he listened to Jake and Mom in the next room. "You can't blame anybody but yourself if your life doesn't turn out the way you want."

I accepted his counsel seriously. Dad and I counterbalanced Mom and Jake. Some nights when I was in bed I heard Mom crying and Dad telling her not to worry about Jake. "We will use good judgment and that will be adequate to handle any situation that arises."

I remember the desperation in her voice when she screamed at him, "You aren't seeing what he's doing! He's not a confused little boy. This is bigger than you know!" She would sob hysterically and Dad would leave the room and sometimes the house. It took me hours to fall asleep on those nights. I didn't know the details of what they were discussing but the tension hung in the air then, just as Edward's words do now.

23 Navigating Family Shadows

When Carolyn delivers the last bag of papers I inquire obliquely if she has looked at any of them. "Only to code them so we can match numbers with names to determine the winners when you return them to me."

"Fine," I reply, closing the door on the possibility that she has noticed anything or anyone unusual. The box for the entries is near the front door of the library, out of sight of the desk in her office. Only identifying numbers are printed in the upper left-hand corners on the back of the first page of each entry. I will ask her about the two threatening pieces by number when I'm finished.

I wonder if I will be surprised by a paper in the bag, she hands me now but I am not. Nor am I very interested in the writing. I throw the bag of them away and keep the three I have already chosen. I will hand them to her in a week and tell her how much I've enjoyed this project. I can't lay it on too thick with her, though. She's astute, having spent years in large universities and larger cities. And I know she doesn't trust me.

Ellie has invited me over for dinner. She fixes a healthy vegetable stir fry with herbs from her garden and grated cheddar. Food was celebrated in our family with pasta, bread, and heavy sauces. Both she and I have revised our eating habits significantly, losing some of the old-world charm and most of the calories. Being with her for dinner brings back the enfolding warmth of family. I stop on the way to buy her favorite Chardonnay and I walk in her cozy home after dark. No dinner smells greet me, the lights are off, and Ellie sits in the dark. She's been crying, a pile of tissues circles her feet.

I kneel by her chair and put an arm around her shoulders. She can't speak, sobs shake her violently.

"What is it, Cuz? Has something happened?"

She raises her head and looks at me through her tears. "It's Deb. She's gone." And she lowers her head in her hands and weeps.

I am dumbstruck. The last I heard Deb was progressing well and looking forward to coming home. I can't believe it. Deb has died? Ellie can't give me details now. I want to comfort her, though. Rosemary tells me to kneel there and just hold her. Ellie's crying intensifies and, I have to admit, I'm scared by all this emotion but I stay with her. After a very long time she sits back in her chair. I move to the other chair and switch on a lamp. I wait for her to speak. Minutes pass.

"They called from the hospital. She was scheduled to be released tomorrow. We had talked this morning about my picking her up. She sounded happy. But then something happened after lunch. They picked up her tray and she was fine but 20 minutes later when the nurse went in to give her meds, she…" Ellie's voice trails off. I extend my legs, cross them at the ankles, and exhale. I examine her ceiling, not as interesting as mine.

I feel sad and very sorry to lose Deb. She was my friend, too, and had consistently been kind to me. I also feel guilty although this sounds like a strictly medical issue. It was because of me she was in the hospital, however, so anything that happened there goes on my account.

Ellie and I sit in the semi-darkness a long time, mostly not speaking, but once in a while remembering a scene from childhood. We are assuring ourselves that we are still here and we are still us. She reminds me of the family reunion in Tenkiller Park with the cold stream and the mud where we caught tiny crawdads. The four cousins howled. We draped arms and legs over each other and lay entangled in the sun. Jake and I told stupid knock-knock jokes. Ellie and her sister Maria groaned and rolled their eyes which encouraged us. This was the only time Jake and I performed, both of us being shy, but we knew our older cousins loved us. They pampered us and we felt safe with them.

Family wasn't always safe. Our grandmother suffered terribly, probably from what is now called schizophrenia, undiagnosed in those days in Malta. Our fathers told stories about her "fits" when she would throw knives, scream, and chase the dog around the yard. Ellie's father roared as he described the escapades. My father became quiet and excused himself. Those reactions characterized the differences in our families. From the same genes the extroverted brother laughed his way through tragedy and the introverted brother ached inside himself. Ellie and I are our father's children. But now she cannot deny the tragedy and I will not withdraw from her.

I sit with her all evening and ask if she wants me to stay the night but she prefers to be alone in her home. Since her second husband Bryce died eight years ago, she has cherished the tiny delights of each day, grateful for the small touches. She has created a sanctuary for herself here which nourishes her at times like this. I hear the door lock as I stumble back to my rental car, only now remembering that I haven't eaten.

No fast-food stands are both a blessing and a scourge, this being the time one is most needed. But I scrounge through the leftovers in my fridge and concoct a sandwich, new to this earth— bits of turkey and ham, fresh spinach leaves, kiwi, sliced oranges, slivered almonds and a touch of dijon mustard. Sweeter than I usually like but it's late, I haven't eaten anything for hours, and all this emotion drains me.

Rosemary tells me I did fine with Ellie and I appreciate the kindness. It's hard to love someone who is hurting so deeply. There is no way to escape that hurt myself. I'm glad I can carry some of it for Ellie and I'm glad to know I'm strong enough. I've always feared that I'm not.

Reminiscing with Ellie tapped a dam of memories that flood my heart. Out of where-I-don't-know, I think about the girl I had a crush on in third grade, Polly. She was beautiful to me with brown curly pig tails, freckles, and a contagious giggle. Her body was round, not yet gender defined, and she jumped rope as long as two people would twirl for her. She proclaimed herself the Jump Rope Princess and made a cardboard crown she wore to school.

The other children laughed at her and her homemade crown, tore it from her head and threw it onto a leafless tree branch where it hung all through the fall. She cried in humiliation and didn't jump rope after that. I witnessed this drama unfold but never said a word. The crown hanging in the tree accused me of being weak. I wished I could have saved her but I didn't dare make a move. When I was on the debating team my junior year in high school, I had pretty well nailed the argument against offshore oil drilling but took an unnecessary stab at Brandon Phillips, my opponent. He was not related to Phillips Petroleum but I inferred that he was and that his arguments were self-serving. None of that was true and I knew it wasn't, but I used the accusation to score points with the young judges. He left the stage tense in frustration and anger. I didn't want to apologize and risk a loss so I ignored him. Again, I decided that another's pain wasn't as important as my own comfort, though any comfort I felt was fleeting.

Little guilts built up to major inaction. Passivity, in almost every way except intellectually, became a way of life. I didn't engage the day exuberantly; I gently skimmed over the surface. By doing nothing, I allowed great harm to evolve. Since I couldn't find peace in my heart, I chose to live in my head. I tried to look appropriate and resisted delving deeper inside myself than my surface appearance.

I see now how living that way sucked the life out of Rosemary. She was fresh, excited, and joyous when I married her. She left me disappointed, sad, and crushed. The fact that I can hear her voice now soothes me and now I listen. Now I see how seriously I should take her and how much I need her sensitivity. I will respect my "relationship" with her now even though she's not here physically.

24 Awakening Desires

This week I want to be very attentive to Ellie, partly out of guilt, partly out of family commitment, partly out of my new-found respect for women's feelings. In the morning I stop by her house with rolls and coffee but she's dressed to go to the gym. "Come with me," she insists and so I find myself in my first- ever yoga class. The instructor glides in, a half inch off the ground, turns around, and… it's Lauren. I cough and cough until Ellie pounds on my back, hissing, "She won't bite," but I'm embarrassed to be seen by her here. No matter where I run into her, I'm flustered and she's cool. Why would it be different now?

Today she's dressed in all white — loose, flowing pants which ride low on her bony hips, a short top with long full sleeves hanging freely over her pants. Her hair is pulled back but not tightly. She is a vision, the iconic yoga teacher. I am swept away. I had thought I was drawn to her but now I am overwhelmed with her beauty and her grace.

She speaks. "Um, Nick? You with us? Glad to have you here. We do beginning poses, don't push yourself. Your body knows what it needs."

How right she is. What I would give for an hour with this woman. But Ellie has warned me and I've brought her enough grief. I do dog poses, frog poses, a snake pose, a tree pose, and what I would name an escalator pose though that doesn't sound very yogic. By the end of the class I'm stretched, pulled, extended, and I've breathed with and without awareness. I feel great and surprisingly energized.

Ellie goes to the grocery store so I walk home. Lauren passes me in her tiny green imported car and asks if I want a ride. And, of course, I invite her in and we share barley coffee and chai tea and I listen to her speak about her disciplines — her meditation and yoga and food regimens and walks and her dream journal. And I'm entranced. I say nothing, however. I'm just the polite cousin of her neighbor. I walk her back to her car, promising to be at the next yoga class.

I collapse on the couch and sigh like a teenager. How foolish balding over-weight middle-aged men must appear when love bites them. I'll be careful, though. No one will suspect. I do, however, practice the poses before the next class. I want to impress her.

Lord, save me. I am mortified by my naiveté.

25 Threads of Deception

Since I fully appreciate the gravity of the consequences which ensue when I question breathing humans, I explore the old newspapers in the library for information. The puzzle of Chase and family intrigues me. I search every paper for two months after the accident and learn very little. I do a Subject search entering Chase's name for all dates since 2006. In 2009 he was named vice-president of a small securities firm in New York. In 2010 and 2011 he was indicted but not convicted on five counts of fraud, just what I've been told.

I transfer to the computer and search his name and the name of his company. I find several articles about him with pictures at society functions in this country and in the Orient. He stands with different gorgeous women, none identified. A good-looking guy with a dark moustache, he mingles with the elite. In some photos he stands with politicians, in others with sports figures. In one he golfs in Japan.

A dealer, no doubt. But what is he dealing? When these pictures were taken his wife had died and he had moved away from his son and his father. His life seemed to make a total break in the early months of 2008. No more California or family. But what? International business, traveling, and, I deduce, a high-powered life. Money drips in these pictures. This guy is moving fast. Apparently, his company has an office in Hong Kong which he visits regularly.

Nothing suspicious is suggested but something doesn't fit. I leave the library unsettled but without knowing why. Carolyn walks in quickly, almost running into me. "Hey, Nick, are you OK?" "I don't know. I'm not sure of anything anymore. Except that I do have your first, second, and third place winners. I'll bring them by tomorrow."

"Thanks, you're a gift. This is a major contribution to our branch and you will be remembered in the Friends newsletter. I'll announce it at Rotary, also. We're always interested in service projects and you have given us a professional service! It couldn't have happened with anyone else!"

I appreciate her appreciation but I'm not sure I want the attention. "It couldn't have happened with anyone else." I'm afraid that line could apply to several unsavory events lately. Whoever Edward happens to be might not like the kudos I'm receiving. Why can't I be as invisible as I've been all my life? But nothing seems to be continuing as it was. What was tedious and predictable is anything but. I can't imagine what might come next and I don't want to speculate.

I walk home with my hands in my pockets, studying the ridges in the unpaved streets. I wander through Sweet Springs. It's been dry and the leaves are brittle, crunching under my shoes. It's dark in the trees and a lizard runs across my foot. I trip on an exposed tree root and fall into a piles of leaves and dried muck. I stagger to my feet feeling clumsy in addition to confused. I wipe my hands on my trousers and stick them back in my pockets.

The next morning, I awake with poison oak and without my wallet. Of course, my identity is missing. Perfect.

26 Isolation's Whispers

This is the week I had wanted to be available to Ellie, especially supporting her in attending yoga classes at the gym, but the poison oak decides otherwise. It covers each hand past my wrists, slides down my neck, and even crawls around my lower legs. Itchy, irksome, distracting, annoying. bothersome, and most inconvenient. My escapades are severely curtailed. In addition to not being able to go to the library to deliver the papers, I don't want to touch the papers and give them to Carolyn.

I also don't want to shop or to be seen. A week's hibernation will suit me fine. I draw the blinds, as though darkness will heal me. I don't touch Hildy which frustrates us both. Even within my home I'm limited about what I can do. When darkness settles I leave for a walk, taking a flashlight. I'm glad to breathe the fresh cool air. I walk the blocks Deb and I had covered and I wish she were with me.

"Oh, but I am," I hear inside my head.

Aloud I respond, "I wish you were walking here with me, Deb." It's dark. No one is around. This "conversation" should be safe. "You told me so much and everything you said made sense. I wish I could talk to you some more."

"I'm here now. Go ahead."

"I'm so sorry you died. I feel responsible and I hate myself for putting you in danger."

"It was a pulmonary embolism that did me in, not the thugs. And, actually, from my perspective, it's really OK. Don't worry about it."

"Ellie is so upset. She loved you, still loves you. Losing you was one of the worst things that could have happened to her." "I love her, too. But she'll be fine. Take care of yourself.

You don't look too good right now."

"I don't want to appear in the light, I don't want to be seen or touched, I feel guilty, I'm confused, and I don't trust anyone. Why would you think anything is wrong?"

"Gee, Nick, sounds like a great way to live." "Oh, yeah, and I talk to people who aren't here."

"That's not necessarily bad. Wisdom is where you find it."

"I'll take any help I can get from anywhere. I just don't want to cause more heartache for anyone."

"That is so sweet that you're concerned about other people's feelings!"

"It's taken me a long time to learn." "You won't forget it now."

"Say, do you have anything more to tell me about Julie's accident? Seeing as how nothing worse can happen to you, I don't mind asking."

"There are some details you'll find interesting. All of them are in the library. You've found some but there are more. Spend time there."

Of course, that isn't an option soon, not until the poison oak clears up. But at least I have some direction, if I can call it that. Talking to dead people for direction. Haven't I come a long way from my days as a respected university professor?

27 Whispers in the Dark

Family I can always depend upon even though this is the time I wanted Ellie to depend on me. Graciously, she picks up the papers and delivers them to the library without touching anything in my house. She also picks up my grocery list.

I keep werewolf hours, quarantined during the day, walking and talking with Deb at night. Her reassurance means a lot. After all, if someone you caused to die can forgive you, how bad can things be? I don't go any further with that line of thinking. As I pass Al's house I notice a light on, the first time I've seen any indication of life there in weeks. I hesitate. I hear male voices seemingly working together. After ten minutes I walk on, feeling self-conscious about standing in the dark, staring at a window. When I pass by again on my return trip all the lights are out. What happened? Who was in there?

Reaching home before 11:00, I find the monster raccoon harassing Hildy. He doesn't scare easily but a loud noise with a thrown rock motivates him to amble away.

I turn on television and fall asleep. Within a minute I'm dreaming. I'm walking over green hills of pot plants. There are hills beyond hills beyond hills. The farther I go the louder the chant becomes but I can't decipher the words. Ta-dum, ta-dum, ta-dum, the plants sing. As I walk over the fourth hill the chant becomes deafening. I feel unsafe but not afraid. Until one plant wraps itself around my leg and pulls me down. Other plants pile on top of me and wrestle me until I am entangled and can't move. One wraps around my throat.

I awake in a panic.

28 Temptation

When my poison oak has improved 95%, I walk to the library, avoiding Sweet Springs. I've used the microfilm records, I've used the computer, and, yet, Deb has told me to return. What is it I'm supposed to see? I walk down all the aisles of books, look over the videos, and sit in the magazine section. I flip through the National Geographics — such fine photography, such exotic locations... and I see Chase smiling at me! On the cover of May, 2009, he's wearing a round helmet, like a WWI soldier, and he's walking through waist high grass in Burma. The caption says he's discovered a new plant and received permission to bring seeds out of the country. The feature article reports that his Experimental Botanical Enterprises specializes in unusual plant hybrids from different areas of the world.

Of course, that's what the pot fields are about. He's experimenting with hybridization. And he must be paying off the authorities to let his experiments proceed. Maybe he's even applied for a license under an FDA regulation and all this is legal. Though it certainly is not above board. Why isn't it better supervised? How could Donny and I just walk out to and through the fields? And if Chase has put so much work into this project, why the destruction of my car?

I call Ellie in the afternoon under the pretense of confirming our yoga plans for the next morning. I tell her about the National Geographic article and my suspicions. She confirms that Chase's EBE owns the pot fields and is licensed. She also confirms that Chase spends almost no time here but does employ a business manager who visits from LA once a month. I'm aware that the more she tells me the more danger she may be in (and I realize that phone conversations are not a good idea) so I cut short our talk and agree to see her at yoga class in the morning.

I'm early but I try to act nonchalant. I stretch although it's awkward for me. I attract some glances but the room fills and the women chatter. I will never understand women's need to talk so much. They talk about what is, and what isn't but might be, or what isn't and probably won't be, or what happened a few years ago, or the dinner they made last night. They squeal when someone wears a bright new headband or leg warmers that match wrist bands. They notice haircuts and ankle bracelets and all of them have painted toe nails. Not just pale pink but purple or green or dark red. This is an entire subculture to which I am not privy, maybe no male is, but I'm getting an up-close glimpse here. I'll observe and learn.

Lauren starts the class before Ellie arrives. Today she is wearing sky blue — tights, leotard, warm ups, and my heart pounds. What power does this woman have over me? I'll be cool, though, and no one will know. I twist and lean and reach and wonder how anyone does this. Maybe male bodies aren't made for yoga. Of course, mine isn't made for basketball or football or baseball, either. I walk and that's the extent of my interest in physical activity.

I stare at the clock the last 20 minutes which isn't good for my neck and spine. I will devise a plan for hanging out with Lauren that isn't so demanding of my body. I think that moving from a sedentary life to an active life so quickly could be very bad for my heart. I'll reconsider this fitness fervor.

As I walk out of class I notice that Ellie hasn't made it at all. Oh, well, she's busy. I walk home and, again, Lauren offers me a ride and, again, she comes in. Today, however, I sit on the couch with her and ask her about Greg and the kids. How unavailable is she, I want to ascertain.

She says all the right things initially — a wonderful marriage, bright boys, hard-working, in college now. They left last year and her life has adjusted to an empty house. Greg travels for business part of every week but they are close, they've been together since they were in high school and, well, things change but still it's great, great, just different.

And I move two inches closer and put my arm on the back of the sofa. And I listen and I empathize and I understand the way no desperate man ever has and it works.

Within the hour we're rolling in bed. And when she says

she feels guilty, I listen and empathize and understand and we roll around some more. Greg is gone for a few days and I promise I will do nothing to interfere with her wonderful relationship and we kiss and she doesn't want to leave and I don't want her to leave. So we kiss some more.

The clock moves into the afternoon and I bring us sandwiches we eat in bed. We snuggle and snooze and when evening falls she insists on leaving. I don't stop her and I tell her I will never make her life difficult but that I find her to be inspiring and lovely and compelling and beautiful and any time she has I am available to her. We kiss some more and she walks into the night. I nap, sleeping three hours without moving. My body is more relaxed than it has been in a very long time.

The phone rings about 8:00 p.m., awakening me. I hear Ellie's voice on the answering machine. She is not OK.

29 Pursuit of Truth

I lunge at the phone when I discern distress but Ellie hangs up before I can grab it. I call her at home but no answer. Apparently, she's elsewhere. I call her cell and leave a message. I'm bothered. I throw dinner together and talk with Hildy while we eat.

"So, anything new with you, girl? That monster raccoon may like you, but I infer that you're not interested, huh? Good judgment. I don't know that he has anything to offer, not anything that you need. I, however, hope I have just what Lauren needs and wants. We'll see. It was a great start and if anything comes of it, that will be terrific and, if not, I have some memories. Isn't life surprising?"

And I go out for my walk with Deb. After a block I can feel her come and I ask if she saw what today brought.

"I did, indeed. You had fun, huh? And about time! You've been too proper for too long. Let go and live a little," and she chuckles at her reference to living. Somehow dead she seems more grounded than when she was alive.

"I found information about Chase in the library but there's still something missing about Julie's accident. I don't know why it happened or what the aftermath was."

"Keep searching," is all she says. No matter how I try to entice her, I can't elicit more "conversation" so I walk in silence, looking at the lighted houses with closed windows.

Al's house is not lit but some rearranging has been done on his front porch. Boxes are stacked and folded lawn chairs lean against the walls. Something is in progress.

I return home, committed again to searching the library for information about Julie's accident. Chase was a presence here and I know there is more to learn about him, but the details of Julie's accident, especially the weeks and months after her accident elude me. Was there an investigation?

Would Al and Chase let it go without one? What about Donny? Where is he now and what happened to him then? This week will be dedicated to answering the Slate family questions.

I try to concentrate on business but as I drift off my thoughts return to Lauren. Her coconut shampoo scent clings to the pillow case. I inhale her deeply and hug the pillow. It was good to have a woman in my life, or if not entirely in my life, in my bed, even for a few hours. I'm happy.

30 Uncovering the Past

Carolyn eyes me questioningly when I enter the library. "Poison oak cleared up?"

"Totally healed. Isn't the body wonderful?"

She maintains her gaze without smiling. Does she know about Lauren? How could she? I have nothing to feel guilty about. She doesn't intimidate me, I tell myself, but clearly, she does. I stumble over my words and trip on the carpet.

"Just investigating that old accident. A piece is missing. I don't know where to find it but I'm guessing that a clue resides in this building."

"Good luck," is her only response and she turns her back and walks into her office.

From my previous visits, I know that the local newspaper holds nothing of interest and a traffic accident wouldn't be reported in the LA paper. There has to be another source. Maybe a local magazine article about Chase or his business or Al. I look through all the Los Osos Journal magazines in 1999, 2000. 2001, 2002, 2003, and 2004 when Chase left.

Citizens are featured each month with a detailed article about their pasts, their interests, and their activities in this area. The usual human interest palaver which I can do without. I didn't realize how many people live here with whom I have so little in common. (I fear that would be true in any town, though.) The magazines paint a picture of Small Town, USA, that fairly glows with healthy well-adjusted folks who want nothing more than to picnic with their families and participate in the community Fourth of July parade. The celebrities-for-the- month bake pies, do woodworking, raise bees, and paint watercolors of Morro Rock. I squirm as I read. But I'm on a mission to discover some history about the Slate family and I will not be diverted.

Nothing in '99 or 2000 or 2001 so I look further back and find an article in 1989. A picture of Chase, Julie holding baby Donny, and Al standing in the background over the headline, The Slate Clan. No mention is made of Chase's mother. But pictures of Chase and Julie's wedding in 1986, Chase in his high school football uniform in 1977, and Al receiving a Chamber of Commerce award in 1965 border the article.

The Slate family had moved to this area in the late 1800s when Grandfather Slate bought cattle and three hundred acres. His empire grew over four decades until he left an operation twice that size to his son, Frederick, in 1919. Drought, poor management, and bad investments during the Depression decimated the family fortune until the acreage was sold to pay debts after the war in 1948.

At that time Al had returned from the Pacific theater, convinced of the opportunities for trade with the Orient. Nothing of that ilk existed here and he developed a thriving venture selling exotic foreign teas, oils, spices, decorative items, household articles, and clothing. He expanded his sales along the west coast, opening a store in Los Angeles and one in San Francisco.

Business mushroomed but his interest in it waned after his heart attack in 1983. Too much success, the doctor had said, according to the article, and Al gratefully ceded his business to his son, Chase. I fill in the next lines with the information from Deb — Al's stipulation that Chase marry a local girl and live here. Apparently in 1988, Chase and Julie and baby Donny were doing their impression of a well-adjusted middle-class family and no one had any reason to doubt that it would continue.

Al, however, had shifted his interest from business and making money before his heart attack to the sewer controversy afterward. One might think he would choose something less stressful like painting watercolors but perhaps that was too tame for him after traveling around the world and developing a successful international career. I surmise that he was accustomed to trusting his vision, his ingenuity, and his business sense. According to the article he studied soil reports, engineering projections, population surveys, partially treated-sewage evaluations, bio-solvent permits, and aquifers. He developed a well-constructed position that the sandy soil in Los Osos will not support a sewer nor is a sewer appropriate.

After the Journal article about the Slate family, Al's arguments opposing the sewer were printed. He had written:

> The plan to put a central collection system accumulating raw sewage in a gravity structure and put the effluent from the wastewater treatment plant into four acres of a large housing development between it and the bay is not a good idea because of problems which don't exist now but could develop. The biggest problem is the random spill of raw sewage, for instance, out of manhole covers, from broken pipes, or as a result of an earthquake. It's not *if* overflow will occur, it's *when*.

> There are numerous reasons why there will be spills from a wastewater treatment plant. This plant is estimated to receive 1,400,000 gallons per day (gpd) in dry weather and 1,700,000 gpd in wet weather. It was intended to put the effluent into an eight acre parcel, alternating four acres with another four over a certain time period (two days, for instance), transferring back and forth.

> The engineer's term for what that would cause is liquification. Sand underneath the sewage liquifies, turning into quicksand. The raw sewage must be pumped out of big tanks and hauled away. Permits must be obtained from the Water Control Board to spread 80% moisture bio-solids (sludge) from the sewage point. 80% moisture sludge should be handled the same as hazardous waste — in lined ponds to keep the material from getting into the ground water.

> A permit to spread bio-solids of less than 50% moisture requires a machine called a scarab,

named after the Egyptian beetle. These scarabs are in an air-conditioned enclosure stirring the 80% bio-solids with other bio-solids (50%) so they will rot adequately to sell as fertilizer.

Regulations say that anything over 50% moisture must be held in a lined pond. Then it can be pumped into a tank trunk, tested, and disposed of it in a sanitary method. Supposedly, the bio-solids would be sterilized before leaving the plant, allowing it to be spread on an open field. However, with 80% moisture the pathogens will begin to grow again. They are very toxic.

Besides problems with the bio-solids, there is always the possibility that the hillside could burst. There are methods for keeping the septic tanks in place and handling spills, a step/steg system to catch effluents — step being a pressurized septic tank, steg a gravity septic effluent collection system. Hydrologists estimate that the water would not get any closer to the surface than 30 feet; however, they have planned five harvest wells on the way down the hill to take care of the subwater from the aquifer. They need to keep it dry so it won't discharge and wash houses down the hill, perhaps drowning somebody in his sleep with quicksand.

Problems which may be created are raw sewage spills, effluent problems, what to do with the sludge, and unforeseen laws coming on the books which won't allow anybody to transport their bio-solids from the waste water treatment plants to another county for disposal. A suspected problem is nitrate from the septic tanks polluting the ground water.

In a county funded report, six professionals specializing in soil science and water treatment stated that Los Osos is built on a sand dune which is a natural filter which denitrifies the water. Most of the denitrification takes place close to the surface. However, nitrates in the soil keep denitrifying all the way down to the ground water which is totally saturated sand. A stratum of clay is a natural aquatard. The water won't run through the aquatard. So, the logical conclusion is that water from septic tanks is not polluting the ground water. Therefore, the primary reason for building a sewer is invalid.

Al's proposal continued with considerations about ESHA regulations protecting the kangaroo rat in one proposed sewer site. Another proposed site was deemed unacceptable because it was too near the community center, the library, and the Catholic Church. A consideration which would affect everyone in town, and maybe in the county, was affordability — a proposed sewer would cost more than $200/month per household in Los Osos indeterminately. And then the streets in town were mentioned. None is paved and apparently sewer proponents vowed to block any move to pave, install curbs or street lights until the sewer controversy is settled since sewer excavation will destroy the streets anyway.

Today the debate still rages and Al's work is still cited as the most complete exposition of the opposition. Thus, Al carved a place for himself as Outspoken Sewer Opponent, his next role in the community. Apparently, as his health allows he still attends sewer meetings.

Now I grasp the history of the Slate family and their impact on the community for over 100 years. I decide to attend a sewer meeting. Surely, there I will meet opponents with strong opinions, citizens with a long-time involvement in this issue, and perhaps someone who has known Al and family. I need another informant who doesn't know me and doesn't yet distrust me.

31 Voices and the Cesspool

Sewer meetings are advertised on makeshift signs staked in corner lots. The sewer opponents hope to gain support for their cause and encourage everyone to attend. I go on Tuesday evening.

The room slowly fills with the most individual, self-contained folks I've seen. These are not the people who hang out at the library — quiet, focused, cerebral. These are colorful characters — long beards, long hair, plaid shirts, work boots, women in long skirts. They wander in singly, seriously, not speaking, each carrying papers in a book bag or satchel or brief case. They sit in the rows of folding chairs, filling the first rows first unlike most meetings I attend where the back seats fill initially. A microphone stands in the center at the front and people choose numbers to speak. The meeting was advertised to start at "7ish" but the moderator announces at 7:20 that speakers will each have three minutes and please, please respect that time limit.

The first gentleman looks to be over 70 with hair curling over his collar. His worn brown jacket frays at the wrists. He speaks precisely, focusing his light eyes on his paper, up at the panel of five Board members, back to his paper. He makes three technical points and concludes that the sewer project should be abandoned. He thanks the Board for their attention as he sits down.

Speaker #2, dressed casually, speaks with energy, punching the air with his right hand while his left hand crunches several pages. He looks to be about 50, without anger but with conviction. He also concludes that the sewer project should be forgotten for entirely different reasons. The third speaker could have been a retired school teacher — proper, soft-spoken, demure in her long sleeves and long black skirt. I can imagine her walking out of the pages of Little Women.

She, too, thanks the Board for its attention and walks back to her seat with her eyes on the floor before her time has elapsed.

I realize that I am focusing on the speakers, not on their messages. Of course, all the messages are the same — the sewer must be blocked. But each citizen contributes his own flair to that dictum. I especially enjoy the fourth speaker, a man in his mid60s with dozens of papers and a black patch over his left eye. His slight accent sounds Eastern European. He gestures slowly with long pointed fingers which have long nails. His collar is buttoned to his chin. A sense of artistry dominates his manner. This is the man I seek. I notice where he sits as I listen to the next eighteen speakers. I mentally checkmark a young construction worker, the middle-aged woman, and the artist as possible contacts. I look forward to the break, before the Board speaks, to approach my new "friends." I feel a bit deceitful and just a tad guilty but then it is not necessarily true that I am the harbinger of doom, no matter what Elizabeth and Les and a few others (including myself) think. Tonight I am just another Los Osos concerned citizen fulfilling a civic duty.

I maintain that air at the break when I mill about as attendees drink strong coffee and agree with each other. I encounter the construction worker as he bites into a donut. While his mouth is full, I open with, "What an interesting town meeting. I'm new here but I certainly appreciate the depth of commitment the citizens exhibit. The sewer really draws some reactions, doesn't it?"

"We've been talking and planning and sometimes screaming about this damned sewer for 20 years! It's the local project. I don't think anyone really expects a decision to be made. What would we fight about then?" He chuckles and picks up another donut.

The fact that he is easy-going and can laugh at community antics tells me I probably won't get any insight into hidden layers of intrigue that I suspect exist. I smile, tip my cap and look for another conversation. The school teacher sits quietly by herself so I approach her. Immediately, her eyes widen and she drops her pen. I retrieve it and hand it to her, our fingers touching in the exchange. Hers are colder than the evening air warrants.

"What do you think will come of the meeting tonight? I haven't attended a meeting before but feelings seem to be running high. Can we expect a concensus, do you think?"

"I don't mean to be rude but, sir, I don't know you. This is our concern. Why are you here? What's your interest?"

I am taken aback by her directness and her personalizing what I had hoped would be a genial non-encounter. I stammer my apology, having no prepared response to this line of questioning. I'm knocked off balance.

"I'm new to this town but now I live here and I want to be involved. This affects me and I want to understand the situation." By the time I finish speaking, two other women are listening. Their eye contact is unswerving and unnerving.

The shorter and plumper smiles and extends her hand. "Glad to meet you. I'm Esther Davis. We want to welcome new blood." She laughs and glances at the still seated third speaker. "Opponents sometimes send spies so we are wary of faces we don't recognize. Other than that, we're truly are a great group!" I laugh with them and take two steps backward, trying to avoid their circle. Unaware, I step into the path of a woman in a white nylon jacket barreling through the crowd in a motorized wheelchair operated by a set of controls on the right hand rest. I've seen these wheelchairs advertised on TV for seniors needing to get around without a car. I am grateful that I didn't land in her lap, having my foot run over being a small enough penalty.

"Listen, son," she booms, "if you really want to know what's going on here, ask me. I can tell you the ins and the outs no one wants you to know and I know where the bodies are buried!" Clearly, she is the person I need to meet. Did she grasp what she had just volunteered for? I won't tell her but I will follow as closely as she'll permit. While the others laugh and shush her, I bend down and offer my hand.

"Nick Sanders, new to town."

"Madelyn B," she replies. "Call me Maddy, everyone does. Honey, I've lived in this backwater town for 48 years and no one gets anything past me. These politicians with their propositions and their proposals and their plans and their debates… it's all smoke. No substance. They're not letting the sewer go through. Hell, they don't want a sewer. They just want to keep us riled up so we don't see the real action. The more we wrangle, the better for them." And the meeting is called to order with the pounding of the gavel.

"May I sit with you, Maddy? I can learn a lot by listening to you." That was honest, right? Nothing to offend.

"Sure, honey, let's move up to the front row. They're going to hear from me now!" She is loaded and ready. My heart races. I watch the drama unfold. Before the gavel lies quiet, Maddy is speaking. Her sandpaper voice offsets the appearance of vulnerability from sitting in a wheelchair. A Texas twang, more pronounced than I had noticed in our conversation, dominates the room. She's performing! Some days my luck is so good I can't believe it.

"My dear Board Chairman and respected Board members, honored Los Osos citizens, and all concerned people here tonight, on this propitious occasion let's not waste time with the nickel and dime petty tussling we usually go through." If she had the chorus she deserves, voices at this point would chime, "Well said, well said!" But she continues without vocal support. "We know, and I do mean we, you and I, all of us know, that the real issue is not the sewer. We've never had a sewer, for Christ's sake, and we've done fine. Why have we let Them set us against each other? Why are we fighting? We've lived here forever and we're neighbors and friends. Why, Helen, weren't we all with you when Joe died? We brought casseroles and invited you over. And Paul, weren't we there for you when you fell off the roof of your garage and your arm was in a sling for two months? Don't we take care of each other?" At this there is a rumbling of assent.

"Darn right, we do! We're in this together and we always have been. So, how can we let Them tear us apart and incite this small-time warfare? Don't let Them do this! This is our town! Let's keep it the way we've always loved it, the way we know we want it to remain!" And now there are shouts of "Hear, hear!" Aristophanes couldn't have written this episode more convincingly. I am enjoying myself immensely.

A man's voice from the rear interjects, "Sit down, Maddy. We know how you feel but you can't stop progress. Get over it. Everyone needs a sewer. This is our opportunity. Don't bury your heads in the sand," he proclaims as he addresses the crowd. At this point fifteen voices rise, hands and arms fly, and the gavel clangs into action.

Maddy turns toward me, raises her shoulders, and exclaims, "Ain't it fun? It's not going to get any better than this so let's go find us a bar stool and I'll fill in the blanks." She whips her chair around and zips out the back door as I scramble to keep up with her. She is half-way down the block by the time I hit the street and she waves her long white scarf, indicating the saloon on the corner.

Inside the Merrimaker I can barely see. Already she is chatting with the bartender whom she introduces to me as Ralph as she sips a Heineken. The Beach Boys wail, "Ba-ba-ba, ba-barber Ann,"and we are transported to the late 60s.

Life was uncomplicated then. No commitments, no major disappointments yet. Life still held promise. The Bad Guys were easily identified and nobly resisted. We were on the side of right and justice. Choices were clear. I feel invigorated just sitting here in the darkness with my new friend. Maddy and I speak a similar, if not identical, language.

"So, Nick, what do you think of our little sewer controversy?" To myself I think it's a Greek tragedy replete with passion and fiery rhetoric. Maddy continues without hesitation, "And all this about shit, for heaven's sake. We're fighting about shit!" She bursts into a belly laugh that fills the bar.

"You just come from a meeting, Mads?" A man's voice rises from the back of the room.

"How'd you guess, Clarence?"

"You're never so happy as when you piss off those geezers and run out. You're a devil, Mads. When they goin' to catch onto your game?"

"Don't you go tellin' my secrets, Clarence. We're having us a good time, just the way it is."

"OK, Mads, if that's what you want. Beats me how you

escape lynching with all the trouble you stir up."

"Don't worry 'bout me. No one would dare target me. Remember Jasper? In the early 80s? Haven't seen him lately, have ya? Nope and you won't, not ever again. He took it into his head to teach me a lesson and, boy, did he get an education!" Everyone laughs at this implicit threat. What happened? I'll ask her later when I know her better.

She's finishing her second beer and beckoning for a third. This woman can belt them down. I don't try to keep up with her; my first sweats on the table.

"So, Maddy," I begin but she speaks without acknowledging me. "There's a few things you need to understand about our little cesspool of a town. See, we look fine on the surface, great at times. We have this unbeatable location in the cleanest part of this fine state. You can surf, you can fish, you can hike in the hills. But you can't live a normal life here." She sits back in her chair and takes a swig from her bottle, setting it down hard. I don't take my eyes from her face. What an incredible statement. I open my mouth to speak but she's not paying attention to me.

"This quaint charming sweet little town is a bubbling cauldron of mishap and mayhem and mischief and worse. Don't be taken in. Don't believe anything you're told. Trust no one. And for Chrissake, don't be stupid. Watch your back." Her last words slur and her head falls to the side as her eyes close. Within a minute she's snoring loudly. I look around, confused, but Ralph is already pushing her wheelchair behind some curtains.

"I'll take it from here, son. Why don't you just head on home now? Maddy'll be fine. I'll see to her." "I'd like to talk to her again. Do you..."

"As I said, son, why don't you head home? Now." He pulls my arm roughly and shows me the door.

Back on the street the fog, wet and cold, kisses my cheeks. I can't see three feet in front of me. Or in back. So I'm not expecting the blow to the back of my head that lays me out flat.

32 Daylight

I see the sun before I open my eyelids and I feel its hot needles pierce my eyeballs. Am I Lawrence of Arabia? I turn my head to the left hoping for shade but my skull threatens to erupt so I lie flat again. I realize I am in a bed and my head is supported by a pillow but it isn't my bed or my pillow. I don't want to open my eyes. The pounding of a giant hammer on a metal anvil inside my head makes it impossible to think. I pray for death to relieve me.

Death doesn't respond and in 20 minutes my bladder forces me to open my eyes to find a toilet. I realize I'm in Ellie's spare bedroom. How did I get here? I stumble five feet to the guest bathroom and throw up before I am in the door. I sink to my knees and fall on my right side.

Please allow me to die, God. I've never prayed before but I can't withstand this pain, so please, show me mercy and let me go. Ellie gasps as she rounds the corner and sees me and the mess I have made in my first minutes of wakefulness. "Nick, let me help you!"

"I must get to the toilet," I plead fearing it may already be too late. She pulls my arm but can't move me. I crawl through the vomit to the toilet bowl where I throw up again. I tug at my pants and sit with my head in my hands. This may be the lowest point in my life. I have never felt worse physically. Every inch of my body and my head aches. I can't remember anything that would explain this misery. Sitting on the toilet, I lean against the wall.

"Nick, are you OK?" She knows I'm not so I don't bother to reply. She wipes the floor and hands me a half glass of water. I am grateful to rinse my mouth. In two minutes, I am ready to stand and to allow her to escort me back to bed. I collapse on top of the covers and raise my arm over my eyes. When Los Osos needs light, it doesn't get it and now would be a good time for the usual clouds and fog. Considerately, she pulls the shades and runs to the kitchen where the tea pot is shrieking so that I think the top of my head will erupt.

She returns with red tea and I tell myself, No more vomiting. I put my hands on my head to quiet the pounding and feel a bulging bandage.

She whispers, "Les called me at midnight, said he'd been tipped that a drunk was lying on the sidewalk in front of the saloon. When he saw it was you, he told me to take care of you so that he wouldn't have to file a report. A couple of the men from the bar moved you here and I bandaged your bleeding head. You had a bad fall. Let's get you to the emergency room. Can you walk? Do you want some toast?"

I don't remember anything and I don't think I can walk. I feel weak and uninterested in food. I hope that if I lie still enough the pain will stop. But it doesn't. When I don't move or open my eyes, Ellie suggests, "I'll call Doc Johnson and see if he'll stop by. He's retired so he's usually available." I am mollified when she leaves me alone.

I must have drifted off. When I awaken the doctor is taking my pulse and speaking gently. "You've suffered a concussion. Someone took a very heavy object to your head and there is swelling inside your skull. It's serious but not with longstanding consequences. However, for a few weeks you're going to need lots of bed rest. I'll give you a prescription for a painkiller. That must really hurt. Don't let the pain get ahead of you. Take a pill every 3- 4 hours. Don't be brave. Just cooperate and rest and let your body heal itself."

I swallow one blue pill without raising my head more than two inches off the pillow. I am so grateful for his kindness and his competence that I try to smile. The pain is too great and instead I drift into unconsciousness and some evil dreams. I sleep and wake and sleep and dream for the rest of the day. I forget who I am and where I am and what all this is about. Not that I ever really knew the latter.

Awakening after dark without the throbbing in my head is such a relief that I feel happy. The house is still and dark but I can hear Ellie in her bedroom. What time is it? What day is it? I stand up shakily and wander toward the smell of tomato vegetable soup in the kitchen. A small covered pot on the stove holds just enough soup for me and I eat at the table alone. Ellie comes out as I finish. "You look better than you have in a couple days. How're you

feeling?" At that moment I realize that after health, family is the most precious gift in the world. I've never loved anyone more than I love Ellie right now, in her nightgown with cold cream on her face and her hair pinned up. She sits with me and I give thanks that I'm not alone. Having my cousin with me and feeling no pain in my body or my head seems like a miracle. Nothing else is important.

33 Trust No One

Back at my house a few days later, reality gels. I still need the pain pills, I sleep long hours, my head is sore and my memory shot, especially short term. I cook simple meals for myself and Hildy and straighten my papers but I don't dare walk alone outside or drive. I am forced to stay indoors and I am fine with that. I read and watch TV and think or daydream. Mostly I want to heal. Doc Johnson was right. Healing is slow.

I make notes and draw maps and try to connect the disparate facts I have gathered. I sketch a picture of the town with the pot fields out by the old train station. The cemetery is on the other side of town. The library and the proposed sewer site are in the middle of the page, not too far from Sweet Springs and the Saloon. Los Osos Valley Road runs past the town, east and west. Everything is in relative walking distance if you have good shoes and strong legs.

Closer to my house is the gym, the grocery store, and Al's home. Someone had challenged me or my car at my home, at the pot fields by the train station, in the writing from the library, in the cemetery, and at the Merrimaker. I had done myself in at Sweet Springs by falling. Presumably, all these facts, except maybe the latter, are connected. I say "presumably" with my fall because I haven't retrieved my wallet yet and that makes me suspicious.

And then there is Lauren. I sincerely want to believe that she is not part of this town but the fact is she lives here and has for years. Maddy said, "This little town is a bubbling cauldron of mishap." Elizabeth hates me, Deb is dead, Ellie is frightened, Les is annoyed, Carolyn is wary and distrustful (I infer), Lauren is wonderful (I want to believe), and Maddy is a font of knowledge but an alcoholic to the core. Does she know what happened to me that night we spoke? Her words come back to me in snippets — "cesspool of a town… you can't live a normal life here… we look good on the surface…" and, finally, "trust no one." Sadness floods me with the last.

I want to trust Ellie because she's my cousin and Lauren because I want to love her and Maddy because I like the way she thinks. I don't want to be alone in this. But I fear that the truth is that I am very much alone. Something's going on here and I may be the only one who can understand it.

The attacks against me have become more potent. I feel an increasing urgency to decipher this mystery. At the same time my head hurts and I can't concentrate. Deb would know what to say. But she doesn't offer a thought. Hildy nudges my hand. I look around the room. What am I not seeing?

34 Anger Sinks In

I spend the next two weeks inside, in bed or close to my bed. I watch television during the day which I've never done. The plethora of reality shows makes me think that the world must be nuts if what is shown on TV is reality.

I wake and sleep and watch TV and dream and I don't know where one activity ends and another begins. Day, dusk, night, dawn, noon, twilight, clouds, fog, everything is fuzzy. And I don't try to make sense of anything. This is not the time for dark outlines or clear separations. I drift in and out and upside down and I tumble and fall and hover and bob and whatever exists this moment is and I don't have to understand. Am I hallucinating? Doesn't matter. I move through time and time moves through me and nothing is as I've known it and that's OK. I just am.

Some evenings Ellie shows up carrying Chinese food in small white cardboard containers with wire handles. I encourage her to talk and to tell me about the world in which I'm not really interested. But I like the human contact and I want to practice acting normal.

She kisses me on the cheek when she leaves and asks if I need anything, and always I say, "Just your good wishes, my favorite Cousin." And she promises to return and I float back into my reverie, not discerning or discriminating, just pleasantly drifting. I lose track of the days, sometimes turning on the television to verify the day and date. Then I turn off the sound and watch the muted people move and gesture. They appear nonsensical. Or is it the world that's nonsensical? Definitely my world is.

Ten altered-state days later and I awaken on Saturday morning, back and alert and almost ready to resume life as a human. I feel like I've returned from a space vacation where I encountered nothing I have known and where I couldn't be as I always have been and now I'm back but I'm not as I was or who I was. I don't know why I say that or how to distinguish me now from me then but I know something has changed.

I walk into the sunlight which, in itself, is jarring. I haven't been outside or breathed fresh air or seen fellow planetary inhabitants for almost two weeks. Is this world new? Or am I? I walk slowly to the bay and back passing Al's house which has a For Rent sign in the front yard. Jimmy rides by on his bike, tinkling his bells when he sees me.

"Where you been? I ain't seen you for the longest… You OK? My Mom said maybe you had finally got yourself killed but I didn't believe it. I knew you wouldn't do that."

"Hey, Jim. Good to see you, too. I've been a little bit sick but now I'm fine and rarin' to go! So, you tell me, what's been going' on? I notice the For Rent sign in Al's yard. Did he move away?"

"Well, my Mom says it was getting dangerous here so his son came and moved all his stuff away last week. That's what my Mom says."

So, Chase has been in town. This is big news. Something serious must be going on. Chase doesn't do anything without purpose or so I imagine from the reading I've done about him. If he wants Pops out of Dodge, he's trying to escape something he's not controlling that he fears. He's growing pot here openly, perhaps practicing hybridization to make it more powerfully intoxicating. He must own the police department, such as it is. He has more money than anyone in town. What could he fear?

And then I hear Maddy's voice, "I know where the bodies are buried." I must find Maddy. I don't want to drive yet but I do want to go out after dark tonight so I call Ellie. She gasps when she hears that I want to return to the scene of my ambush. She protests but I promise that I won't drink and that we won't stay long. She has serious misgivings which I appreciate but, in the end, she agrees to go with me.

We walk into the Merrymaker before 8:00; only one couple sits in the back booth. Ralph washes glasses and looks startled when we approach him. "What can I get for you two this evening?"

"Just some information for me. Anything for you, Ellie?"

"I serve drinks. I don't dispense information. I don't know

a thing and I don't say what I do know."

"I was severely hurt in front of your fine establishment two weeks ago and I think you know who did it. I think you know all about it and, maybe, you played a part in the escapade, a very big part." I can feel Ellie's anxiety as she places her hand on my arm on the bar.

"Come on, Nick, let's go. Don't do this. Please, Nick."

I pull away from her and walk around the corner of the bar to the service bar with the moveable counter. I move it up so there is no impediment separating Ralph and me.

"I need some answers. I only have a few questions and we can do this quickly and easily or… but let's not go there. As Ellie says, we're all friends and we can work this out." My heart pounds in my chest.

Ralph motions me to a table and he follows. "OK, I'll give you five minutes but then you must promise to leave and never come back here. I don't ever want to see your face in my bar again."

"It's a deal," I agree. "Just tell me who knocked me out. You pulled me out the door. Were you working with someone who took over when you tossed me on the sidewalk?"

"I swear, I had no idea anyone was out there. I knew I wanted you out of my bar 'cause Maddy was talking too much. She tells secrets that folks around here don't want told. She wakes up the next morning and don't remember a thing but everyone's heard her. She's the only one doesn't know what happened and she's glad to talk again. She don't realize that she's getting people hurt. Look what happened to you. I don't know who did it, but I bet it was 'cause of your interest in Maddy's stories."

"I don't believe that you don't know who was involved. I think you know exactly who decked me and you knew he was planning on doing it and you helped him. I think you're in on this all the way." He stammers but I raise my voice.

"I'm not an idiot. You may have the Sheriff on your side, carting me away without investigating, but you will not dismiss me. I could have died! I'm still suffering and who knows how long that will continue! You owe me big time,

Buddy, and don't think I will forget it!"

At that moment Les walks in and sits down with us. "You boys holding a meeting?"

"Why, Les," I say. "We're reliving the good old days, like the night two weeks ago when we were both here but only one of us walked away. You were here that night, too, weren't you, Les? What a coincidence! And we're all here again tonight! This is just grand!"

Les speaks immediately, "Now I don't want you gettin' no bright ideas, Nick. Let it go. You're recovering just fine. Doc Johnson thinks you'll be good as new. Let's just get on with life and move forward."

"No, I need some answers. I've seen the pot fields, I've had a rock thrown through my window, I've had my car set on fire, and I've been assaulted. I deserve some answers. How does everything fit together? Oh, yes, and I heard Chase was in town last week. Now isn't that an interesting development? What do you make of that, Les? You're the Sheriff. Our safety is in your hands. What guidance can you give us?" I know I am pushing it. Ellie fidgets. I want Ralph and Les to squirm, too. This isn't only my problem.

But it takes less than a minute for Les to assure me that, indeed, it is. He rises to his full height, thrusts out his chest, and declares, "Nick, either you go along with us or you leave. This is our town. We're happy. We do things our way and we get along just fine. Now if that's such a big problem, well, there are about a million other towns you might like better.

"Oh, yes," he continues, "and don't threaten me. I don't cotton to that kind of treatment. Now I'm declaring this bar closed to the public as of right now. So, get yourself out of here and you and Ellie watch where you're walking 'cause we sure don't want any more accidents, do we?" And I am as rudely ushered out as I had been the first time.

35 Lost Connections

Ellie is nearly hysterical when we return to her house. "Nick, what are you doing? Do you want to get us killed? I have never seen anyone make enemies faster than you do!"

"Don't you see, Cuz? They are both in on it!"

"In on what? I swear you are losing any semblance of sanity. Just relax. Don't antagonize everyone. Play nice. You can do that, can't you?"

"Play nice? They knock me out, they blow up my car, they write threatening notes in the library papers…" But I hadn't mentioned that before and Ellie looks up, startled. "What threatening papers?"

"When I was reading the entries for the writing contest, I read one that described my death. Well-written, too, but I didn't choose it."

"Be serious, Nick."

"Believe me, I am very, very serious. And did I tell you about seeing my baseball cap in a new grave at the cemetery?"

"Nick, get hold of yourself! This is way too crazy! You are more bonkers every day. This has got to stop. Now we are going to live a normal quiet life without accusing everyone of plotting to do you in and we will smile at our neighbors and we won't have any more crazy talk. Do you understand?" She is using her oldercousin babysitter-in-charge voice. And I realize I've lost her, too.

36 The Ground is Stone

Sitting in my home over the next few days, I feel more alone than I ever have. Losing Ellie's friendship and the trust that she would always be there for me splits my chest open. I don't love Ellie any less and I don't hate these townspeople. I feel like an alien. How can I think so differently from all of them? How can the world look one way to me and the opposite to them? I feel like a puzzle piece in the wrong box. I have no hope of communication with anyone here. And I can't turn off my brain. Something pulls me forward. Something demands that I be involved even though everyone loudly repels my incursions. I am out of step but I must keep marching.

As I sit on my couch with Hildy snoring on the floor, I think about what it is to be human. Chase's experience must be 180 degrees different from mine. He has money and power and, from the pictures in the mags, I guess he also has beautiful women and respect. Does he feel uncomfortable inside himself? Does he wrestle with guilt or despair or, yes, loneliness? My experience of loneliness is profound but it can be met and satisfied. It doesn't seem that that will happen soon but I know it's possible. But what about Chase? Is he lonely the way I am? Does he need friends and confidants? Does he want to talk in the middle of the night? I can't imagine it.

My fantasies about Chase all have to do with power and invulnerability. Is it just me? Do I need to believe that he is so different from me? Although, I must admit, I am different from the me who drove into Los Osos a few months ago. I have layers of feeling I've not known before. However, I believe that Chase is not crippled with feelings, not slowed by conflicts. I imagine him to be decisive, cold, and invincible. I wonder if he can make decisions without caring or hesitation. I don't call that strength and I don't call my new-found sensitivity weakness. We're living at different poles but I believe that I may be able to understand him. I know he'll never understand me. In that way I have an advantage.

Surely, he and I must have something in common. Neither one of us fits in here — I because I'm actively not wanted and he because he has greater ambitions that pull him away. We've both lost our wives. I didn't want to lose Rosemary. I don't know about Chase and Julie. We both have family who live in Los Osos. Ellie is perturbed now but I know she'll recover. Chase may secretly be involved with his father and his son. Otherwise, we're both loners, doing life in our own peculiar ways.

My brain cramps. I wander into the kitchen, willing to clean as a distraction from the tangle of thoughts I can't sort. A tiny mouse scampers across the floor and dives under the baseboard. Another consideration for tomorrow. Suddenly, I'm tired and confused. I lie on the couch and turn on the TV. Within two minutes I'm dreaming.

I'm climbing near the top of a snow-dusted mountain. I'm alone and I'm carrying a flag on a pole. I need to plant it at the peak. I'm breathing hard and my chest aches. I must complete my mission but my body cries in agony. I slip and fall and resume my climb. Night is descending. I must secure the flag and then hurry down the mountain. I'm not safe. I circle the peak but the ground is stone. I can't force the pole into the rock. It's essential that I claim this mountain with the flag. I don't know how and I'm getting desperate. Darkness blankets me and the wind screams and blows me off my feet. I tumble. I can't catch hold of anything which will right me. I lose the flag and I roll and fall and realize I've left the mountain and I'm falling in air. I don't panic, though. I quit struggling and my fall slows.

A giant bluebird flies by and carries me by the neck of my jacket to her nest, a huge pine needle bowl in an immense pine tree.

In it are red easy chairs and rugs. We sit comfortably with our feet up on fluffy ottomans. She's my friend. I just didn't recognize her.

I awaken in the middle of the night. The silence around me comforts me. Hildy's snore vibrates the air. I sit up and realize I am pleased. I don't know why or by what. I'm just satisfied to be here. I wonder if Chase ever feels like this.

37 Chase

After my dream I lose some urgency and some fear. My differentness isn't a problem, just an interesting fact. I view myself as someone who has something to offer. Whether or not it is recognized and appreciated is unimportant. I have a contribution and I am making it by being me. What a relief!

Not so tied in knots, I relax through the day, doing what presents itself — some weeding and sweeping and napping and letter writing. E-mail has destroyed the poetry of heartfelt communication so I indulge in some slow, considered descriptions of my days for the few friends in Pennsylvania who might be interested. John and Abigail Adams maintained a relationship over years with their dedication to letter writing. I can't imagine that happening these days but time was more generous in the past and I allow myself to drift back there. I describe the scents of Sweet Springs — piney, molding, dank — and what G.M. Hopkins would call the "dappled sun" in the marsh. Life is poetry. Living is the challenge of the poet. And living in some meaningful way is my challenge now with everything around me falling apart.

I move more slowly through my days and notice details I hadn't seen before. I watch a spider weave a web between the oak tree and the fence and snare a gnat which he devours immediately. I notice a woodpecker attack the same oak. A lizard darts about anxiously. All this life proceeding without my attention. All at its own pace with its own rhythm. Each little thing doing its unique part. And I have my part, too.

The phone rings but I don't jump to answer it. These days I don't welcome loud noises or fast movements. Answering machines were invented for me and I use mine. Unfortunately, callers don't always, but I figure if they don't leave a message they don't want to hear from me. No message with this call so I continue into the bedroom and put away laundry. Doing household chores grounds me. I've always appreciated neatness but I've never tried to create a welcoming home. Now that's all I have so I invest my energy here. Putting the last socks in the drawer and hanging up the shirts, I imagine that I am Chase, not that I imagine he nests. If he were in my situation now, what would he do?

First of all, I realize that he would never be in my situation. In my imagination he's always the initiator, never the victim. He's low-key and subtle, maybe not tranquil, but never showy. He doesn't draw attention to himself (as I have unknowingly done on several occasions).

He pulls strings and manages situations and seemingly succeeds, if success is measured by doing what he chooses and maintaining the goodwill, or at least respect, of the locals. He's apparently unconflicted and, I suspect, unreflective. I think that because I am very much neither at this point and I assume he's nothing like me.

I want to know him better.

38 A Funeral

Another week inside my house leaves me restless and curious about what is happening in the world. I walk downtown every morning, passing Cad's and the gym. On some days I pass the barbershop and wave at Elizabeth. She doesn't return my gesture but I want her to know that I acknowledge her and that I am not retreating. Of course, the Saloon isn't open but I look in the dark window and toward the community meeting rooms down the block. My walking acquaints me with the town layout and pace and lets the townsfolk see me maintain a routine. Regulars at the newspaper stand and the coffee cart recognize me. I'm engraving myself into this scene in my humble way.

I pass Carolyn buying something grandé and steaming and greet her with sincere enthusiasm. "How are you? I haven't been out much. Are you back to normal after the writing contest?"

"Normal? No, Nick, things are not normal. You know what's happened, don't you? Didn't Ellie talk with you?"

I'm perplexed. I've been allowing Ellie her space and haven't talked with her for more than a week. What's so big that could have happened in that time? I shrug my shoulders.

Carolyn continues. "Al has died. He was hospitalized at Stanford Medical Center and was diagnosed with a rare illness resulting from years of drug dependence."

"I had no idea. He was such a foundation in this community, too, and such a contributor to the sewer debate. All of you must feel his loss intensely. I'm so sorry." I'm pretty good at spontaneous sincere empathy.

She shifts her drink to her other hand. "Yeah, yeah, that's true, but you don't get what this means for our community."

I agree. "No, I guess not. Is it more than losing a valued friend and neighbor?"

"You did all that reading in the library, right? You have read about the position of the Slate family in Los Osos. You know there is a history spanning decades of their different interests and business ventures. You're a bright guy, Nick. Put it together!" And she hurries away in the direction of the library.

I'm shocked at the news of Al's death. Donny didn't tell me any of this. And where is Donny? It hasn't been that long since I've run into him. He can't be too far away.

So, Al was at Stanford. Interesting. I walk toward my home, stopping at the grocery to buy some strong coffee and to pick up the local rag. I pass Lauren leaving the gym. Yes, this is the time her yoga class breaks. She doesn't see me, head bent down and arms cradling a bulging gym bag. She, too, seems to be in a hurry.

I call Stanford Medical Center and ask about Al Slate. "No, I'm not exactly a relative, just a very concerned friend. I heard he died and I want to know when." I am told they can't give any information, NOT ANY. "I'm a friend of his grandson's." And I hear a dial tone.

What about a funeral? If the Slate family is so influential there must be a big funeral scheduled soon. I peruse the Bayside News and find what I'm seeking. The funeral is this afternoon at 2:00 at the Catholic Church. Yahoo! Everyone I've ever wanted to meet will be there. Maybe the perps who have already marked me will be in attendance. I haven't anticipated an event this fervently since I moved here.

39 The Church

On this Thursday afternoon the church is packed. Light streams in the tall windows, stained green and red and yellow at the top. Two sections of blond wood pews face the simple altar and two sections of pews on the sides face the center of the church. Every seat is taken.

I stand in the back and try to melt into the dark stone wall. When other late comers stand in front of me I succeed in becoming invisible. From my vantage point, peering between two padded shoulders, I spy Ellie in the far corner and Carolyn in a side seat. As far as I know, neither has seen me.

Then I start looking at the others there. This is the most high-powered crowd I have seen assembled at any function in Los Osos. Lots of middle-aged men in business suits. They must not be from here; no one wears a suit here. In the front pew, draped with ribbons (to indicate the family section, I presume), sits Donny with his hair slicked to the side, looking uncomfortable with his suit jacket buttoned. The man next to him I recognize from the pictures in the library as Chase. He has aged since his days tramping through Burma. He looks worn and tired. Over 50, he's done a lot of living, as they say.

More people arrive and folding chairs are hurriedly set up in the aisles. Couples separate to find seats but many folks arrive singly. I recognize a few Cad regulars, a couple women from the gym, and Elizabeth. This event must warrant closing the barbershop and most other business in town. I think I see Ralph from the Saloon but he slumps in the corner of a pew and I lose his face.

At 2:15 the organist plays something classical, slow and dark, and the chatter ceases. I don't recognize the piece but it effectively creates a somber mood. The young priest in dark vestments processes behind two altar boys waving bulbous metal containers billowing incense. The chains clank ominously. It's hard to breathe the smoke and several women cough. The priest blesses the crowd from behind the altar, facing the congregation.

"My brothers and sisters in Christ, we are gathered here today to send our beloved friend, Al Slate, to his righteous reward. We know that death is not the end. Truly, it is just the beginning. Let us kneel and remember Al, each in our own way, for a few minutes."

The mourners clumsily move to their knees and grip the backs of the pews in front of them. Many cover their eyes with clasped fingers. I hear a sob and some nose blowing. Those of us in the back lean against the wall. In five minutes the priest asks the congregation to sit and he reads some generic prayers about the soul of the deceased joining its Father in Heaven.

Then he closes his missal and looks out over the group. His hair is thinning but he has a pleasant face. He seems sincerely committed to being here. I wonder if he really knew Al or if this is his first assignment and he has just read the instructions for How to Lead a Funeral Service. When he starts talking, I feel ashamed of my cynicism.

"I've known Al for just over two years but, I admit, not as well as most of you. As you know, this is my first assignment out of the seminary and I came here, 2,000 miles from my home, with some trepidation." A few people snicker. I surmise that he is well-accepted now. "So, being the president of the Board of Directors, Al was one of the first parishioners I met. I remember the first day I saw him — he had just come from a sewer meeting and smoke was still curling out of his ears — and I prayed that he would be on my side." More snickers. "He was not someone I wanted to offend." Nods of agreement. "But he was generous with his time and energy and information. He welcomed me and soon I felt at home here. I still appreciate that gracious reception. It meant so much to me when I had no confidence and no experience to rely on."

He moves away from the podium for a minute and looks at a spot above the crowd and then closes his eyes and clasps his hands. "Take our brother, Al, and protect him on his sacred way, all you Angels and Saints." A few more minutes of silence and he raises his head and looks over the group. "Please, this is your time to speak. Any memories about Al you would like to share, any thoughts about our lives together, anything that would acknowledge this momentous passing? Please let us share our grief and our celebration of Al's life together." And he walks to a chair on the side of the altar and sits, head down, eyes closed.

Three minutes pass and an older man from the front pew on the left side walks slowly to the podium. He looks to be Al's age, a bit creaky but alert. His suit has served well for thirty years I infer from the cut. "Well, you all know me," he touches the outside corner of his eye with the back of his hand. "Al was my best friend. He was the one I talked things over with. He knew more about me than my wife did, bless her soul. Al was the kind of guy you knew you could trust. He was honest. If he thought it, he said it. And if he said it, he meant it, 110%. I loved that old man. And I miss him already." A tear runs down his cheek as he stumbles back to his seat. The room is still. Everyone waits. Who will speak next?

A slightly younger man stands in the pews on the right and walks to the microphone. He's had some experience speaking publicly I suspect from his self-assured demeanor. "Well, I am so proud of our town for showing up on this occasion." I ask the man next to me who this fellow is and he replies, "The mayor."

"Al and I, we had our differences, but I always respected him. I didn't agree with him and some of you remember the Town Council discussions he conducted until 2:00 in the morning. He felt strongly about his beliefs and could always defend them. With Al, you knew where he stood. A man like that you have to respect.

We've been arguing for years and I'll miss our exchanges. He kept me on my toes."

Before the mayor is seated Elizabeth is at the microphone. "I guess I knew Al in a way no one else here did. Sure, he could be blustery in public but the Al I knew was as gentle as a kitten. He liked simple things. And he was a good, strong, uncomplicated man. He treated you right and he expected you to treat him right. But what most folks didn't know about Al is that he had a big heart. Yeah, he argued a lot but sometimes he'd cry. He missed the ones he loved. Granted that wasn't a big number, but he could love and when he did, he gave it his all." She hesitates and then adds quickly, "I know." And she leaves the podium without looking up.

Two minutes pass and Donny walks awkwardly up the steps to the microphone. From my limited view I think I detect Chase's arm reaching out after Donny as he stands but Donny is on his way. I've noticed that about Donny — when he has an idea, he acts.

"My Granddad was the best. He loved me. He wanted me in his home when my Dad didn't want me." Twitters and chirps fill the room. Donny doesn't notice and continues. "My Granddad was the best. He told me about how things are really done. And don't never trust that mayor, he said." Louder chirping. Chase rises and moves toward Donny. At the same time Maddy appears from the extreme right and moves to his other side. Each takes one of his arms simultaneously.

"Donny, you honor your Granddad, just the way you're doing," Maddy says into the mike. "Now you go right ahead, son. I know your Dad is proud that you tell the truth." Did Chase blush? The congregation stirs. Donny moves a step closer to the mike, Maddy's arm around his back. I realize I have not seen her stand before and I had assumed she couldn't. But clearly she is in control here. I, and I assume others, hold our breath realizing that something remarkable is happening. The priest doesn't look up.

Donny continues, "When my Mom died, I was young then, and I felt pretty lost for a long time. You know, a guy needs his Mom." Maddy holds him closer. "You go on Donny, we all know what you mean."

"Well, me and my Mom, we were best friends, and when she died I just about died, too. I'd never been alive without her. She helped me with everything." I can see Chase pull at Donny's arm but Maddy's presence is overwhelming. She leans around behind Donny and whispers loud enough for us all to hear, "Chase, please help me. I fear I'm about to collapse with these old legs. Please take me back to my wheelchair. Thank you, son."

What could Chase do? We'd all heard her plea. So, the two of them move away from Donny, Maddy leaning heavily on Chase. Donny has the microphone and the attention of the whole church. We can all hear Maddy ask Chase to move this and adjust that and push her out the back because she really needs to get some air and get much closer to the bathroom. She is a joy to watch. Evidently, Chase is unprepared for her mastery and polish. If you don't know Maddy, it looks like a feeble older woman instructing a caregiver. But if you do, you know you are watching local history in the making. We know this moment will be recounted for years.

Meanwhile, Donny rambles on about his grade school days with his Mom and their nature walks. Smiles dot the room and intermittently a giggle escapes. Donny enjoys the attention and speaks louder. "My Mom taught me how to identify plants and which plants are poisonous and which plants are not poisonous but you don't want them near you anyway. Like my Dad's experiments behind the train station." The group gasps in unison and, suddenly, I think I understand why Julie died and why Chase hadn't protested. God bless this crazy boy.

"Mom and Dad didn't always agree and she told me it was OK that married people don't always agree but she told me to always tell the truth and she said that sometimes my Dad couldn't quite figure out what the truth is but that I should always love him anyway." Laughter bursts from a few young men and the priest finally looks up. I hope he won't interfere with this superb show but he probably is unaccustomed to such audience participation and, frankly, delight. Chase has been out of the church this entire time, no doubt due to Maddy's shenanigans, and as he walks in the back door at that very minute, I can see the shock and fury on his face. Only a few of us in the back witness his expression before he turns and strides out.

Apparently, the priest has caught sight of Chase's second exit and realizes that something very very unusual is occurring. He stands up, walks to Donny, puts his arm around Donny's shoulders, and thanks him, gently but firmly pushing Donny away from the microphone. He motions to a man in a dark suit in the front row to help Donny back to his seat. The priest starts to speak but an air of amusement has replaced the heaviness of the service and all he can do is to remind us of the profound transition of a soul returning to God's welcoming arms.

At that the crowd erupts in applause and stands up. The priest looks confused and hurries off the altar. I rush outside in hopes of catching Chase but snag not a glimpse. I don't want Ellie or Carolyn to see me so I walk away quickly, looking back in half a block at the crowd, whispering among themselves.

40 The Unexpected Ride

Walking home, kicking stones and thinking about what I've witnessed, I don't notice a car slow behind me. "Hey, Nick!" I turn expecting a friend. Later I would wonder why. A man in sunglasses emerges from the passenger side and opens the back door. "Let us give you a ride."

"No, thanks really, I'm just three blocks from home." But by then he drags me into the back seat and I know surely that this is not a friendly visit. I fall against another man who rights me and introduces himself as Chase Slate. The car picks up speed and I hear the doors lock. The windows are tinted black. So, this is the introduction I sought.

"Nick, may I call you Nick? I feel like I know you. You've had such an impact on my home town and I've heard all sorts of stories." His voice is modulated and smooth as fine brandy. I *was* being watched and he did have informants.

"Why, Chase, I am delighted, yes, delighted to make your acquaintance. I've heard so much about you, too. Not the least being today." He shifts his position and I can feel his indignation. Good, he isn't so cool that he's impervious. "But, Chase, let me offer my condolences on your grievous loss." Apparently, this is too much because the next thing I remember, I awake in the dark with a splitting headache.

I don't know how long I had been out — hours or days — but I recognize the concussion symptoms and I don't like having my head used for batting practice. I'm getting too old for this. If it happens one time too many I won't be coming back, not all in one piece.

I lie on a hard surface and see light under a door. As I sit up my head screams and I fall back on the board with a loud groan. The door opens and a huge male figure, backlit, opens the creaky door and enters the room. "You're not goin' anywhere so jus' get comfortable." His voice is rough.

"Actually, sir, I think there may have been a mistake. You see, I am not the person who reserved these fine accommodations. In reality, I should probably vacate the premises forthwith" and a hairy hand covers my mouth.

"Will you shut up! What do you think is going on here? We're not playing games and this ain't no movie. So, don't give me none of your fancy talk. Now I got to give you food iffen you wants it so all I want to hear is yes, you want some grub or, no, you don't. So, just say one word, yes or no."

In addition to intense physical pain and the insult of being held against my will, I'm offered "grub." Never before in my life have I been offered grub. But, really, why not? I'm famished.

"Yes is the word you await, kind sir."

"I told you to shut up!" And reflexively I draw away from his raised arm. He departs, closing the door, leaving me in semi- darkness again. This is not what I would call a welcome development. No, it's closer to a disturbing and worrisome state of affairs. Like an unseen fork in the road leading to a deadly waterfall. Or the steps after the Danger, Turn Back Now sign. By my own actions I have entered an unknown arena. I have no experience here. I don't understand what these fine gentlemen want. And I must do something to end the clanging in my head. Where are the little blue pills now? I wish I could just pass out. But I am hungry.

The grub is better than dog food (I presume) but lacks embellishment. The best thing about it is that it puts me back to sleep. I don't know how long I sleep but my beard has more than three days' growth when I stir. My head doesn't hurt as much but my muscles ache. I don't want to soil myself and I need a bathroom desperately.

I stumble and fall getting up and this time when the door opens a woman walks in, asking what I need. I tell her a bathroom before I look at her face. She opens the door and points. As I walk past her, I notice it is Lauren.

41 Captives

The bathroom is off a large main room. When I emerge from the bathroom, I join Lauren sitting in a grouping of brown suede chairs. Beyond the sliding glass doors and multiple windows I see a eucalyptus grove. Inside I can look down a row of rooms, one opening to the next, and see office desks alternating with seating arrangements. The angle of the sun indicates that it is mid- morning. I can't see anyone else here besides Lauren. She is as beautiful as always though the circles beneath her eyes are darker. "So, where's your husband? Traveling on business? And you're just looking for a diversion?"

"Please, Nick. Don't make this harder." I almost laugh.

"No, I don't want to inconvenience anyone."

"This could all be over very quickly. Just cooperate with them and we can return home." I guess from the landscape we are still in Los Osos but I don't recognize this particular terrain.

"Well, you know that the last thing I want is to upset Chase and his goons. I was just walking home, just like I do every day, and I was abducted. I am the victim here. I am not the one causing the problems."

"Nick, listen, there is no more wiggle room. You can be smart and you can be cutting and you can be accusatory, but, Nick, you can't win. Please don't make this harder."

Not ready to concede that victory is lost I ask, "Have you been in on this all along? That day at my house? Was that a setup for this?"

"Nick, please, this is where we are now and both you and I want to get out of here intact. And, to remind you, there are others who could be hurt by your choices." Is she threatening Ellie? How dare she?

"Just don't pull my cousin into this. She has no idea what I'm doing or what is going on. Leave her alone."

"Don't tell me. Chase calls the shots and he will do whatever he needs to. You know he's a dangerous man. I won't say more but you are intelligent and you want the best for everyone. So, don't be hardheaded. We could end this all quickly if you say the right word."

"What are you doing? Who are you?" And I stand up and walk to the windows. In each room is a sliding glass door. I can just open one and walk out. I pull on the handle and immediately sirens scream, dogs bark, and a helicopter whirs overhead.

"Now do you understand, Nick? You can't leave this place. You can't escape. There are too many of them. It's no use. If these doors open without the alarms being dismantled, any person leaving the house will be shot. It's completely guarded."

The complexity of this operation impresses me. And frightens me. I must think about this, but right now I'm hungry and I smell awful. Suddenly, I want a shower. I had noticed one in the bathroom and I tell Lauren I want to use it. She agrees and says she'll lay out clean clothes on the bed.

Twenty minutes later I feel renewed. I don the black sweats she's left and towel-dry my hair. I shave with the electric shaver which does a poor job of removing my beard. She's serving thick soup and black bread and I sit at a round table with her and eat. The food is delicious though I would welcome a piece of beef.

"How many days has it been since the funeral?" I ask.

"Not many. You haven't lost much time. That's not what you need to worry about."

"Oh, yes, and what is it I need to worry about?" As much as I was drawn to her before, I'm starting to hate her for betraying me. "Nick, we've all told you gently, leave well enough alone. Well, you wouldn't. Now you see where that has brought you."

"I don't agree with your premise that I am responsible for the ill-fated actions of the last however many days. Yes, I do remember being asked to back off but you have to agree that with the attacks against me, that would have been impossible. I was threatened and my friend Deb was killed. No, I do not back off in the face of such aggression. This is not civilized!"

And I stand up, tipping the table so that my empty soup

bowl tumbles and shatters on the stone floor. I won't apologize. This scenario is outrageous and unconscionable and I will not cooperate. Submitting to these oppressors, whoever they are, is completely out of the question. How could Lauren even suggest it? She picks up pieces of the earthenware bowl and wipes the floor. She clears the table without speaking and retires to the kitchen. I walk the length of the house, noting the wires in the glass and the lights. My heart throbs. I have no ideas about how to proceed.

42 Daydreaming

Lauren and I are the only two in the house. Twice I test the alarm system by leaning against a glass door and both times the sirens and dogs and helicopter react. I am convinced this is a fail-safe system.

I avoid Lauren for two hours, pacing and doing sit ups, push-ups, and a few jumping jacks. I can't concoct even the first step of a plan. As dusk falls, I sit in a chair near where she does needle work. She doesn't look up.

"So, what's the plan? Are the others coming? Is a big move in the works? What?"

"It's up to you, Nick. You can have whatever you want to eat, you can do anything as long as you stay inside these walls. I am completely available to you." She lowers her eyes. "But until you agree to back off and to leave this area and to drop your investigations, you can't walk out of here. We'll make it as comfortable as we can, but you won't have access to books, computers, newspapers, television, or telephones. As long as you want to live here by these rules, you are welcome to stay."

"And Chase can hear everything we say and do, I'm sure. Can he watch us, also?" I look around the ceiling for small cameras but I don't notice any. "So, this is my prison complete with a guard." At this moment, Lauren disgusts me.

And then I realize that I can't simply agree to follow their rules and they will release me. They will never trust me. I already know too much. At this moment my death seems inevitable.

Does anyone know I am missing? Ellie and I weren't talking much and she might not realize I'm not at my home. What about Hildy? Will someone hear her whine and feed her? If anyone enters my home, they'll know I'm gone. I had established a walking routine but I doubt anyone in town would question my absence. What have I done? And what is being done to me? This can't go on indefinitely.

Why do "they" hate me? Why am I such a threat to them? What might they lose because of my presence? I've suspected intrigue since I moved here but the depth of this resistance confounds me.

In addition to my head, my brain aches. This much thinking is normal when I'm normal but I'm badly damaged now and I can't function very well for very long. All the sleep I've gotten, probably from drugged food, has been a blessing. Both for me and probably for Them, too. They can't kill me. That would eventually incite serious trouble as long as Ellie is around. And they can't let me live free and unregulated. They are as constrained as I am. They need to watch my every move, prevent anything that will draw attention to their undercover operation, and, yet, not destroy me. They must know they will never win me over. So, they and I are in a similar cramped situation with some glaringly different details.

I retire to the bedroom which has been cleaned. If it weren't imposed without my consent, this wouldn't be a totally bad way to live, for a week or two, anyway. I snooze, waking often and drifting off again. My sleep world is action packed, lots of running and high walls.

I awake convinced that I will accept these lovely accommodations as they are and not try to force a change. I'll allow my health to improve and my strength to return. Will I take advantage of Lauren's "availability"? Doesn't interest me at all right now. Another indication of how I am not myself.

So, the next few days are spent waking, eating, improvised exercising, a little talking, and lots of sleep with and without dreams. Since I'm not pushing myself, I'm not discouraged. Lauren doesn't push me, either. In fact, she doesn't initiate any conversation. She always responds but I set the tone. Some days I am hostile to her, inquiring about her husband and her sons and what would they say about her now and where do they think she is, after all? Sometimes I catch a fluttering in her eyelids but she doesn't argue with me or defend herself. That makes the taunting not much fun. And I'm not proud of myself, either, for that kind of adolescent behavior.

A week has passed and, while I am detained against my will, I am comfortable physically. My days are half reverie and half wakefulness. I observe the most interesting fantasies floating through my head. I am always the Hero. I vanquish dark forces with a laser slice from my well-aimed saber. I am an efficient, sure, confident, and benevolent warrior. I like my movies and I like me in my movies.

43 Tears of Prison

With the release of my efforts to change my situation, I appreciate the minutes of each day. Of course, I don't let on to Lauren and I don't treat her well. The invisible They must have chosen her for this position because of our interlude. They know I am vulnerable to her but the longer I stay here the more I wonder about her vulnerability. Not in relation to me. Much as I would like to believe it, I don't harbor illusions that I am important to her. Something is important to her, though; why else would she be in this position? They used some kind of leverage to "convince" her to accept this assignment.

As the days pass pleasantly enough for me, I watch Lauren. She busies herself around the place, cleaning and cooking and whatever it is she does with her needles. Her mornings are focused. She does the routine maintenance work daily and she even cleans the windows twice a week. She dusts and vacuums and waters plants and organizes drawers of kitchenware. Her brisk work pace dissipates later in the day when I sense a rising restlessness. In the evenings she does her needlework for a while and then stands up quickly, throws her work aside and walks around the house. Not going anywhere, just expending some frustrated energy. When she loses her concentration at those points I become very quiet and very, very observant.

"Need to do some yoga?" I ask as she starts on one of her purposeless jaunts. She ignores me and leaves the room. I crawl to the floor and feign a stretch. I lean to one side and the other with one leg extended and then the other. Within a few minutes she's back and I notice that she notices what I'm attempting. I continue, with rounded back and lifted head, two transgressions I know she can't tolerate. She bites.

"Keep your spine straight, breathing out as you reach your nose to your toes." I suspect that committed yoga instructors don't abide sloppiness even when they are not officially teaching. I make little mistakes and soon enough she's on the floor, also. We stretch and release and breathe. I follow her lead and she guides me through her workout. Of course, I can't keep up with her but after a few minutes she isn't thinking about me. Her movements create a beautiful composition. Her whole body responds to her inhales and lengthening and her exhales and bending. Fluid motions. No pressure. Experiencing the moment.

When she finishes, she looks up, somewhat surprised, as her awareness comes back to the room and to me and to our situation. For an hour she was elsewhere and I could tell it was good for her. The muscles in her face have relaxed. I sense that she might be available for conversation but instead I thank her and leave.

Thereafter, every morning and every evening I attempt a yoga pose. When she sees me, she joins me and we go through her routine without speaking. In the morning she salutes the sun. In the evening, she practices Rishi's posture. Even without discourse I discern that her sentry role melts. Her walk is slower and her shoulders more relaxed. I don't want to approach her too soon. I want to be assured of a sympathetic reception before I make any move. So, we practice yoga together and I always thank her and leave the room. I actually think I'm getting better. I know my middle-aged muscles feel more flexible.

Now I'm Cool Hand Luke. I show no interest in her and I don't ask for anything. I hope that my lack of emotional intensity coupled with my new-found commitment to our yoga practice may intrigue her. Twice she has corrected my posture with a light touch on my back and shoulder. I don't look at her but simply continue. We're shifting positions. I'm more comfortable with this situation and she seems more dissatisfied. I want this reversal to continue.

It only takes another week and even in the mornings she's not able to focus. She's great during our yoga times but otherwise she's agitated. I ask for some tea after morning yoga and when she places it on the table, I ask if she will please join me. She does and I'm ready.

"I've watched you become more and more restless and while I greatly appreciate the yoga time with you, I've learned so much that I've needed and didn't know that I needed, I notice that you are not OK. Something's missing for you and it's showing. You have demonstrated such concern for me and I can't pretend that I don't see you gradually… well… disintegrating. I think you're losing weight, your needlework isn't progressing as it was, and… you just don't seem yourself." A tear rolls from her right eye down her porcelain cheek to her perfect chin. My arms want to reach out to her but I hold them stiffly at my sides.

"You've helped me with more than you'll know, and I can't pretend that I don't notice your pain." I'm good, I think to myself and immediately feel embarrassed by my craven callousness which in reality is just a front. Really, what I said, I meant. I am just afraid to mean it.

She looks upward to the light fixture and holds one finger in front of her lips. So that's where the microphone is. I point outside, asking in pantomime if we might walk and talk. I made a gesture crossing my heart, assuring her that I won't run. I think she will dismiss this suggestion, but she rises from her chair, turns off the lights and flips a series of switches behind the drapes. "Quickly, come outside and stand ten feet from the door," she whispers. I do as I am instructed and she goes back in, manipulating the dials and switches.

I stand on mounds of decaying eucalyptus leaves. There are no paths or tracks anywhere in sight, just thousands of trees. "We can only be out here for ten minutes before someone will suspect something," she whispers. "There is nowhere to run. After ten minutes if we are not back inside and I give them the closing signal, they will find you with their helicopters and shoot to kill. So, let's be careful."

Now I allow myself to put an arm around her shoulder. She relaxes and leans into me. "It's my family. They don't know where I am. I didn't think you would last this long. They told me I had to do this, be your caretaker and do whatever you need, or they would kill Greg and my sons. My consequences for getting involved with you."

"And now you can't go home."

"And Greg must be worried to death." She cries deeply, pitifully, sorrowfully as I hold her. She is more a prisoner than am I.

And, thus, the tide has turned.

44 Against the Tides of Fate

We go outside for ten minutes every morning and every afternoon and talk a little more freely. I want to ask about this organization that has blackmailed her into betraying her family but she is overwrought. She is anxious and fearful and guilty and regretful. If she hadn't mastered her yoga, she couldn't have endured the tension. Twice she comes close to asking me to capitulate; I can tell by the pleading tone in her voice. The fact that she doesn't makes me wonder if her suspicions about "their" reactions are the same as mine. She is effectively trapped. Any move either way seems to promise someone's demise. My Hero needs to emerge from my dreams and enter real life.

Before dawn the next morning I hear a vehicle drive up, drop off a load, and depart. I open my bedroom door but don't turn on the light. In a few moments Lauren comes out of her bedroom, goes through the ritual of the switches and the dials, opens the front door, drags in a box, repeats the switches and dials procedure, and closes the drapes. She leaves the box sitting in the middle of the room as she heads to the bathroom in her bedroom.

I grab the cardboard box, pulling the top off and ripping the sides. It is filled with food. At the bottom of the box lies an envelope with her name on it. I tear it open without hesitation and read, "We see what's going on. You have four days to complete your mission. Don't think you can escape."

When I stand up and turn around she is standing in the doorway. If she had held a gun pointed toward me, she would not have appeared more menacing. I feel her fury and her desperation. She is my adversary, no warm feelings present. She is a mother lion whose cubs have been threatened. She is ready to kill or to die or both.

We look at each other for two minutes without speaking. I

hand her the note. She reads it and throws it on the floor.

"OK, Nick, you have ruined my life. I must try to reclaim some small part of it, if that's possible." Are her eyes swollen? Has she been crying?

"I'm sorry," I say. "I've truly loved you. I want to help you now. Even more than I want to help myself, I want to help you."

"Oh, Christ, no. Just be quiet. You've done too much damage! You have to go. They will kill me now if you don't give them what they want. You've ruined everything! How could you! I was kind to you and I made a little mistake and now I will never finish paying for it. And my family will pay for it. And it's all because of you, swaggering into town, just thinking about yourself." She weeps hysterically.

Without thinking I grab her and slap her, just hard enough to get her attention, not to hurt her and I take over without even realizing what I am doing. "Before the sun comes up we must get out of here. Do what you do with the dials and switches, put on your best jogging shoes and meet me outside in one minute. This is our only chance. We've got to run for it."

Dazed, she follows my directions and we are among the eucalyptus in two minutes, the dew enhancing their spicy scent. I know we have to make good time before the light allows the helicopter to observe us. I pull her to the right but she pulls me to the left.

"No, Nick, this way. Follow me as fast as you can." She leads me through trees and around trees and over tree roots. We slosh through piles of leaves. The running is difficult and we each slip many times but, panting hard, we make progress. We run the equivalent of half a mile through the trees when we hear the sirens and the dogs. Lights flood the house from a floating helicopter but we aren't near. Unfortunately, there is no cover where we are except the trees and the darkness which is fading. The sound of the ocean is louder, waves breaking but not close. Of course, we are in Montana de Oro. If only we could get to the beach. Apparently her thought, too, because we race through more trees, then over open ground, and huge boulders, ending in the water with the sun peeking over the horizon. In the water we wade along the coast until we find a cave we crawl into. My lungs and heart are grateful for the yoga practice. We listen to vehicles racing, alarms screaming, dogs yelping, and we wait, barely breathing.

Now Lauren and I are truly in this together.

45 Asylum

We shiver in the small cave for what must have been three hours, not daring to emerge until we hear voices talking and laughing. We clamber out, bedraggled, but fade into the small crowd. We tell passers-by we have been swimming spontaneously and act like honeymooners. One couple camping offers us hot coffee and another gives us a ride in the back of a pick-up out of the park toward town. It is good to be anonymous again.

But how are we to re-enter our lives? Now Greg and Ellie may be in danger. We have to think carefully without wasting time. No doubt The Organization (as I think of it) is alerted to scout for us. Whom can we trust to hide us without endangering themselves? They will watch each of our houses and Ellie's home and office. We are not safe if we are seen.

We jump out of the pick-up at the edge of town. I am glad to walk outside. I haven't walked any distance for as long as we've been in the house which I am guessing is a month, maybe longer. Lauren is walking quickly and smiling. We are free but need to be more careful than we ever have been in our lives. Consequences will be immediate and fatal.

Where to go? We see more drivers and joggers and bicyclists and now we really don't want to be recognized. We cut through some fields and climb a couple fences and wander into the reserve near the golf course, west of town. Lizards and bunnies run from us. The sage smells fresh. We climb over the sand dunes to the bay and borrow a row boat tied up near 13th Street and row to the coffee house. This is too public for me but the tide is out so we can't hug the shore. We dock, tie up, and scurry into the neighborhood. I feel sure we have been spotted; I can only hope that it is by an uninterested neighbor.

We are close to Lauren's house, my house, and Deb's house and decide to try the latter first. Ellie's real estate sign stands in the front yard but no one is around. We jiggle the doors and windows and find a window in back we can jimmy open and climb through. I have never been so glad to collapse. We are inside, safe, and unwatched. We are also filthy and take turns in the shower, borrowing clothes left in drawers. Deb would be happy to help in this small way. We are worn out and immensely relieved after our escape. We fall asleep on the living room rug.

The front door opening wakes us and late afternoon sun spills in. Before I am completely alert I hear Ellie's voice. "I was afraid I'd find you both here. I'm glad you're safe but I could kill you for scaring us all." Lauren asks about Greg and Ellie assures her that she will phone him when she leaves. Greg has called Ellie every day wanting news. He's still out of town.

"How did you know to come here?" I ask.

"With the commotion so early this morning and the report of two strangers in the Chambers' row boat, I wondered if something was up. I've been to both your houses, but don't worry, I was careful, and I wondered what I would do if I were in your situation. I have to come by here every few days to check on the place so no one is suspicious if my car is here. I just tell them I am cleaning the place out. Which I am. Slowly. So, if you two need to hide for a couple days maybe this is as good a spot as any."

Kinder words I haven't heard. She continues, "After sunset I'll bring some groceries and let the neighbors know I'm working here. I hope you'll be safe." Her voice trails off. She looks from one of us to the other and back again. "I truly hope you both will be safe. OK, see you in a couple hours."

So, we have a resting place of sorts. We're not free to use the lights but we are inside with beds and toilets and someone else's clothes. I'll ask Ellie to bring some of my pants and shirts when she returns.

Ellie returns after 9:00 pm with clothes and food and a fear surpassing our anxiety. "You can't stay here. They know you're here and you're not safe. Eat and change clothes and then we must go."

"But why…" Lauren starts to ask and then stops herself. Why, indeed. Why any of this? We eat chicken and fruit greedily. "I've opened a new escrow in Salazar Hills. It's a lovely estate, gated, with an acre surrounding the house. Let's get you there now. The family has just moved out and the furniture will be there for another month or so. It will be just like living in a home." She lowers her voice. "No one must see us, though."

Ellie drives away without lights as Lauren and I huddle on the floor of the back seat. She turns on her lights downtown and heads into the hills. She stops at a gate, punches some buttons which release the gate, and we drive into a neighborhood of extravagant houses. No street lights apparently are permitted here and as she drives we peek over the back seat. No cars on the roads. Lights glow in some houses but a serene silence blankets this neighborhood, unlike any other I've seen in Los Osos.

Up a winding driveway, we approach a colonial house with white pillars — out of place in a coastal meadow to my way of thinking but a welcome sight nonetheless. Lauren and I run in the door before Ellie turns on the lights and we are delighted to find ourselves in a family home with family pictures and throw rugs over the carpet and a piano. The house is imposing but I can't tell how large it is. I can discern the outlines of a long-curved sofa, two large chairs with ottomans, silk flower arrangements, and a couple floor lamps. I have seen pictures of model homes like this in magazines but this one is real and lived in.

Ellie goes outside to bring in her For Sale signs and points to a blaze tickling the night sky in the direction of Deb's. "They will think you are inside and that now you're dead. Maybe if they believe you're gone, we'll have some space and time." She isn't even surprised.

46 Secrets of Los Osos

Before Lauren arises the next morning, I sit with my feet propped up on a sand-colored leather ottoman, gazing at nothing in particular. This magnificent house sits on the crest of a hill with no other houses at "eye level" and spectacular views of Maeve Binchy rolling hills in two directions, downtown Los Osos in a third, and the bay and, farther out, the ocean in the fourth. The autumn hills are covered with dried grass and nearly leafless trees. The few fishing boats in the bay are quiet, probably already returned from the morning's outing. Downtown crawls with miniature cars, none moving fast. A west coast rendition of Walt Whitman's America.

Two lanes circle the complex with smaller paths to driveways. Each driveway leads to a house, 3,000 - 6,000 square feet. Every house is grand in its own way. The neighborhood mixes colonial, neo-classical, and southwestern home designs. The homes are what real estate ads would call "tasteful" but I would describe as "excessive." The amount of money in this neighborhood alone is more than I've seen in all of Los Osos. I notice one rider on a beautiful pale palomino crossing the hills. A few long cars slink toward the gate. Otherwise, the only movement is natural — the breeze in the trees, the clouds drifting, and the eagle hawks soaring.

Lauren walks in rubbing her eyes and stretching her arms in her borrowed pjs. "What a trip," she whispers. "Our very own manor. Just like in a novel."

"Jane Austen didn't have it this good. Let's explore." And we set off through long hallways, five bedrooms, four baths, two kitchens, a pantry, a music room, a library, and what must have been a pet room. The house is decorated in muted earth tones but has been lived in, evidently with more than one child.

Nothing — the furniture, the wallpaper, the window shades — is in perfect condition but the overall impression is one of comfortable indulgence.

After we traipse through the main floor and the upstairs, we find a small closet in the kitchen with a staircase down to a wine cellar. Here it is dark and very cool. Lots of wine racks line the walls but not many bottles remain. This room is as large as my apartment's living room with two small wrought iron tables and chairs which I couldn't imagine anyone using due to the temperature. Unlike the other rooms, this room is dusty. Very interesting. It doesn't seem to be an extension of the family quarters but maybe the adults needed a place of their own. Probably not used much, though. Lauren investigates the corners and alcoves while I stand in the middle of the room and turn in a circle, taking it all in, my first private wine cellar. This lifestyle resembles nothing I've known.

"Look, Nick," Lauren says excitedly and holds up a piece of folded yellow paper. "A pirate's treasure map." It is drawn with crayons in a child's hand. I smile and turn away. "But wait," she continues. "On the back there are some words: 'It isn't that they can't see the solution. It's that they can't see the problem.' What could that mean? Is this a game to solve a mystery and find a treasure? Maybe there was a party and this…"

But I'm not listening. I recognize the quote from G. K. Chesterton and the beating of my heart quickens. I don't have a coherent thought but I feel a release of some tension as though something right has happened, even if I don't recognize what the rightness is. "… they can't see the problem." Of course, why hadn't I understood that?

"Come on, Lauren, we have work to do," and I pull her up the stairs. Emerging into the sunlight of the main floor shifts our brain waves from the subtlety of the dark cool cellar with its chance clue to the harsh delineated logic of mid-day.

Up here what does "they can't see the problem" mean? The Los Osos residents can't see the problem that Chase presents? Too prosaic. I say as much out loud and Lauren responds, "They can't see the problem because it isn't a problem. They see it but they don't define it as a problem." I suspect that she doesn't know what she said or why she said it.

"What are you talking about?" I ask impatiently.

"A problem is not a problem unless you make it so." That sounds like Alice in Wonderland to me. It's easy for me to dismiss Lauren as flaky when I'm cerebral and focused. When I'm open to her, those same qualities entrance me.

And that in itself is what she's talking about! It's putting two ways of seeing together to appreciate the total picture. Not just my way, not just Lauren's, not just Chase's, not just the locals. And a curtain lifts!

What do we have when we put it all together?

I don't have any definite indication of crime, just a lot of hushed transactions. I don't know of particular ongoing malfeasance before I entered the scene but someone or something has made my life uncomfortable since I've been here. If I approach this differently and take "their" perspective, I would say, "Life has been great and just as we've molded it. This outsider crashes our party and threatens to deprive us of what we've worked to create. He doesn't know what he's doing but we stand to lose."

By viewing the situation in those terms, I can appreciate their position and accept it as tenable. I say to Lauren but mostly to myself, "I assume that the life that has existed here for years is satisfying to the citizens. In fact, it is more than satisfying; it's the best they can imagine." And I hesitate. Why would it be the best they can imagine? But Lauren answers my question before I ask it.

"Life here hasn't always been easy. We've suffered through territorial disputes with the ranchers, massive land acquisitions by the federal government for railroads and the power plant, and, worst of all, skirmishes with the giant oil corporations who want to drill right off our shoreline. That offended all of us, but how could we protect ourselves when international law decrees that we have no rights beyond three miles? Now three miles might seem pretty far, but, in the case of an oil spill, it's nothing. We were looking at the possible loss of our beautiful county and our pristine shoreline and the unspoiled countryside and, eventually, our way of life. We don't want to be owned by a corporation. We want a simple clean life."

And now it all makes sense. Why couldn't I see it? Chase is the savior who has rescued this county from potential ruin. He has the money to buy any favors he wants. He has the business and political connections to negotiate any deals he needs. That's why he has the support of the community. And, if he has to use underhanded methods once in a while, well, that's better than living without protection. The locals allow Chase free rein in return for a "guarantee" that life will go on.

Chase takes care of the citizens and they conceal him. I smile in recognition of the beauty of this arrangement. But when I look back at Lauren she glares at me.

"Now you understand, Nick. We can't let you destroy our home and our lives.

47 Escaping Control

"This arrangement has existed for more than a decade, hasn't it, Lauren? Or did it start with Al many decades ago? Did it arise with the import business?" One little piece of information leads to another. I am unraveling a knitted blanket by pulling one thread. "So, how much do the residents really know? Did you know that Julie would be killed? Do you know why she was? And, anyway, where is she buried? Are all of you partners with Chase & Co. or do you just entrust him with the mission to safeguard your comfort and let him work out the details?"

Lauren gazes at me impassively. She doesn't attempt to answer any of my questions. In fact, I don't know what is going on with her at all. She seems an empty shell. Nothing elicits a reaction. This isn't the Lauren of our yoga days when she was worried about her family. Her soul has gone somewhere else.

"You ask lots of questions, Nick, but not the right ones. That's why you're dangerous and must be contained."

I smile disingenuously. "Contained? Is that what you're doing, containing me? I thought you and your friends were trying to kill me."

At that moment I hear Ellie's voice behind me. "We've told you over and over, Nick. You must be more careful."

"Are you working with them, too, Cuz?"

"You're alive, aren't you? If I hadn't whisked you away last night, do you think we'd be having this conversation today?"

I turn to look at Ellie. Her eyes are dark and her shoulders rounded; she looks tired.

"You were in on all this, weren't you?" I ask. I realize my cousin knows much more than I thought she did and she has known it for a long time. I look at her wonderingly. Do I know her? Is her real estate business part of this larger operation? Can I trust her? Will she be honest with me? Now I question if she ever has been. Suddenly, the world I thought I knew has shifted. "So, you betrayed Chase & Co. for me. Is that it?" I look at both women. "You took a risk to save my neck and now you'd better be very sure no one doubts you. And completely sure that I don't expose you by showing myself." My voice gets louder. "Is that right? What do you plan to do? Keep me locked up here for months, bringing me food at night? What's the next step, hmmm?"

Ellie and Lauren exchange glances. Are they are working together? Knowing them each as I do, I don't imagine that they have detailed plans that extend much beyond tonight. They are not plotters. Both have spontaneously betrayed Chase for me. Are they aware of their precarious positions in relation to The Organization? I'd bet that they are both concerned that I will endanger them unintentionally.

"Ladies, don't worry. May we make a pact, just the three of us? There is no one else, is there? Are you in cahoots with others I don't know?"

"No, Nick," Ellie responds. "It's just the three of us right now. But at some point, probably pretty soon, Greg will be back and Lauren's sons will be home. And, as far as Chase is concerned, Lauren and you are dead. We must not arouse his suspicion."

I need the women to trust me, although I realize that trust comes in ounces in this town. "I will guarantee you both that I will take no action. I will not cause any problems and I will not plan anything." Their glances bespeak doubt and maybe antipathy.

Ellie stands and replies, "Nick, we really are beyond words. We cannot chance a sighting of you by anyone in this area. You have a track record that tells us you are not trustworthy, that you think only of yourself, and that your words are meaningless." Pretty strong language from my Cuz. "From this point on, we make the decisions and we call the shots."

"Am I to endure another period of incarceration?" I ask, trying to sound light. In reality, I am very upset by Ellie's tone. I've never heard her like this.

"Nick, you don't get it. You've put us in incredible danger. Lauren and Greg will have to move away from here if we can manage that. And I will never again do business in this town."

"So, what are you suggesting? That you kill me gently and gracefully rather than have Chase & Co. do the deed viciously?" "I never wanted it to come to this, Nick. I tried to dissuade you. I wanted to help you. But you are so damned independent. You just won't cooperate with anyone." And she withdraws a syringe from her bag. As she approaches me, I step backward.

Does she think I will allow her to inject something into me?

"What are you doing? You're my cousin. We're on the same side. I just promised you my loyalty." I speak quickly and somewhat breathlessly.

"This isn't permanent. I just need to know you'll be out of commission for a couple days. In the end you'll come back, good as new, just without the memory of a few things. You'll be fine, though, and you can walk away and start a new life anywhere you want. It's for the best, Nick. Trust me."

But I surely don't trust her when she approaches me with a needle and I won't allow anything to be plunged into my body and I'm not willing to lose the tiniest bit of memory. No, whatever her plan, I'm not participating. I shove the ottoman in her direction and she falls over it, the syringe piercing her own arm. She looks at me with her wide brown eyes for ten seconds before she passes out.

I'm frantic and want to call an ambulance until Lauren reminds me that Chase will kill us all if he finds out that I'm still alive. "It's not permanent, Nick. She'll be back. Almost as good as new."

How can these people be so cavalier about their friends? I am delirious with worry and Lauren explains to me that Deb had supplied phenobarbital to induce a short-term coma. "We've used it before," she adds. My mouth drops open as I stare at her. Are there no moral limits to what is done here?

48 Opportune Time?

I sit by Ellie's bed, listening to her breathe. Guilt overwhelms me. What have I done? How could this happen? I retire from an honorable position, make a reasonable move, act without impure motives, and leave a town in ruins. My wonderful cousin is in a "coma" and, although Lauren assures me, she'll recover, I wonder. I am so glad our parents can't see this. However, Uncle Sammy would have some advice. Never one to be disarmed by gentility, he always said, "Plan your next move. Don't let them catch you napping."

As I sit with Ellie and wait, I think about Al. He was a promoter. He envisioned something that didn't exist and he created it.

And I think about Chase. I'm guessing that Chase feels vulnerable about something of which I am unaware. Maddy says she knows where the bodies are buried. What does that mean? I want to find her and talk to her but I have to keep her away from the booze. The bar and the sewer meetings are the only places I know to encounter her. The latter is safer for me. While Ellie is blacked out, I may have a chance to move. Lauren is no longer my caretaker but she may feel responsible for Ellie, her link to Greg. She surely can't go back home and she can't see Greg until Ellie returns to us.

Lauren busies herself in other parts of this huge house. I don't know where she is or what she's doing but I can hear her singing lightly. She's not distressed. She probably feels better than she has in weeks knowing that her family is safe.

Ellie was worried. She senses danger in Chase. Does she know something about him that the others don't? He inherited his house in the early 1980s when he married. He had grown up there as had Al. Al let him and Julie live there and when Julie died and Chase moved away, Al moved back in and has been

there ever since. Donny has lived there off and on with Al since his mother's death. Lots of family history inside those walls. What else is in there? The house is still boarded up but Ellie is not handling the property.

I bet I can worm my way in. I want some time alone in that house. Better to do it before Ellie "wakes up."

49 The Mysterious Plot

That night I tell Lauren I want to sleep near Ellie and I improvise a bed on the floor of her room. An hour after Lauren retires when I hear nothing inside or outside the house I snatch Ellie's car keys, release the emergency brake, and coast down the hill. The fact that nothing goes on here works to my advantage tonight. I park two blocks from Al's house and, with a flashlight from Ellie's glove compartment, I walk there. I don't try the front door. I slip past the overgrown bougainvillea and around the corner of the house.

No lights are on and I assume the house is vacant. When I hear voices, I freeze near an open window in back and try not to breathe. The voices fall slightly and I fear they have heard me. But in two minutes they resume. All the voices are male — maybe three or maybe four. They are planning something. Some merchandise is being moved and secrecy is essential.

"Ya can't do it this week. Folks is still on guard from the explosion and the fire. We have to let things die down."

A soft spoken but urgent voice implores, "We don't have time. I agree we must be careful but we must also be swift." I realize when I hear the last word that I don't often hear the word "swift" spoken. Someone has been to college.

"Gentlemen, please," and with those two words a chill inch up my neck. I recognize Chase's voice from the funeral. Same authority, same presence. Those two words tell me that he is clearly in charge of this gathering. He wants something done. What? He continues, "We must be smart. People are tense. We can't tolerate anything out of the ordinary. We must blend in. Remember, we're almost finished. This is the biggest transaction we've ever..." and a raccoon spies me and shrieks. He runs through the backyard, knocking over small flower pots.

I coil into a ball on the ground, crouching behind a hedge. I hear the back screen door open and someone steps out onto the landing. A male voice grumbles, "Lousy raccoons.

Someone should shoot the pests." My heart beats like an enraged percussionist on a snare drum. I fear it will give me away but apparently it isn't audible beyond my ears. Hunched over, trying not to breathe or flinch, I can't hear. I don't move for what seems like hours. I wait until everyone leaves. Where had they parked? I don't hear cars drive away.

I sneak back into Ellie's bedroom and sleep for a few hours on the floor, awakening stiff and unsure of what I heard. I don't know what is going on but it sounds like a major undertaking. Chase is in town and is directing. Something big is happening. But what is it?

50 Maddy

I can't think of anyone I can reach out to except Maddy B. Her honesty encourages me to trust her. Personally, I love it, but I imagine she can instill hate in those who fear that she might tell their secrets — Chase, for instance. Her skillful manipulation of Chase at the funeral must have infuriated him. She effectively neutered him in public. Did he take revenge? Will he? Is she still alive?

I turn on the TV just to listen to something other than my own thoughts for a few minutes. The local cable channel carries last night's sewer meeting, an especially enthusiastic engagement. I count 48 attendees, half of whom want to speak well beyond their three-minute limit. The male chair and the female vice-chair handle the crowd by looking at the clock and only responding to time, not to any arguments. Was this simply an opportunity for the locals to vent? Maybe with no one listening? Or caring?

I've heard that just talking, whether or not anyone listens, is valuable, though that concept never made sense to me. I demand that folks pay attention when I speak. I've lectured to thousands of students and then tested their recall of my words. My words.

Now I can't speak aloud and I don't want any attention. And the manner in which I perceive and reason is proving to be grossly inadequate in navigating my way. I used to be an authority. How far I've slipped.

The camera scans the restless crowd and I think I glimpse Maddy B. sitting in the back. She's talking and laughing with a couple old geezers. So, she's not dead and she's not silent. The first hopeful news today.

51 Stealing Fire From Heaven

It's been two days I've been watching Ellie and praying for strength for her soul and forgiveness for mine. Those Catholic roots are like fescue — they never die and they appear when you're not expecting them. I want to be totally rational and unemotionally agnostic. And I can be, most of the time. But the stress of these weeks and months has shredded any intellectual vestiges in my pastiche of a personality. And I'm reduced to that quivering boy who has always lived inside me, though formerly shrouded by competence and position. Now there is no more hiding.

Paradoxical to say that here today. I can't go out except at night but that can be dangerous, too. I can't call anyone or buy a newspaper or take a walk. I can't do anything normal. This world is one which doesn't allow me to function. What can I do?

I can't move but I can think as I have been doing, overtime. I can write and create my own world with my own rules on paper as Kipling did. I can expose an underworld of evil as did Poe or I can imagine a world I can impact beneficently as did Cervantes. How would these three authors approach my situation?

Kipling would use imagination and creativity. He was not bound by what had gone before; he created life. He would tell me not to limit myself. Poe knew the depths of evil possible. He would tell me to be aware. Cervantes would tell me not to lose my dream.

Have I ever had a dream? I've had anxiety and unsureness which led me to circumscribe my choices to those someone else had already made. Rosemary accused me of lacking imagination. That wasn't it exactly. I lacked confidence that I, Nick Sanders, could personally contribute anything new. I could only see myself as an efficient steward of what already exists, not the developer of something unimagined. If someone else thinks of it, I can refine it. My job is to modify, adapt, and alter.

Not relevant in this situation. I need to steal fire from heaven but I need to be a bit more god-like to complete my task. I haven't thought of myself as a god. I am humble. But now I must be powerful.

52 Lauren

Ellie stirs slightly and vocalizes softly. Lauren seems unconcerned, preoccupied with reading Henry Miller in the other room. "Listen, Nick," she calls, "What do you think of this: 'Most of us imagine that we are traveling in a straight line, whereas the truth is that we are moving in circles.' Do you agree with that?"

Not answering a direct question directly, I ask her if she does. Immediately, she replies, "I think it's probably more true than we'd like to believe. It seems that in our 20s we have lots of things we want to do. We can see what's wrong with the world and we want to change it. We protest or sit up late talking about a new society or envision a way of living that doesn't damage the environment. And then in our 30s and 40s the responsibilities of daily living and working and raising a family swamp us and we're glad to just get by."

She sighs and looks down. "Sometimes I wonder if I've sold out. I wanted to contribute something and I thought yoga and meditation and spiritual evolution were my path." I notice a slight flush in her cheeks. "So much for my commitment." She's quiet for a moment and continues softly. "When did I lose my way?"

I move next to her on the curved sofa. I can feel her sadness but mostly her confusion. She really is one of the good souls but also one of the lost ones. I want to console her but realize that would minimize her struggle. This existential angst is the human challenge. And, really, isn't that exactly what I'm thinking about these days, too? I reason and deliberate but Lauren gets it in her gut. I'm learning to respect that.

"It's not easy," I offer. "I, too, had thought life would be closer to a straight line, but since I've come here it seems more like one of those roller coasters that loops up and around and down and half the time you're hanging with your feet over your head. I sure don't know what's what anymore."

She moves a half inch closer to me but I won't let this degenerate into something sexual, though it could do so in about two seconds. I say "degenerate" because what is happening now between us and inside each of us is monumental and noble and sacred. We must respect that.

We must let an otherworldly source guide us. I'm quite sure my mind has no worthwhile advice to offer at this point. Nothing I have done in the past will suffice to meet the challenges of the present circumstances.

I don't know what to do but I know what not to do — anything I did before. I've moved on and time has moved on and we're doing something bigger now. I just don't know what in particular that is. But I know we'll find out if we can maintain our alertness.

So, we sit and we wait and we don't talk or touch and the sun goes down. And something in me feels stronger for our mutual commitment.

We are ready to take a step we've never before taken in our individual lives and there is something about our celibate partnership that allows that. Lauren and I each yearn to be more and to do more than we've ever been or done. We're finally ready to be tested. We each want and need this test. We need to grow out of ourselves.

Suddenly, I want to tell her what I discovered last night on my secret escapade. We're in this together. We're traveling similar personal paths. We're joined in some way. Because of each other, we find ourselves here.

"Lauren, last night after you went to bed, I slipped out. I went to Al's house. I thought there might be some information or something there." I hesitate as her mouth drops open.

She doesn't speak so I continue.

"I want to tell you what I discovered." She closes her mouth and leans toward me, interested. "Chase and a group of men are planning an operation. I heard them. Well, I didn't hear all that much but I heard that something is coming. I don't know what or when but I know it's soon."

She doesn't counsel me to back off as Ellie always does. No, I had surmised, accurately, that she is now ready to take the leap she hasn't previously dared to take in her life. Before I can say more she responds, "We must stop them." She is ready and available.

"But I want to act before Ellie rouses," I continue, "and that may be a matter of hours." She nods her head vigorously. We both love Ellie but we are compelled to move.

"I saw Maddy B. on TV at the sewer meeting last night. Do you know her?" I ask. Lauren lets out a laugh. "Who doesn't? The neighborhood eccentric?"

"Did you see her at the funeral? The way she disarmed Chase?" Lauren nods and smiles. "Why is she still walking around and still attending sewer meetings and still active? Why hasn't Chase leveled her?"

"Maddy B. is a fixture in this town. She's been spouting off about this or that for almost two decades, since her husband died. This is what she does. We all love her; we just don't know if she's really all there." And Lauren taps her forehead. "But we take care of her because she's ours."

"When did her husband die?"

"Why he was in the car with Julie. Didn't you know? He suffered damage to his internal organs and languished at home for some days before passing on."

Why am I still surprised by these ton-of-bricks revelations? Why wasn't it mentioned in the newspaper obit? Another layer of intrigue. My curiosity spins into determination and amps up to fifth gear.

"Lauren, we must talk with Maddy. I want to see her tonight. Do you know where she lives? We need to find her before Ellie awakens." I talk fast and my mind races and my heart pumps and I'm on my feet before I know I've stood up. Lauren is with me.

Thankfully, it's dark. The fog blots out the moon so the blackness is complete. We coast and then drive and turn down some unpaved streets near the Elfin Forest, a romantic name for a little scrub brush acreage. The houses here are old and small. I wonder how some of them remain upright. Lots of wood but not much brick, these places were built more than eight decades ago.

Lauren directs me to the end of Pine Street, walking distance to the entrance of Elfin Forest where the boarded walkway meets the unpaved street. It's after 10:00, but there is a light at the back of the house. Lauren knocks softly and calls Maddy's name but gets no response. We walk around the side of the house and, through the window, see Maddy asleep in a recliner. Lauren knocks on the window insistently until Maddy opens her eyes. She doesn't recognize Lauren at first but she's not alarmed. And then we spy the empty vodka bottle at the side of the chair.

"Maddy, it's me, Lauren. I need to talk to you."

"Door's open," Maddy replies and closes her eyes. The place reeks of alcohol as does Maddy.

"Lauren, we can't do anything with her like this. Let's take her back to the house with us. We can keep an eye on her and get her sober." I look at Maddy. "I need this woman sober."

Lauren coaxes Maddy to lean on her and leads her to her wheelchair. Lauren tells Maddy that she needs her help in the car out front and pushes her wheelchair out the door. Maddy stays conscious long enough to fall into the back seat. We return to the house and let her sleep in the car. She's too heavy for us to move without her participation. We'll have to catch her when she awakens, as soon as she awakens, and explain the situation.

Lauren and I look at each other. We have two unconscious women on our hands and a mystery to solve.

53 Scars of the Past

I sleep fitfully, fearing I won't hear Maddy and she'll awaken and make a ruckus. Ellie makes little sounds in her sleep but doesn't open her eyes. Lauren disappeared into her bedroom but emerges, glorious, at dawn. She's slept better than I have. And she's ready to talk.

"Good morning and isn't it a blessing that we have such a beautiful day?" Lauren beams. "Let me make us some breakfast and I'll tell you a story or two." I'm cheered by this offer and I smile appreciatively.

In less than ten minutes she places scrambled eggs, bagels with jam, and hot tea on the table. We sit, cohorts in crime, or, hopefully, in preventing crime. We're more comfortable together now than when we were in bed, having reached a mutual goal of rising to a new level of integrity. I know I'm different and bigger and more myself than I've ever been. And I'm ready.

She begins, "Maddy lost Joe as a result of the accident. Yes, Joe was in the car with Julie. You see, Joe was Julie's father. He had been drinking and Julie was driving him home. No one is clear about the details after that — how the car spun out of control — but it was a huge tragedy for this town. Maddy never recovered. That was when she started drinking." Unbelievable.

"Maddy is or was Chase's mother-in-law?"

"Yes, and he has been indebted to her since that awful accident. Rumor has it he supports her and sends a physician to look in on her and give her vitamins because Maddy will not put the bottle down. Chase dotes on her. You saw how she treated him at the funeral. He will let her do anything to him and say anything."

And we hear Maddy call from the garage. Lauren springs up and rushes to the car, retrieving the wheelchair from the trunk. In ten minutes they are both in the kitchen.

"Maddy, how are you feeling? Do you remember coming over here last night?" Lauren is solicitous, searching

Maddy's face for a clue to her mental state.

Maddy growls, "Give me some aspirin. Or a drink. Whatever you got closest."

Lauren pours orange juice and leaves to search for aspirin. Maddy and I sit at the table, Maddy with her eyes closed and her head in her hands. Me, leaning back in my chair, watching her, waiting for the next move. I'm having fun now! Whatever develops will be great. Finally, some details are fitting together. Lauren returns, opens a giant-sized bottle of ibuprofen and places two on a napkin next to Maddy's juice.

"Thanks for coming, Maddy," she continues, acting the part of the hostess. Maddy looks at her sideways and swallows the pills.

"Didn't have a choice now, did I?" And she looks at me.

"You remember me, don't you, Maddy?" I ask. "We spent an evening at the Saloon a while back."

"I know I've seen you. Oh, well. I don't worry anymore about what I've done I can't remember. I can't do anything I'll regret anyway. More's the pity." She looks around the kitchen. "Where are we, anyhow?"

"We're in Salazar Hills. For a few days we have the use of this gorgeous home. Isn't it fun?" Lauren puts on a good show.

Maddy isn't buying it. "What's going on? You don't want me. I have nothing to give you."

And I jump in. "Oh, but you do, Maddy. You may be the only person in the world who has what we need." She looks interested. "We're investigating the goings on around here. You may have noticed things are getting more tense and more unpredictable and more explosive lately."

"You can say that again! That fire the other night — I knew Chase was up to his tricks. I could see his fingerprints all over the dirty deed. Fits his m.o. perfectly."

"How do you mean?" I ask sincerely and respectfully. I'm thrilled with her responsiveness. She is a font of knowledge and she's bubbling. She's not even uncomfortable with us here. How quickly she adapts.

"Chase, he doesn't stay around here much. So, when he is here, his presence is felt. You don't see him on the streets but you sure do feel him!" And she chuckles to herself as she looks down at her hands. She's becoming quiet. I don't want that.

"Lauren was just telling me you're related to Chase, so to speak." "Not anymore. And I never was really. It was a bad mistake. The worst mistake of my life. I'll never forgive myself for letting him steal my precious daughter." Maddy's eyes tear as she looks around the room. Is she looking for alcohol?

Lauren pulls her chair closer and puts her arm around Maddy's shoulders. "It's been awful, hasn't it? And for so long." Maddy leans her head on Lauren's shoulder and cries softly.

"You'll never know," she whispers. I watch the two women interact with kindness and gentleness. I remain a silent spectator.

It's only a few minutes before Maddy sits up straighter and looks around, grabs a paper napkin and blows her nose loudly. "I'm so glad you're with us here, Maddy," Lauren continues.

Maddy finishes with her nose blowing and tear wiping. "So, you serving breakfast? 'Cause I sure could use some."

Gleefully, Lauren rises. "Coming right up." Lauren cooks and I ask Maddy gently probing questions. She seems eager to tell her story. She tells me about growing up on a farm in Wisconsin, an only child with a distant father. She watched her mother die in an accident with a tractor her father was operating. She said her father wouldn't talk about the incident but he moved them both to the west coast to escape the scene of the horrible event. She said he didn't talk much after that and that she raised herself while he drank on the front porch. One day in her senior year in high school she came home and found him rocking in his chair as always but this time he didn't wake up. She said it was a relief to be away from him. In less than a year she married Joe, a neighbor and a classmate.

Lauren sets Maddy's plate in front of her. Maddy leans back slightly and purses her lips. For a moment she is quiet. She picks up her fork and taps the plate but continues talking.

"Julie was the best thing I've ever done. She was beautiful and alert and cheerful. She loved everyone. A happier child you've never met." And Maddy again lowers her eyes and grows quiet.

"Joe and Julie and I were living on acreage owned by Al and Joe was trying to grow grapes. He'd buy new plants every year but they never produced anything worthy of being sold. And, even though he was trying to make alcohol and sell it, Joe bought so much alcohol we couldn't pay the rent on the place. Al carried us as long as he could, years actually, but he had bills to pay, too.

"One night Al came over and wanted to talk with Joe. They told me to take Julie and go to the back bedroom (she must have been twelve then) so they could have some privacy. Al stayed for more than an hour. I didn't know what they were talking about but when I came out both men were happy and smiling. Al said not to worry about the rent, everything will work out. Joe didn't say a word, just headed for the bottle under the sink and drank 'til he passed out." Maddy's face contorts and she plays with her fork, pushing scrambled eggs around her plate.

"Well, it was years later before I learned that on that night Joe had sold our daughter to Al. No, it wasn't as uncivilized as it sounds. He had made a deal with Al that when Chase was ready to marry he would convince Julie to marry him. That was very important to Al. And Joe said it was fine because the Slates were a good family and Julie would always have what she needed and Joe and I could keep the farm. Really, there were no losers. Or that was the way Joe put it when he told me years later." She shakes her head and closes her eyes for a minute.

"Well, I wouldn't hear of Julie marrying before she was 18. She was such a sweet girl. Really, she didn't know anything about the world. Why, she'd never been out of the county. But when Al snapped his fingers Joe told Julie that her marriage had all been arranged. At first she protested but she was naturally meek and soon enough gave way. The marriage went off without a hitch, but Joe and I never had a peaceful night after that.

"Julie didn't complain but she didn't look happy anymore. I seldom saw her smile. She worked hard at teaching school but she lost her spark." Maddy sighs deeply.

"When she became pregnant we rejoiced in hopes that a baby would give her back the life we thought we had stolen from her. And, actually, it did. Donny was a beautiful baby, too beautiful, perhaps. He was big but he didn't grow the way boys do. He didn't gain his coordination, he could never play sports, and he was always slow. Julie didn't care. She devoted herself to him. Donny became the center of her world. So, when Chase started traveling, she barely noticed. It was Julie and Donny. Chase was just a figure in the background. There were stories about his overseas exploits in the papers but she really didn't notice. Donny saved her from a marriage she never wanted."

Maddy looks around the room again. "Hey, you wouldn't have, maybe, a beer, would you?" Lauren shakes her head and says, "Sorry. Can I make you a drink of fruit and juice and protein powder and vitamins?" Maddy scrunches her nose, shakes her head, and says, "Water will be fine." Perhaps she doesn't eat, I think. How does she survive? How has she survived all these years?

"Maddy," I interject, "I hear different stories about the car accident and about Julie's death and I didn't know until yesterday that Joe was in the accident, too." Lauren's eyebrows arch like mountain peaks but Maddy isn't offended. Lauren shakes her head but Maddy speaks, unaware of Lauren's consternation.

"I guess I had something to do with that." My ears Spocked. "I wasn't there, of course, but I never forgave Joe for the deal he made using our precious daughter as currency. After she moved out we slept in different rooms, sometimes not speaking for days. I hated him. He destroyed the best part of my life but what could I do? I couldn't support myself. I couldn't work. I couldn't leave. So, I made his life miserable. I punished him every way I knew how and, you can believe me, he felt it. He paid for that despicable deal until the day he died. Unfortunately, Julie died with him."

"What do you mean, 'unfortunately'? Did you... know

something about his death?" How do I gently, without offending, ask if she murdered her husband?

"Well, that bastard Joe used to go drinking at the bar out of town. It's not there now, but it was back in the hills, down Los Osos Valley Road — the Scream Catcher. He'd go down there every night, after he'd been drinking all day and drink more with the low-lifes who'd hang out there. He turned into one of them— scum, lower than scum." She did hate this man who was her husband.

"Well, he made me sick. I'd had enough of him and I didn't want to smell his beer breath another night. So, yeah, I had the guys at the garage jiggle some wires and unhook some hoses. I didn't tell them why. I told them I wouldn't drive it and I'd be back the next day so they could finish the job." Her head falls into her hands with her elbows on the table.

"But that night, it had never happened before, the bartender called Julie to come pick her pop up!" And Maddy wails. "Oh, why? Why that night? It would have been fine if that damn bartender didn't interfere. But he did. And, of course, Julie would do anything for her father. She got out of bed and drove her own car over there and left it to drive her father home in his. They had loaded him into the back seat of his car and locked the bar and left." Maddy bawls as if she hadn't mourned her daughter's death from years ago.

"And so, my plan worked. Perfectly. Except it killed the wrong person. I hated Joe for ruining our daughter's life but it was because of me that she lost her life entirely!" Maddy shakes her head as tears fall on her chest and on the table. "I can't forgive myself for killing my beautiful daughter. I will never forgive myself."

In my mind I finish her sentence: And, so, that's why I drink.

54 Teaming Up

Wow.

I didn't expect any of this. So, the car accident wasn't intended to kill Julie and it wasn't engineered by Chase. Al had played the Devious Manipulator earlier but not in this incident. Maddy sobs with her head on her folded arms on the breakfast table. Lauren's shell-shocked expression tells me she didn't know any of this. Suddenly, everything has again shifted. I don't have any idea what to say or where to go with this new information.

I stand up and leave the room, intending to walk circles through the house and allow my thoughts to settle. I do two laps through all the bedrooms and halls when I hear Ellie stirring. Not what I need now; at the same time, I want her back and whole and OK. I enter her room and approach her bed. Her eyes are opening but she's not focused. Softly, I ask, "Ellie, are you OK? Do you feel all right?" She is groggy but knows who I am.

"Where am I? What happened?" And she closes her eyes again and breathes deeply and evenly. Is she asleep? I watch her for three minutes before I continue my pacing.

I want to deal with Maddy now but when I enter the kitchen she's snoring, her head still on her folded arms. Lauren sits without moving, her face blank, eyes dazed. Three women in this house with me, none of them functional. Don't I have the touch?

It's just a minute before Lauren speaks. "That's some tragic story!

I didn't know. I would never have imagined. Poor, poor Maddy!" "I'm sure no one here has heard what Maddy just told us," I surmise. A colossal secret! Lauren says sincerely, "I will never breathe a word of this to anyone. Anyone. It's incredible. This poor sad woman carrying all this with her, alone, for so many years. My heart breaks for her." Yeah, I think, murder is a painful secret to keep.

Aloud but to myself I mutter, "I wonder why Joe wasn't

mentioned in the newspaper obit? He didn't die but he was there at the scene of Julie's death."

I could have jumped out of my skin when I hear Ellie's voice behind me at the kitchen door. "You don't give up, do you?" I race to her side and guide her to an empty chair but she is steady and doesn't require my assistance. Lauren smiles and hugs her.

"Are you feeling, OK? I'm so glad to have you back!" What is it with these women? They can do unconscionable things to people they call friends and still act like they love them.

"What day is it?" Ellie looks around. "What happened?" Lauren pipes in, "Let me fix you some eggs. That will be good, won't it? Some scrambled eggs with a little cheese?"

Ellie gains better orientation by the minute, meanwhile Maddy dozes and snores. Lauren stands at the stove beating eggs as though this is a normal morning in a normal household. What a bizarre scene.

Ellie speaks. "Now I remember — the fire, you two staying here, the syringe. That's what did it, isn't it?" She looks at her forearm but sees no marks. "I've had the wildest dreams. Of course, it looks like you two have been busy, also." She looks at Maddy for two minutes but doesn't remark.

"I dreamed I was in the Amazon and there were huge beautiful birds with dazzling colors who would shriek and call to each other. They communicated in their own parrot language. They were organizing a take-over of the jungle. They wanted to destroy all humans who had mistreated them and their homeland." She sits back and seems to be thinking about something. Then a clearer consciousness clicks in and she says, "What have you two done? What's going on?"

Lauren places food in front of her, removes Maddy's plate, and becomes engrossed with her work at the sink, turning her back to us. Ellie stares at me.

"Well, it's a lot to tell," I stammer. "Eat your eggs while they're hot and we can talk later." Ellie doesn't move, just stares at me, daring me to dance around this one. I owe her some straight talk for her three days lost.

"Well, I made an interesting discovery at Al's house the other night. Chase is in town and he's planning some big operation. Maddy just told us…" Lauren scowls at me over her shoulder. "Maddy told us a lot about her life here. She provided some missing facts. But we need to know more. Lauren and I…" But again I stop when Lauren turns around and slings spears at me with her eyes. Her facial features are so expressive. She dries her hands and sits at the table with us. As she sits Maddy stirs slightly with the movement of the table.

"Ellie, you and I have been through a lot," Lauren says in a deferential tone. "We've been friends for 15 years. We've known each other through some pretty hard times and we've been there for each other, haven't we?" Ellie's demeanor softens. Lauren continues, "Yeah, we have. But I want you to know something about me that you maybe never have known. I haven't. I've realized in the last two days that I haven't been living my real life. I've been doing what I thought I should do and going through the motions and acting the part but I lost my soul somewhere along the way." Her eyes tear. Maddy turns her head but her eyes are still closed.

"Ellie, I love my family, but I haven't ever been really . . . you know, really living my life from the inside. I've tried to do the wife and mother thing like everyone else but I've been going through the motions, as they say, and I can't do that anymore." She pauses and uncrosses her legs and shifts position. Bored isn't quite the word for Ellie's expression but she is not engrossed by this confession. Maddy raises her head, her eyes open but unfocused. Lauren barely notices.

"I wonder if that's true for all of us. Have we just been pretending? Have we really known what's going on but didn't want to acknowledge it?" She sighs and looks at the dish towel on the table. "Honey, I love you, Ellie, but this life we're living… it's crazy. It's made us all crazy. We believe things we know in our hearts can't possibly be true but we go along with them. Just to fit in. But nobody here is happy! And, more importantly, nobody here tells the truth!" Her voice drops. In a loud voice Maddy chimes in, "Amen, Sister!" She sits up and leans back in her chair.

And Lauren proceeds. "You know it and I know it and, if they would only admit it, this whole screwy town knows it! Ellie, you and I love this place. This is home! We love the characters who live here with us and we know they're crazy but we really do love them!" Maddy looks at each of them but neither meets her gaze.

Lauren continues, "But, Ellie, it's up to us — the four of us at this table — to stand up and speak the truth. Too much is undercover. Too much is ignored. Too much is, well… lied about. You know what I'm talking about." Ellie looks away and I believe she does know what Lauren is talking about. I also know that I don't. Maddy attempts to stand and raise one fist. "Right on! It's about time!" But she slumps back in her seat. She's interested in this conversation but physically weak.

"Ellie, this is the time for us to act," Lauren says with her characteristic sincerity. "We have to do something to save our wonderful town. We can't hide our heads any longer. Please, won't you tell the truth with me? Together we can make a change. Together we can turn this town around. We can save these people's lives. You know that's the right thing. We can help! Please, Ellie! Please, do this with me."

Maddy waves an imaginary flag. She is in. Ellie is silent for a few minutes, looking around the ceiling and the walls. Tears roll down Lauren's cheeks slowly. She looks steadily at Ellie and holds her hands folded in a prayer position in front of her face.

55 Scratching the Scars

I have to hand it to my Cuz. She's no marshmallow. The Maltese blood that runs through our veins won't let her be duped. Lauren's feelings carry her. Ellie leads with her skepticism. I admire her for that.

"Did the world change while I was asleep? Has the earth shifted on its axis?"

"Actually, that's a good way to put it. What we've done in the past, we can't do any longer." Lauren is satisfied with herself.

"What's this 'we'? You may have had an epiphany but I've been out of it."

"The truth is we've all been out of it. Forever. Living here we've changed. Don't you remember how you were when you first moved here? You were eager and outgoing and ready for anything. You were an adventurer! You opened a real estate office having had no experience in real estate and you trusted. No, more than trusting, you knew it was right and you didn't doubt yourself. You proceeded and doors opened and business worked and life developed and you were happy!

"Don't you remember those early days? You didn't make much money the first six or seven years but remember when we'd run into each other at the ice cream shop on summer evenings? My boys were little and your Bryce was still with us and life was uncomplicated. We didn't have much but all of us here together felt so privileged, like we've been given this incredible opportunity, this little bit of paradise for ourselves. No one else knew how special this area was and we didn't advertise it. We just loved what we had and appreciated the hills and the shore and each other. Life was simple. We were happy.

I know you remember that, Ellie. Don't you?" Maddy looks askance at Ellie and snickers.

Ellie responds stiffly, "I worked really hard to get my business going and things were tight for a long time. It wasn't peaches and cream." Clichés bug me. Why can't I ignore them? "Of course not, but we were whole. What we thought, what we did, what we wanted, what we dreamed. It was all so normal. And happy! We knew each other. We helped each other. We cared what was going on. We didn't have secrets." "OK, Lauren," and Ellie pushes against the table until she's standing. "You want to talk about secrets? Let's do that. And let's start with you. Any secret you want to share? Hmmm?"

Suddenly, Ellie has taken control of this conversation. Her brown eyes bore into Lauren's. Lauren squirms in her chair and examines her cuticles. She makes noise but she doesn't speak words. Maddy is silent, mesmerized by the force of Ellie's thrust.

"OK, so a lot has been swept away. If I'm asking for honesty, I'll have to go first." Lauren stands now, too. "When my boys were young, wanting to give them everything, I took them to kiddie soccer and T-ball and cub scouts. Isn't that what you're supposed to do? Expose your kids? Well they got lots of exposure. Unfortunately, Greg wasn't involved — business, long hours at the office. So, the boys and I shared lots of time. "I grew to know their coaches and teachers. I just wanted everything to go well for them. Maybe I became over-involved. My motives were honest, at least initially. Brian didn't do well at soccer his second year. The first year was great, so this was a surprising development. And, naturally, I consulted his coach." "Yeah, naturally," Maddy adds. "I remember that coach.

How many marriages did he ruin? Four? Five?"

"Well, I didn't let him destroy mine," Lauren adds with some exasperation. She looks perturbed and defensive, not how I've seen her before.

"No, you sure didn't. But it was so close some of us were taking bets. I lost $10." Maddy giggles. Still standing, Lauren crosses her arms. She speaks firmly, "That was a terribly sad time for us but we survived."

Ellie interjects, "Come on, Lauren. You said you wanted honesty. You were the one who had the affair. You were an adult. You made a choice. You were not the victim here.

Your husband, your sons, and, to an extent, the school suffered because of your selfish actions. Do you want to be honest or not?"

Lauren drops her head into her hands and cries. Ellie continues, "The reputation of the school was smeared, we lost our coach and we didn't have soccer for three years after that. Yeah, your marriage survived. Of course, that was when Greg started traveling so much. Any connection? Huh? What do you think, Lauren?" I haven't seen Ellie so vicious, not in adulthood. She could skewer her friends in junior high, making fun of their weakness in front of a group who laughed until the victim cried. I forgot how icy her heart can be.

Lauren gasps. She is broken, she can't defend herself. She is guilty. Nothing more to say. I can see that she just wants to move on. "That was a terrible mistake. I'll never forgive myself."

And Maddy laughs. "Forgiving yourself for that one seems minor compared to what followed!" Lauren blushes and Ellie zeroes in with her laser focus. "Yeah, Lauren," Ellie offers. "What about the sixth-grade teacher? And who was next? The tutor from the college? How old was he?" No one is laughing now.

"I never slept with anyone under 18," Lauren protests. I am shocked watching and listening to all this.

"No, not that you knew was under 18," Maddy laughs accusingly.

"He told me he was 20," and Lauren's voice trails off.

"Yeah, and you're as naive as we are," Ellie jabs. Her friends glare at Lauren.

Lauren sinks into the chair, her elbows on the table, her head in her hands, beyond tears. I am overwhelmed. Is she? Is this the Lauren I fell for? Apparently, other men respond to her the way I did. I was naive thinking I was her first dalliance, maybe even that I instigated it. What is real?

Ellie is hot now. "Yeah, Lauren, let's tell the truth. A good idea. What did happen with Donny? Anything? Why was he prohibited from entering the gym? We all like Donny. Why does the owner of the gym hate him? Any ideas? Hmmm, Lauren?"

And Lauren explodes, pounding the table with her fists. "I did nothing in that case. I swear it and I think you already know it's true. I did nothing with that boy. I never touched him."

Maddy chimes in, "We know you didn't touch him." Were her eyes twinkling as she smiles broadly? "No you weren't the one doing the touching. We completely agree with you on that one."

Lauren protests. "It wasn't my fault! I couldn't stop him. I didn't make him do it. I never led him on. He got no encouragement from me. So, he had a crush on me. Is that my fault?"

"No," Ellie offers. "And it wasn't your fault that he sat on the curb in front of the gym playing with himself and repeating your name, either. But, really, Lauren, don't you think that's the height of tacky?" Ellie can draw blood with her sarcasm. "Singing about Lauren, his love, in public. How did Greg react to that? I'm actually surprised Greg hasn't sued for divorce. I bet he could get custody and a settlement with your fine record." I expect Lauren to run out but instead she walks to the far side of the room and slowly returns. She stands at the table and breathes for a couple minutes while the rest of us hold our breath.

"I admit I've lived a lousy, selfish life. I hate myself, OK? I've thought about offing myself but I can't do that to my sons. I've caused them such pain. I'm going to live honorably from now on. I don't expect you to understand or believe me or support me but I will do my best and if I'm all I have, well, then, I'll make it on my own. I just don't want to hurt anyone else." Lauren stands looking at the table, holding the back of the chair, her hair falling over her face. She doesn't ask for forgiveness but I want to tell her that I forgive her, even though I've just learned her story.

"Lauren," I start, "We all make mistakes. You do have quite a list but you are still here and we are still here and I think what is important is that we go on together. Isn't that right? Why don't we just move on now?" I look at Ellie and Maddy who stare blankly back at me. I want to wrap this up.

"Yeah, Nick," and Ellie focuses on me. "I bet you would

like to just move on. Certainly, you have no secrets. You've led such a praiseworthy life." I feel betrayed in public even though no details are spoken. "What's the matter, Nick? Getting a little antsy?" Is she smirking? How can she turn on me so easily?

I feel the blood drain from my cheeks. "Be very careful, Cuz. I don't think you want to do this." And I look at her menacingly. But there's no stopping Ellie.

"I should be careful? Is that what you are cautioning me, Nick? I should be careful?" She is taunting me and I know this won't end well. Why is she so hateful?

"Ellie, we all have a past…"

"That's for sure in your case, huh, Mr. College Professor. Finally made yourself respectable, huh? Left us immigrant trash behind? That's the term you used, isn't it? Immigrant trash? Well, that's certainly not you any longer, is it? No, you're not any kind of trash now. Not so that anyone knows, anyway. Of course, you don't let anyone know you too well, do you? Not since Rosemary.

"What a beautiful woman she was. First, you quit talking to her and then you essentially deleted her from your life. Think her depression had anything to do with you? How many suicide attempts did she make? Those long sleeves hid her scars but everyone could see right through her eyes and she wasn't in there anymore. You killed her soul. She just tried to finish the job. You were so smart and you knew just how things should be and you knew exactly what you would and wouldn't do and you didn't need to listen to her, did you? No, you were the smart guy. She was just little wifey. You sexist asshole pig. You present this perfect facade to the world and you kill the people who love you most."

That takes my breath away. I'm reeling but I won't protest. I've thought the same things about myself but no one has ever said them aloud. I'm surprised Ellie knows this and humiliated that she will expose me publicly.

Maddy speaks, "Whoa, boy, you've got your own story, too. Tell us. We're all confessing here today. Come on."

I can't just jump into this and spread my insides all over the table but I can't allow Ellie to lacerate me, either. I take the offensive. "It seems to me you're in no position to be hurtling accusations."

But it's Maddy who stops me. "Nick, we're all in this and we're doing it together. We didn't sign on for True Confessions but that's how it's developing and now it's your turn and you've got to come clean. Come on, Nick. What have you been hiding for so long that you've lost your wife and your humanity? Tell us."

Suddenly exhausted, I can't think of a distraction and, really, I don't want to. My deepest regret which I've never told anyone has burned a hole in my stomach for decades. I want to disgorge it. I want to throw up and be free of the suffocating pain that ended my life or what could have been my life.

"OK, listen. I haven't said this before and I don't know if I can say it now." I look down and brace myself. "I dearly loved my brother Jake when we were kids. Life at home was strange with our parents but he and I bummed around and rode our bikes and delivered newspapers and threw the pigskin. That's when we were young. As we grew up — in junior high and then more in high school — he drifted further and further into his own world until finally, I couldn't pull him back. But that was OK because I was thinking about college and preparing for a career and for my own life. I couldn't wait to get away from Middleton. I thought when I left home I would re-create myself and be the man I wanted to be, no more the wimp everyone ridiculed. I could make myself somebody.

"Meanwhile, Jake was deteriorating. Now we know it was the schizophrenia overtaking him but then we thought he was just getting weirder and weirder. He wouldn't talk to anyone and sometimes he would walk around the streets for hours without looking where he was going. We'd ask him at the end of the day where he had been and he wouldn't know. Or wouldn't say. He wouldn't say much to anyone. No one could get through to him any longer.

"Mom wouldn't give up on him, though. She worried about him and read books and consulted doctors but nothing made much difference. If he were prescribed medication, he would take it for a while. When he started feeling better, he'd think he didn't need it anymore and quit. Then his paranoia would burst and he might act violently. He wouldn't sleep or bathe and his appearance would slip.

"I didn't want him around me when he was like that. He embarrassed me and I hated the jeers I received from the other kids at school about being the brother of the loony bird, having sicko genes, and turning into a monster one day myself. I had always hated being held back by my family's reputation and here it was happening again! I had to get away from him. He wouldn't let me help him, but, in reality, I couldn't help him. I was just a kid."

Ellie interrupts. "You were a self-centered punk. You could have protected him but you were only thinking about yourself. You didn't think about how he was feeling or what he needed. No, your only concern, as always in your life, was with yourself.

What did *you* want? Well, you made it abundantly clear that you never wanted to be part of our family. You didn't want to be his brother. You never showed him any loyalty. Or any of us for that matter."

She's right. I hated being labeled "immigrant" and I hated not being like everyone else and I hated the kids' references to the Mafia. I just wanted to be normal and to be accepted and to be appreciated and I thought the way to do that was to be like everyone else. And Jake sure wasn't part of that picture. I thought I could never have what I wanted until I excised him from my life. He wasn't doing anything with his life. He never asked for my help. Why shouldn't I go ahead and make the life I wanted? Isn't that the American dream? Isn't that why we are here? If Jake doesn't want that, well, I wish him the best. But, really, what can be expected of me? Dad didn't worry about him. Dad didn't even seem to notice him. He just did his work and polished his shoes and read his books and said, 'Your life is what you make it.'"

"So, what was that summer after your freshman year of college like? Tell us, Nick," Ellie mocks me, just like the kids did in high school. I look at my hands folded on the table and don't speak for a long time. But I know I must.

"I was home for the break and we were a family again. Mom tried to make it a normal home but Jake was crazy and stoned much of the time and Dad was off in his private world. After a year of proximate normalcy on a college campus, I couldn't stand it. We were pretending and that's all we were doing. No one was telling the truth. Mom had given up on that and was just trying to live day to day. It was bizarre being in that house.

"And one night I couldn't stand it any longer. We were finishing dinner, another dinner where Mom made pretend conversation and Dad read the paper and Jake babbled disjointedly. And I said, 'Enough! There is a major problem here and we need to talk about it. We are not an average family and we can't pretend any longer that we are. Crazy Jake here is the joke of the neighborhood.' I could have continued but my father shouted as I had never heard him shout before, 'That is enough. I will not have that kind of talk in my house.' He hit the table hard and he left the kitchen and spent the evening in the garage working with his tools. Or that is what we thought he was doing. Jake went to his room and smoked and Mom cleaned the kitchen. All as if nothing had happened.

"Well, about midnight after we had all gone to bed, a shot awoke us. It was very loud and very close. We found Dad's body in the garage. He had shot himself in the head and lay face down in his own blood." I can't control my weeping, seeing that horrible scene again. The trauma of that night has been buried in the pit of my stomach and has laid there rotting. Now, for the first time, I have gotten it out. I cry harder than I have ever cried in my life. I don't want to hold back anything any longer. It has cost me too much. My body shakes and jerks. I fall to the floor and hug myself in pain. I think I will die from the anguish. I don't care how I appear; I don't even think about that. All I want is to reclaim myself.

I must have cried for more than 20 minutes, on the floor, thrashing around. When I finally calm down and sit up, first on the floor and then at the chair at the table, the women all have tears in their eyes. They look at me with understanding, not pity. Lauren puts her arms around me but I don't reciprocate. After another five minutes we look at each other.

Ellie is still crying. "I didn't know that! I was told he had a heart attack. I never knew! I'm so sorry, Nick."

"Can you understand now, Cuz? The one time in my life I let go with my feelings and my words, my father committed suicide. Because of me. I am responsible for my father's death." Another tear works its way down my face. "I know that's not really the truth but that's how I felt for years. So when I'd see Rosemary lose control, I couldn't tolerate it. It brought back excruciating pain. I am so sorry for what I did to her. I owe her another lifetime and if I could get it for her I would. I destroyed her life and my life in addition to my father's. Am I the biggest monster walking around?" I smile wryly to let them know that really, I'm OK.

We're all silent. Until Ellie's cell phone rings. I haven't heard that sound in a while. She takes it in the living room and Maddy and Lauren and I look at each other and at the table. I'm guessing that they, like me, can't believe what we've been through the last twelve hours. The intensity of our time together is like nothing I've endured in my life. I'm about to speak when Ellie rushes in.

"That was Carolyn. She had left messages for me the last three days and when I didn't respond, she alerted Les. They have been looking for me but they assume that you two are dead." She looks at Lauren and me. Maddy pipes in, "What about me? Does anyone care where I am?" She chortles.

Ellie continues. "Carolyn wants to meet with me. Says she has important information. Wouldn't share anything on the phone. I'm leaving now to meet her at the library. I don't know what this is about but I don't want to sharpen suspicions. I'll be back as soon as we're finished."

I stand and hug her. "I love you, Cuz. You're the best Cuz a jerk could have." Her eyes tear as do mine. "OK, now go away." And she leaves, moving rather quickly for someone who has lain still for three days with no food. The telephone always did energize her.

The three of us stand and tidy and keep to ourselves the rest of the day, reading borrowed books and watching sewer meetings on TV. We use our time and space to restore our own foundations. After having been torn apart and exposed to each other, we want privacy.

175

56 Live and Let Live

It is after dark when Ellie returns. She carries bags of groceries and clothes. She seems perplexed and preoccupied. After supper I ask her to come into the library with me.

"What's going on? You're not all here," I ask her.

"Nick, I'm worried. When I went to the library, the door was locked even though it was during work hours. Carolyn heard me bang on the door and she let me in. She took me into the back office and there around her round oak table were Elizabeth, Chase, and two of his business partners. They were meeting about 'the next step.' I think they wanted to see me to detect any indication of my hiding something. I have to tell you, I was afraid. Scared to death. Something hung in that room around all of them. Something shadowy, like an indoor fog, a foreboding presence. I so wish Deb were there. She could identify it. There is something evil brewing but I don't know what."

"How long did you stay? What did they ask you?"

"I was there more than an hour. I kept crying; it wasn't hard after your news. They thought I was mourning the death of a relative — you, and a friend — Lauren. I encouraged them to think that. They asked if I had seen you two and I said no, I was waiting to and hoping to but that after the explosion at Deb's I was sure you were both gone. So, I told them I had been at home crying most of the time and doing some business when I could. Carolyn asked why I hadn't returned her calls for three days and I said I was too upset. I'm getting better at crying on demand. I sure did a lot of it this afternoon. I have the worst headache." She rubs her forehead with two fingers.

"They didn't see you come here, did they?"

"I'm sure they didn't. I went home and then to the bank and the post office and the grocery store and back home and I tried to look like any other citizen going about the details of daily life. I couldn't tell that anyone was following me. I thought of calling Les to guard us up here but he's already in Chase's pocket." As she tires, Ellie looks frazzled.

I want to understand this situation. "What about Elizabeth? What is her role in all this?" "I don't know. She didn't speak, she just looked stern and made notes. I don't know what she was thinking."

"What did Chase say? What went on at that meeting?"

"They were very secretive. The two men who wore sunglasses didn't speak. It was just Chase and Carolyn who directed the conversation and they were careful. They didn't ask me anything too direct but they wanted information. I could tell they were curious and I was afraid they suspected something so I focused on crying and grieving and being unable to concentrate. They bought it, at least a little; they quit grilling me after 20 minutes or so. I was sweating. I didn't want to give away anything but they are so smart that I don't trust I can outwit them. Not for long."

"Do you think we should move? Or keep on the move?" I ask.

"I don't know what to think. This is all so confusing and so scary and so crazy." She shakes her head and looks so tired.

"If only we could make some sense of any part of it," I reflect.

We hear Maddy guffaw in front of the televised sewer meeting. "Let's join her. Maybe she can clarify this situation."

On the TV screen protesters with signs stand respectfully in the back of the meeting room. "Dissolution Delays the Solution" and "Down with the Sewer Board" are the most prominent. Maddy points and chortles. And we notice Donny carrying another sign,

"Live and Let Live."

"What does that mean?" I ask no one in particular.

Maddy replies, "That's a leftover from the days when his father was lobbying for rights to run his experiments. Donny must want to be included." I wonder why Chase doesn't keep a closer watch on him, especially when he's in town. Chase must know he's vulnerable now. He's here. Some folks know he's here. For some reason he doesn't want more people to know his whereabouts. But letting Donny run loose seems a huge risk. Of course, that's what Donny usually does so maybe if he weren't visible, folks would wonder.

The thought occurs to me that we need to enlist Donny. Of course, Lauren and I are unavailable. Maddy won't be questioned about being at the meetings or wanting to talk with Donny. He is her grandson, isn't he? I am still amazed by that connection. We've got to get her to this meeting before it ends and she must leave with Donny. Ellie will have to drive her and we can only hope she isn't noticed.

I suggest my plan to the women and they agree immediately. Time is precious so Ellie bundles Maddy and her wheelchair into her car which isn't quick or easy and they head off into the night. Lauren and I watch the meeting on TV and pray that Donny doesn't leave.

In 20 minutes the camera pans the crowd and we notice that Maddy is in the back in her wheelchair. Ellie is not in sight. Good. The camera returns to the speaker and the board. Intermittently, it surveys the crowd and each time we see Maddy a few feet closer to Donny but laughing and talking with whomever she is near.

The meeting continues until almost 11:00 and we have lost sight of Maddy and Donny. We go to our separate bedrooms sure that nothing more can happen tonight.

57 The Dragon Speaks

The next morning's light seems unusually clear and bright. I sleep late and the world is alert when I open my eyes. Something about the freshness of the day inspires hope. As I make coffee I remember Donny and Maddy and I wonder how last evening turned out for them. And where they are and how they are. Something tells me all is fine. Is that just a wish?

In an hour Ellie arrives lugging her open house gear. "This will give me an excuse to be around here today. I'll put the signs up in front of the house so my car won't be questioned but I didn't advertise it so I don't plan to receive any lookers. The residents here won't suspect that I'm not really expecting anyone."

I ask about Maddy and Donny and Ellie tells me they are both at Maddy's. "It's always a question of how long Donny will remain any one place but Maddy said she'll try to keep him around all day. He trusts her and if he knows anything she'll get it out of him. I told Maddy what I knew from the library meeting so she'll take it from there." We look at each other. Neither one of us knows what to do at this point but wait. We need facts and details from Chase and Carolyn but we risk giving ourselves away if we're too aggressive. So, we sit back but we don't relax.

The minutes and the hours of the day crawl by as on scraped and bruised knees. We can't concentrate. Lauren nervously offers one unrealistic theory and potential plan of action after another. I give her credit for imagination but after the sixth "Maybe they . . ."

I suggest we do some yoga. Ellie joins us and for a few minutes we all focus on something other than our fears. The tree pose Lauren holds for a long time. Both Ellie and I collapse into a tired shrub position but Lauren stays erect, her eyes open but her gaze unfocused.

We leave the room with her standing motionless and make tea in the kitchen. Ellie calls Maddy on her cell phone but hangs up within a minute. "Chase is there now," she whispers. "Maddy isn't afraid of him but she's using Donny as leverage. She told me so last night. Donny won't leave her even if Chase insists and Chase knows that. He has damaged his relationship with that boy so much that there really is no relationship. They each distrust the other but Chase is afraid of what Donny can do to him. I don't think Donny is afraid of Chase. Sometimes he hates him but mostly he ignores him. Between Maddy and Chase, Donny will always choose Maddy."

I remember the scene at the funeral. I wondered how Maddy could be so effective in directing Donny and confounding Chase. Apparently, Donny is one of the few people in town Chase can't control. And I'm betting Donny knows something we want to know. How to get to him? And how to get him to trust us? We'll have to stick with Maddy. Since he trusts her she must always be present wherever he is for the next few days. He seemed to feel comfortable around me when we were getting acquainted but he thinks I'm dead now. I hope he does. I'm afraid he'll say everything he knows. That's good if he's talking to us. It's bad if he's talking about us. That means we can't let him know the truth about Lauren and me being alive and then let him leave. Once he knows we're still around, he's our prisoner. What's another way to think about that situation? I don't want to be the Enforcer but I'm afraid not to be.

Lauren floats in and in her most transcendent tones announces, "We will prevail through surrender. That's our next move — to surrender." Ellie and I look at each other. I grimace but Ellie counsels me to wait and to consider what Lauren says. "Nick, what choice do we have? We're holed up here. We know we're running out of time. We still don't have a clue what this mess is about. We can't fight Chase. Why not consider surrender?"

I don't know what to say. What does surrender mean? Right now, we know that Chase is at Maddy's and I'm pretty sure he's there sans compadres. I know Maddy and Donny are with us in spirit. The only danger is from Chase's cohorts who might show up unexpectedly.

"What do you say, Nick?" asks Ellie. "Shall we head over there now?"

My first thought is that by doing so we give up our only advantage, surprise, but maybe we are using this surprise to propel the plot to a higher level. What could be the downside? We could get killed for real. Definitely worth a second thought. "How about inviting Les and the Rotary folks and the Cad's crowd to meet us there?" I suggest to Ellie. If we have an audience Chase won't act. I've noticed that about him. He relies on secrecy. We'll blow his cover and then with the town looking, we'll confront him with — what? I still don't know.

Ellie is on the phone before I've completed my sentence and in ten minutes we are in her car heading to Maddy's. On the drive over I consider my life, realizing that this may be the last evening of it. I've come a long way and furthest since I've moved to this little town. My life has been uprooted and thrown in the air and I don't know how the pieces will fall. But it all seems right. Whatever happens tonight I know that we — Lauren and Ellie and Maddy and I — we're all acting in integrity. We've looked at parts of ourselves we didn't want to see and we've shared our secrets and we survived. So what if we don't live through the upcoming encounter? We've shown up and we've done our best. What more is there?

As we approach Maddy's, cars line the streets. Some drivers have parked and become walkers who march silently. We join them since we can't make any progress in the car. Neighbors acknowledge each other but there isn't the usual gay chatter. An aura of solemnity shrouds the group. Ellie nods to several folks who thank her for calling.

When we reach Maddy's door, we see more than a dozen people inside her house already and at least twice that many heading in this direction. I'm giddy with excitement. We trusted and now something is happening. I don't know what but I know it's right and we're ready.

Ellie enters first and holds the screen open behind her for Lauren and me. Chase is standing with Donny across the living room and his eyes pop when he sees us. He sputters and puts his drink down. He is surrounded by townsfolk whom he knows but he appears to be distinctly uncomfortable. He shifts his weight from foot to foot and looks around. There is no exit, though. People crowd the kitchen behind him and are still coming to the front door, even though they can't enter. Is he sweating? I don't know Chase but I'm guessing he's seldom this surprised.

"Chase," Ellie opens, "Good to see you again. Our little conversation yesterday was cut short so I thought we might have more to say to really clear the air. That's OK with you, isn't it, Chase? With your only son and your mother-in-law and all your friends here? We just want to chat. And let me thank you in advance for being so available and welcoming."

Ellie's on top of this situation, she's suave, she's orchestrating the meeting. And she's clever. She must know that Chase is seething inside and that he will kill us all if he gets the chance. Our safety lies in numbers and she has called out all her friends, acquaintances, business contacts, and, yes, Les, too. I don't see him but I expect he will show up eventually. With all of us watching, Les can't deny what's going on.

Maddy speaks. "Thank you all for coming! I really hadn't expected a party or I would have saved some booze for you but you all know you're welcome here. We're friends, aren't we?" And she looks hard at Chase. "Aren't we, son?"

For the first time he speaks. He has regained his composure. "It's so great to see all of you! I had no idea. I wish I had known you were coming."

"Yeah?" someone from behind him yells. "Why? So, you could leave town?"

Another disembodied voice adds, "Anytime you're here something goes wrong for us. Then you disappear and we're left to clean up the mess. If we can. What can we do about Deb's house? And, for that matter, about Deb? Hey, what do you know about her?" This reference to their loved and departed neighbor riles the crowd. Voices become louder. Shouts punch the evening air.

"You know, there is a limit to what you can do, Mr. Chase Slate. There are laws and those laws are for you, too, not just us," another unidentified crowd member offers.

Maddy addresses the crowd which has been growing angrier with each statement. "Friends, let's calm down now," she says. "Our neighbor Chase is here for a visit and you know he doesn't often stop by so let's give him a good Los Osos welcome and listen to him. He probably has lots he wants to tell us. Go on, Chase. What's going on in the world? What have you been doing?"

She pats the arm of the sofa next to her as though Chase will follow her lead and sit like a miniature poodle obeying its master's command. Chase doesn't budge. His fists are gripped and his jaw is set but no words come, not for over a minute. Silence hovers uneasily like smog on a September morning. Finally, he speaks.

"I'm glad we have this opportunity to visit. There have been some misunderstandings and it's great that we have a chance to correct them."

Another voice from the back. "Quit your lying, you sonofabitch. You've brought an element to our town that never existed here before and we don't like it. You can't use us for your own amusement and then ignore the damage you create."

A roar of approval follows this statement and indiscernible comments fly through the air. The tension is palpable. I delight in such candor. Now maybe I will learn the truth. And the town will, too. Apparently, everyone isn't on his side as I had assumed.

The noise falls to a muffled din and we look at Chase who doesn't speak. He's looking at everyone and I'm guessing the gears in his head are whirring. Has he ever been on the spot? I gather that his father protected him and directed his way. I presume that his business contacts appreciate whatever it is he does for them so much that they don't interfere. He truly has led a golden life or so I think until he speaks.

"Friends and neighbors, we're in this together. We all love this area and our homes here and our lives and we want the best for each other and for our children and for ourselves." A jeer from the back is silenced by some who want to hear

Chase's words.

"I haven't been around much the last 15 years. You probably thought I was out in the world making big deals and trekking through deserts and forests and hobnobbing with politicians. Yes, I've done my share of that but there has been more. I've never forgotten what we have here. And I've always planned to return."

"Yeah, sure. After cocktail parties in Washington and dinners in Hong Kong, who wouldn't want to come back to Los Osos? Sure, Chase, we believe you," another voice from the back calls.

"I understand, I understand," and Chase raises his palms as if to stop an onslaught. "But there is lots you don't know. You don't want to listen to me now but you must. Give me that consideration. Please." The crowd calms and all movement stops. Chase pivots a quarter turn and walks a step closer to the corner of the room. He turns back, inhales deeply, and talks to the ceiling.

"I've probably had the best life of anyone who has ever lived in Los Osos. I was lucky to be born into a family with generations of land ownership and leadership in community affairs. I thought I was special and those of you who remember my teenage years know that I didn't always use my privilege wisely." A few twitters sprinkle the group.

"Losing my wife was harder than most of you knew. I presume you thought it was just an arranged marriage, that it was my father's plan to keep me in line. It started out that way and I wasn't a good husband at the beginning." He looks at Maddy and walks over and takes both her hands and kisses them, whispering, "I'm so sorry."

He continues, "Julie really was a saint. You thought I was glad when she died but I was heartbroken. I fell into drinking and drugging. My father got me out of here so I wouldn't destroy myself and everything I touched. I threw myself into work and money and the fast life and used those distractions to get away from myself.

"The harder I worked the more success I found. Then it was easier to find better drugs and more women and bigger adventures. Money opens doors and I walked through doors

I hadn't known existed. You've read about my exploits. I can tell you stories you won't believe. But what you didn't read about was what it was like being me. It's funny, when you have everything, no one wants to really know you. Everyone wants to drop your name or have you at their parties or sign a contract with you but no one has ever treated me with the tenderness and caring that Julie did. I've met a thousand women and not one has offered me the gentleness that resided in her heart."

I find myself moved by his descriptions of his loneliness but immediately I jerk myself back. This is a hugely wealthy international businessman and I'm feeling sorry for him? He's good. This is why he's so successful. He intuits what people want and gives it to them.

Someone yells, "We're weeping for ya."

"OK. I know I don't deserve anything from you. I've been self-absorbed and self-indulgent and I haven't thought about too much besides what I want. I've acted like a jerk. I've used this area, you're right, and I've benefitted splendidly. And I haven't given back my fair share. But I want to do that now."

"Wait a minute, Chase," Ellie intrudes. "We're so glad you're sharing with us but let's not rush over the details. What do you mean you've used this area? I don't understand." An image of a metal fist in a fuzzy glove comes to mind.

Chase looks away and then back directly at her. "I finagled a deal to use the land behind the old train station for growing my crops."

"Yeah, Chase, some crops. Thanks for spreading illegal drugs around openly so our kids and anyone else can indulge. You've made us real popular."

"I hired guards to watch the grounds." "The biggest losers around."

"OK, you're right. I mishandled that deal and didn't provide adequate oversight."

Ellie steps forward. "What do you mean 'hired guards' and 'oversight'? What you were doing was wrong. Wrong. Illegal and immoral and a danger to those of us who live here. Do you have a conscience, man?"

Chase's shuffling indicates that he wasn't expecting this barrage. I admit that I wasn't, either. Ellie has turned into an unrelenting truth-demander. Other voices volunteer their agreement.

"You're right," he says a bit defensively, still anxious to move on. "It should never have happened and I'm completely to blame and I regret my actions."

"What, Chase, what do you regret?" Ellie pins him down like a butterfly on display. "Are you sorry about the kids who stole the pot in junior high and became addicted and didn't finish college? Do you regret the corruption of the police force in this county so that we know we can only buy justice? Do you miss the time away from your very own flesh and blood, your son Donny, who grew up without a mother or a father? What is it you regret, Chase?"

Donny steps up with the mention of his name. He may not always grasp the details of a discussion but he certainly can pick up on the tone and tonight he wants to participate. "Yeah, Dad," he starts vigorously but clearly doesn't have his next line ready. "Yeah,… what about me?"

"You're my first son." The crowd buzzes. First? Is there another? "You're the most important…" but the laughter is loud and the scorn unyielding. No one believes that Donny is important to Chase. Cheap sentiment doesn't fly here.

Maddy wheels her chair over to Chase and puts her hand on his wrist in a gesture that is somehow condescending. "Son, you've made a marvelous opening here but we are not anywhere near closing. No, this train has just left the station. And we're all on board for the duration. Which may be a very long trip if Ellie gets her way." Maddy giggles.

Now Ellie is standing, facing Chase who is standing, looking around, people on every side. He won't dare excuse himself for any reason. He's on the spot and he can't back down and he can't wriggle away. He's got some fast talking to do. I'm delighted.

He wrings his hands and looks at the floor for most of three minutes. No one flinches… or even breathes loudly. It's time for the truth. No excuses, no delays. We're all here. We're looking at him. And he knows this is it.

He inhales deeply, raises his head and appears two inches taller. He squares his shoulders and his chest expands. Now he is the formidable figure I expect. His fear and uncertainty have evaporated. The bold aggressive innovative businessman stands before us.

"My friends, and please indulge me with that term, at one time we were friends, weren't we? Many of you grew up here with me. We've gone to school together and played football together and sent our children to the same schools. We've made a life here." A voice from the back interjects, "Until you ruined everything."

"I admit I have definitely influenced the growth and development of this area. It's in my genes, I suppose. My family wanted to make this county something special. My great- grandfather saw potential here and invested his fortune. My father worked tirelessly to introduce new trade and business. My father encouraged me 'to bring the world to Los Osos.' He thought so highly of our town and our people and the serenity of this area. He loved the beautiful unspoiled hills. He said we had some of the best farmland in the state right here. We have Monarch butterflies and sand dunes and eucalyptus groves and white beaches and deer and…"

The same voice contributes, "Yeah and now our very own variety of pot. Thanks."

"My marijuana experiments will revolutionize medical treatment for chronic pain conditions." Snickers and snorts fill the air. "I understand how you may doubt that, but there will be news in the next two years and our work right here will be mentioned for contributing to a breakthrough in understanding the growth and death of cells. Don't believe me. You will read it in the papers and hear it on television.

"And that's my concern now. When this news breaks what will happen to our precious little town? We will be flooded with media types from all over the world, we run the risk of being inundated by international organized crime, and I'm afraid we may lose the life we treasure. I tell you my work will be big and this town will benefit but now we are at a crossroads.

"As of this minute I'm ceding ownership of the land to the city of Los Osos. I will maintain control of the use of the land and the planting and the harvest. When the experiments move to the next level and the drug companies are involved, then it's your decision how to proceed. I will steer the ship until then.

"Do I have your support? Los Osos will become an international center for medical research and drug development. Our economy will be assured of eternal solvency. We can buy as many sewers as we want and complete all the repairs to the streets. We will have nothing to worry about ever again. This is the legacy I'm leaving Los Osos."

"And what about you, Mr. World Traveler? You figuring on moving into an old house near here and settling down?"

"I don't blame you for questioning my motives. I like the life I've lived since moving away from here. I like the glitz and the power and dealing with the corporate decision makers. But don't you see how it will serve all of us if I maintain that role and you produce the world's most healing medical marijuana? I'll do the outside work and you do the inside work. We'll be a team. I'm offering this town an opportunity tonight it has never had and never will again.

"And it's strictly up to you if you want to accept my offer or if you want to reject it. But if you don't take it, I will develop this product myself. So, you see, in the end something big will happen here. Do you want a piece of it or not? I'm offering you an opportunity. You decide what you want."

I was not expecting this turn of events and from the loud murmuring I hear around me, I assume that no one else was, either. Small groups talk among themselves debating the advantages and detractions of this out-of-the-blue proposal. The crowd's fury has melted into curiosity and considered possibility and imagination. This is a civic moment, an evening the residents will remember for decades as The Night Our Town Assumed Its Place in the World. And Chase propelled us all to this righteous height. I say "us" hesitantly because though I have not been accepted as an insider here, I certainly have been caught up in the excitement of the moment. And, after all, I do live here now.

Small groups chatter among themselves, both inside Maddy's house and on the streets in her neighborhood. After an hour they straggle away still twittering in the dark. Ellie and Maddy and Donny and I chat in the living room. We didn't see Lauren leave but when we leave, she is gone. Her house is near. After all the excitement and with Chase knowing we're alive, she probably decided to go home and resume her "normal" life. Who could blame her? We all feel that way. We want to just be normal. And maybe better than normal if and when this news of Chase's pans out.

Ellie and I drive to her house. My physical exhaustion distracts me from the gnawing at the edges of my mind. I fall asleep on her couch before she makes tea.

58 Town Savior?

When I awaken the day is bright but the gnawing continues. With my eyes closed I zero in on my agitation. Everything was wrapped up too neatly, too quickly last night. This town has lived with an uneasy peace provided to them by Chase for months and years while he has lived who knows where. Then he blows into town and several disasters erupt in quick succession. Folks are shaken and very upset. When given the unexpected opportunity, they confront him as they never have. They leave their role as unquestioning recipients and direct their ire to him, something I'm guessing has never happened here before. He does some fancy dancing, promises them the world, and everyone leaves mollified. Again, he positions himself as the town savior and those who just minutes ago were outraged muffle their voices and withdraw.

I'm not buying it.

I'm all for tying up loose ends. In fact, there is little I prefer. But these ends have been tied way too tight, way too facilely. And why is Chase always the decision maker and never the one questioning and open to learn? He's always in control. That fact alone amazes me because that is the opposite of my experience since I entered this town. My life has spun into orbits way out of control and I've adjusted. And grown and learned.

59 Out of 'Prison'

Waking up the next morning early I feel almost joyful. I'm not dismayed by the overcast sky and the wet breeze. Ellie makes one of her famous vegetable omelets and I make raisin toast and life looks possible, even good. I leave to walk to my house, no longer afraid of being seen. I feel like I've been let out of prison. I love breathing the fresh air, swinging my arms, hearing birds and dogs and cars, participating in the morning scene. I even wave to strangers. This is a good day.

I haven't been home in weeks now, not since before my "imprisonment" with Lauren in Montana de Oro. Abruptly, I think of Hildy and am ashamed I haven't worried about her. My front door is unlocked and standing open an inch and, cautiously, I enter. The living room is as I left it, papers strewn and a coffee cup on an end table.

I walk into the bedroom and my heart stops and then races. Hildy's body has been stabbed fifty times. An upright sword pierces her chest. Her dried blood spatters the sheets and the walls. A bloody finger has written "you're next" on the wall opposite the bed.

I ache for her suffering and death and for my responsibility in it. I don't know how I'm responsible but I know that it's because of me she was cruelly murdered. I am mortified. I sink to my knees and sob over her cold body. This awful deed was done days or weeks ago. My grief sickens me and I vomit until nothing is left in me.

Even then I keep retching.

I'm not afraid for myself. I'm infuriated and determined. I will find whomever did this. I've never understood revenge the way I do at this minute. Someone will pay. The phone rings but I don't move. I can't and I don't want to. Nothing will take me away now. Ellie's voice on the answering machine tells me to call her immediately. But I want to bury my dog and clean my house and restore sanity to my life. It's been too long. I'm not even sure I can reclaim sanity as I've known it. Too much has happened.

60 Unescapable Storm

After placing Hildy's broken body in a sheet, I wash and scrub and disinfect, trying to make this place new again. I can't eliminate the odor of death, however, and shadows cling to the old paint. A dastardly incident happened here and I can't expunge that fact. Life will never be the same. I can't know such violence, even second hand, and live with the guilelessness I brought when I came here.

For most of my life I could manage to understand what happened to me, to put words to it, and to make sense of the events of the days and the years. Reason served to interpret my experience. There was a relationship between what I did and what happened to me. Logic evaporated when I drove into Los Osos. I didn't realize that until now, however. No known rules of civilized society have applied since I've lived here but my obtuse mind refused to acknowledge that reality. How could it? I needed life to make sense and I would mentally mold it to the exigencies of my circumstances to extract meaning.

Now there have been so many blows and such severe ones that I can't not see that I'm caught in a drama staged by an unseen but commanding director. Clearly, this director is of the hard knocks school of life — learn from experience and endure any severe experience that's required to learn. But learn what? Is all this craziness choreographed for my benefit? Is there meaning and order which escapes my rational view?

Rosemary could find meaning in clouds. I ridiculed her endlessly about her slippery analysis but now I'm getting the sense that I need to develop an appreciation for slip-sliding and forget the Teutonic two-step. I can't find comfort in rigid surroundings or unbending rules though formerly they had provided me haven in an emotionally stormy world. Now I'm standing in the storm and there is no cover and no escape and there's rain in my eyes and it's OK. I can do this. In fact, there is nothing else I'd rather be doing.

Am I crazy? Not specifically so, but I am different from how I've ever known me.

Ellie rushes in. "Lauren is missing. No one has seen her since last night. She didn't go home."

I can't get away from my own tragedy which, to my annoyance, Ellie doesn't notice. "At this point we don't know anything is wrong with Lauren. We do definitely and without doubt know that a terrible murder happened here," I say impatiently.

In response to Ellie's wide circle eyes I quickly add, "It's Hildy. Someone killed her and wrote on the walls in her blood threatening me." Ellie relaxes which annoys me further. Hildy's death to me is like losing a child. Sort of. I was responsible for her and she suffered because of me. I am now suffering. Of course, I hadn't thought about her for a month. Nevertheless, her violent death pains me tremendously. I can't worry about Lauren now. She's probably OK.

Ellie makes some impotent sympathetic sounds but I'm way over the line. I can't be easily consoled and I won't be distracted. Hildy's murder is an unconscionable and cowardly deed. Someone who knew I was detained entered, apparently without any trouble, and killed an old pet. How much lower can I sink? He threatens me anonymously and violates my home. But he doesn't make himself known or ask for a fair fight. I will squash him like an ugly cockroach under my heel.

I have purpose to my days and focus to my agony.

61 Breaking the Chains

A switch flips in my heart with Hildy's murder, coming as it does after weeks of craziness and confusion and hiding. My stress level must be off any scale ever conceived. I can't muster the energy to be excited or scared or ready to act about anything other than Hildy. I sincerely hope Lauren is safe but I can't think about her now. I wish Maddy and Ellie the best but I have nothing left to give. I must take care of myself and my broken heart.

Funny to say that my heart has broken over an old dog who was dying anyway but maybe her death is symbolic. She lived with me through much of my adult life. When I planned and worked and succeeded, Hildy was there. When I received tenure, she was the first one I told. The awards I earned hung on the wall near her bed. Everything that's happened to me, she witnessed. And now she's gone and in some strange way so is the first part of my life.

My sadness is bittersweet. I want to break out of the bonds that have held me so tightly. I don't want to live with that same fear and anxiety that wrapped my heart in heavy chains. Wistfully I say goodbye. How could it be otherwise? That's all I've known. That's the only me who has walked the earth. I've outgrown him but I do love him and I appreciate his pain and fear. I'm burying him along with Hildy.

It's time to grow up yet some more and I will do it but I want to take some time to sit quietly with my thoughts and my grief. I mourn the losses which I chose — my votes for safety instead of risk-taking, my erring on the side of conservation rather than expansion, my denial of my passion in the service of respectability. I have lost so much and it was all by my own choosing. No one else could foreclose on my life the way I have. What was I thinking? Didn't I realize what a tremendous gift it is to make a mistake and say, "Oh, well, I tried?" By wanting to be like everyone else I curtailed my individuality.

In the early days of our engagement Rosemary told me that my soul was a beautiful rose but the thorns surrounding it were long and sharp. I found her poetry enchanting but didn't seriously consider her imagery. Now I'm so aware of those long ugly thorns and I want to cry because the first part of my life has been about sharpening the thorns, not about nurturing the rose.

Have I been thinking at all? Not really. I did what I presumed would carry me to safety and accomplishment and prestige but the rewards from my choices seem hollow in comparison to the cost to my aliveness. I've sacrificed so much and I didn't even recognize how I was killing myself. I thought being accepted was preferable to being unique. I thought fitting in was more important than trusting my own vision. I thought anything outside me was more valuable than the chaos inside me. So, I signed my own death sentence willingly and proudly. And I felt good about murdering my soul; I thought my pain would lessen. I chose numbness instead of honest living hurt. I opted to be a robot instead of an evolving person.

Looking at Hildy's body I see what I did to myself.

62 Solace

I spend the next few days alone, not answering the phone or watching television. I just want to be by myself and with myself. I straighten and arrange and nest. Having a home means more to me now than it ever has and I savor my moments here. I'm glad I miss Hildy so much and I bless the tears I cry for her. I'm not completely dead inside. I vow that I will cry as often and as much as I need to for the rest of my life. I won't fear my feelings and I won't hide from the consequences of expressing them. I promise myself that I will always check in with my heart before I make a choice and I will only choose what enhances my aliveness no matter how anyone else reacts.

I practice checking in with my heart. I listen to the urges I feel there instead of to the direction from my thoughts — a major redirection. Often, I call on Rosemary to accompany me in this journey into the dark regions inside myself. I so appreciate her now. I wish I had when she was with me.

I slow down. All this running and hiding and confronting and disclosing has worn me out. I need to regenerate and my heart is the pump. I move slowly and I remember old times and I think about the past as though I'm sorting out the elements of my life and putting them together differently. I see what's around me differently and I see myself differently. I have so much more to me than I've ever known and so much more that I can pursue. Although I've retired, I feel like the world is now opening to me. And, finally, I'm ready to open to the world and to myself. After a few days of solitude, I can say I've experienced several moments of peace.

I like that feeling and I want it more.

63 How and What

As I sort and re-sort and reorder and reconsider, I sense the concerns about Chase and Donny and Maddy churn below the level of my awareness as though they are sorting themselves out, too. I don't shine my brain's logical light there. I just trust that something will emerge in due time. I can be patient. After all, it's not my problem to solve or my challenge to understand. It's just something happening in me which I watch. Nothing to be anxious about and nothing to control. I don't know what is supposed to happen anyway so I can't critique what is happening. I just allow. Since I don't know otherwise, I trust that all is OK. Waiting is the how and I don't know the what but I know it will be fine.

I read and walk and work in the yard and chuckle as I watch myself. I must look so ordinary and yet I feel uniquely defined. And patient. I can be patient with this life process because I'm in my own skin and inhabiting my own heart and soul and, thus, whatever happens is right for me. So, I look to life to teach me. I catch myself saying, "Thank you" to no one in particular because I feel such peace. I've never been this satisfied. I'm not striving or looking to the future or worrying about what might be. I'm simply present. That's a relief after these weeks of breathless activity. I just want to breathe.

So, I do. And once in a while I cry and sometimes, I find myself laughing. I sleep well, better than ever. And I live my life with no plans really. I let life come to me.

64 How and What

As I sort and re-sort and reorder and reconsider, I sense the concerns about Chase and Donny and Maddy churn below the level of my awareness as though they are sorting themselves out, too. I don't shine my brain's logical light there. I just trust that something will emerge in due time. I can be patient. After all, it's not my problem to solve or my challenge to understand. It's just something happening in me which I watch. Nothing to be anxious about and nothing to control. I don't know what is supposed to happen anyway so I can't critique what is happening. I just allow. Since I don't know otherwise, I trust that all is OK. Waiting is the how and I don't know the what but I know it will be fine.

I read and walk and work in the yard and chuckle as I watch myself. I must look so ordinary and yet I feel uniquely defined. And patient. I can be patient with this life process because I'm in my own skin and inhabiting my own heart and soul and, thus, whatever happens is right for me. So, I look to life to teach me. I catch myself saying, "Thank you" to no one in particular because I feel such peace. I've never been this satisfied. I'm not striving or looking to the future or worrying about what might be. I'm simply present. That's a relief after these weeks of breathless activity. I just want to breathe.

So, I do. And once in a while I cry and sometimes, I find myself laughing. I sleep well, better than ever. And I live my life with no plans really. I let life come to me.

65 Challenging Status Quo

It's a long walk from my house to Maddy's but after this time alone I'm ready for some company. I trust Maddy. She's shown me her tender spots, she doesn't make excuses for herself or try to make herself look good, and she's straightforward. It's not that she doesn't have anything to hide; she doesn't try to hide what's unseemly. She's a drunk. She knows she's a drunk. She'll tell you she's a drunk. And then she'll drink to underscore the truth of her words.

As I walk over, I hope she's not done herself in for the day yet. It's still early. When I round the corner, I spy her leaning over her potted plants on her front porch. As I approach, she sits up and smiles broadly. "Good to see you, Nick. You doin' OK?"

I climb the four steps and notice she's been pulling grass from her plants. "I'm OK now. I needed some down time and I took it and I'm coming back. How're you doing?"

Maddy's cheeks are flushed and tiny beads of perspiration dot her hairline. "For an old broad I'm pretty darn frisky. It's good for the rest of you that I can't get out of this chair or else I'd be running you around, tearing up the place, creating some havoc!" She laughs and I'm glad to be with her.

"Well, then, you're just the old broad I want to know." It's good to be light-hearted for a moment. I appreciate that Maddy is consistently upbeat and positive. I know that she carries her bushel of pain but she doesn't impose her sadness on anyone.

"I've missed hanging out with you," I say. She looks at me quizzically. "And, yes, I have some questions," I add. She sighs and sits back with a smirk. We know each other. At this moment there is nothing I wouldn't tell her. But I want her to tell me some secrets.

"Mads, I don't know if you remember the first night we met. We went to the Saloon after a sewer meeting and you made some pretty interesting comments." Her expression indicates no recognition. "You said that the sewer controversy is just a cover-up, that all this hullabaloo is really about something else." No response. "I infer that you don't remember saying those words but maybe you can recall the gist of our conversation — that some special interest groups have designs on Los Osos." Again, her eyes cloud. "OK, the words you said to me are 'you can't live a normal life here' and then you said something like what appears to be isn't necessarily the truth. Do you know what you meant?"

"Son, I can't recall the details of what must have been a beautiful evening but I can tell you some facts now. This sewer hubbub is just flak in the air designed to waylay the unsuspecting who think the sewer really is a concern. It's not. It never was and never will be. Oh, sure, we'll get a sewer some day and then everyone will say, why did we fight about it so long? Well, I'll tell you why we fight about it. 'Cause when we stop fighting we lose our town." She looks at me solemnly.

"Why, Mads? What could you lose by actually having a sewer? Doesn't every town have a sewer?"

"It's not the sewer, Nick. It's the transformation of our little town into yet another beautiful coastal village without a soul. We've been pretty isolated here. Yeah, we're on the map but way out of traffic. And with that seclusion we've been granted the space and the time to develop and live as we like. You noticed it as soon as you drove into our little haven. We don't have to succumb to the pressures of an urban area, we don't compete, we're almost backward if you think about it.

"But for us it isn't being backward. We can live without the consequences we'd have to endure in a bigger area. We can think how we think. We may not be well-informed about international politics but we know our neighbors. And, basically, we care about each other.

"Nick, think of it this way. You go to sleep and when you awake you find yourself in a beautiful garden, a paradise unlike anything you've ever known. You can stay in this paradise if you agree to forget the larger world you formerly inhabited. If you agree to accept that — that the rest of the country and the planet doesn't matter and that how things are here is all that really counts — you can stay. But you must accept those facts. You can't straddle both worlds and you can't bring much of the larger world into this one. Now, that isn't too high a price to pay, is it? To be comfortable every day? To live a nice life? Who wouldn't agree?"

"But, Maddy, there isn't a table where you sign a contract when you drive into town accepting those conditions. No one says that. No one talks about that."

"And that's the point, Nick. Everyone has agreed without even knowing what they were doing. And then they do it again every day. The blinders aren't so limiting if all they keep out of sight is what you don't want to see anyway. And, so, we focus on what we can handle and what we want to think about and we choose not to engage with the rest."

I pause and close my eyes for a minute before speaking. "That's why I received such an un-welcome. I didn't play the game. I didn't accept the rules. I asked too many questions."

"That's it, Nick, and don't forget the blinders. We like our blinders. We want to play our sewer game. We could tolerate the pot fields as long as they weren't made a focal point. We could pretend there wasn't any harm done. We're fine with our sheriff's department, such as it is, since we don't acknowledge any crime. You see, we don't have any problems and we all agree on that fact and then you show up." She smiles warily.

"I see. And then I show up. I point out some things you don't want to recognize but then you had to and that upset the state of affairs and that old denial hasn't been the same since." "No, Nick, it hasn't and I don't know if we'll be able to reconstruct it. Too much has happened."

I laugh. "Do you want to continue pretending that what is isn't? Making up life as you go along?" I can't believe she is serious. "Don't you prefer to see things as they are and to know what you're dealing with?"

"Think about it, Nick. Really how much can any one of us control in our lives? We can make little decisions, the kind of car we drive or what we eat for breakfast, but in the larger scheme are we really more than automatons? Are we here for some master puppeteer's amusement? Is there meaning to our days? Maybe or maybe not, but here in Los Osos we make the best of our time. Who can really find satisfactory answers to those eternal questions? So, we enjoy our days and the little things we find to occupy our time and we're OK. Isn't that enough?"

I am astounded, first by this shoddy logic and second by the facile solution. And she sits there and looks at me with no ambivalence.

66 Wait, Surrender, Trust

I'm back where I started. What I suspected, Maddy has confirmed. Now everything is the same, it's just out in the open. I haven't changed a thing here and no one wants me to. Their resistance to me is understandable. But they were straight with Chase the other night at Maddy's. How can that evening be forgotten? It can't.

As I wander home I wonder. Ellie can be so direct. These last weeks she has spoken honestly and openly when no one else was telling the truth. Maybe that sense of detecting insincerity was always behind her taunts, she just didn't know what to do with it. She can be powerful when she sees the facts and speaks them. She tells the truth.

I haven't always done that. When I was young, I didn't see the truth. Later, I didn't always want to acknowledge the truth when I was hoping it wasn't so.

I think of Chase as someone who bends the truth to fit his needs. That show at Maddy's! That upset the status quo in this little town. The buzz the days following was about how he will save us, what a great guy he is and always has been, and how we can trust him to protect us. It seems too neat to me but I am willing to reconsider my judgment of him as a villain. I can't tell the good guys from the bad guys any more.

I detour to the library. The bathrooms are at the front door which is architectural genius to my way of thinking so I stop briefly. Emerging, I open the door into Carolyn's form rushing past and I whisper loudly, "Speed limit 65." She turns but, characteristically, doesn't greet me enthusiastically. "What's with you, Nick?"

"Just thinking and walking and trying to fit puzzle pieces together but I'm not getting a picture. How are you with jigsaws?"

"I've done a few in my time but I gather you speak metaphorically and your real concern is… Why don't you just ask me what you want to know? You don't search me out unless you have a reason." I am glad she doesn't say "ulterior motive" but I trust that's what she believes and, actually, that's true.

"The library writing contest. How do I make sense of the threat I received among the entries?"

Carolyn stands straighter. "What threat? I know nothing about this."

"The intent was very personal and very explicit — a story about an English professor moving west to be near his cousin and dying. I don't know who submitted that paper but I'd like to. If someone threatens your life, Carolyn, wouldn't you want to know more about it?" I don't want to upset her and I don't want to alienate her but I do want her attention. I want her to realize that I'm serious about uncovering this mystery.

"Bring me the paper and I'll do my best to take care of it. I know most of the patrons and maybe I can decipher a clue."

I'm glad she's not emotional but I wish I could read her just a little. Something in me believes that she has a direct line to Chase so whatever she knows I expect him to know within a couple days. This threat was sloppy work, not what I would expect of him or her. I've made my move; now let's wait and see what's the response.

I've learned to be still, to wait, to surrender, and to trust. I've also learned not to push. Especially here. Goal orientation is not a virtue and efficiency is mistrusted. I expect to read a plaque in some government building: "We go along to get along." But there is something that bothers me. I can't identify it today but I trust that tomorrow it will be clearer. I can't even formulate the problem. I've learned that reality here has many layers and unimagined depth. Anywhere I am today will look different tomorrow so today's problem may be tomorrow's condition. And maybe even a condition I learn to appreciate.

Something else I've learned: be grateful, even if I don't feel like it. It's wiser in the long run.

67 Blinders

Ellie and I sit at the Hong Kong restaurant. I've developed a great appreciation for their almond chicken. Ellie talks about real estate but I want her take on Maddy's words.

"She said, 'We like our blinders,'" I tell Ellie. "Can you believe it? She said that everyone who chooses to stay here accepts limitations and, actually, prefers them! Is that crazy?"

"It depends upon what you mean by 'limitations.' We think that people who choose to live in smoggy, traffic congested cities are limited. We can't understand how they would choose to tolerate something so clearly bad for their physical and mental health. But millions of people live that way and want to continue living that way. If you offered 100 people a chance to move to Los Osos, how many do you think would accept your offer? Maybe one, maybe none?"

I consider her statement. When I count my colleagues at the university, I can't imagine one of them accepting such an offer. I wouldn't have moved here 30 years ago when I sought distraction and activity.

"But what about blinders? Maddy contends that blinders are for ignoring what you don't want to see."

Ellie hesitates and looks at the corner of the ceiling. "Are blinders a limited blindfold or an aide to focus?" she murmurs to herself. She continues in a louder voice as she looks at me. "We're not really any different from most humans in the U.S. today. We do our best, we want our lives to count, but we're not always sure what that means. Is it being a helpful neighbor or is it calling a stranger on a perceived misdeed? Should we hate Chase for planting marijuana or appreciate him for contributing to medical knowledge and our well-being with his experiments?"

"He's a small time con man who only has his own interests at heart," I mutter dismissively. The more I think about his benevolent gesture at Maddy's, the more convinced I am he's not to be trusted.

"Now, wait. I can understand how you want to paint him in shades of black but try to look more dispassionately. He was a rambunctious kid in a tiny town. He lost his mother too young and his father didn't know what to do with him. He ran wild, creating minor mayhem until he was married, and you heard what he said about his time with Julie."

"Yeah, I heard," I nod, "but I don't trust him. He's too slick and too slippery and he doesn't stick around long."

"That's true, but so what? You're ready to convict him and you don't even have a charge against him. You don't know that he had anything to do with the rock thrown through your window or the writing contest entry or the cap in the makeshift grave. You can't pin anything on him definitively and, yet, you've already condemned him in your mind. Even at that meeting at the library, I don't know that anything evil actually transpired."

"You said you felt it! You said it hung in the air!"

"Try taking that to court. That's one thing about this area. We give folks the benefit of the doubt. We grant second, third, and fourth chances 'cause we know that life is hard and we can't get it right the first time. Or the second and maybe not the third."

"No one granted me a second chance. I was vilified before I was known. I received so much hate."

"Hold on, Nick. You scared a lot of people. They didn't know you or what you were about and they felt threatened that you, a stranger, could deprive them of a life they love and the only life they know. It may have looked like hate but I'm guessing it's fear."

"Pretty potent fear. Fear with an aggressive edge."

"Yes, when folks feel pushed, they come out fighting but really, and I ask you to be very honest here, Nick, really you haven't been damaged."

I can't believe she says this! I haven't been damaged? What is having my car burned? And my head bashed? And my dog killed? And my freedom of movement curtailed for weeks? Am I to excuse these deeds as misunderstandings? I think not!

"OK, OK," she continues, acknowledging my umbrage, "I know it's asking the unthinkable for you not to take all this personally." And with that statement I explode.

"You're very right, Cuz. It is asking way too much. All this feels very very personal to me. I think it is designed to scare the bejeebers out of me, personally. I think it is not a coincidence that all this has happened to me. Yes, I do take it personally. And I think I have every reason to." I lean back in my chair, cross my arms, and sigh. I can't believe that she is cautioning me after what I've endured.

The fortune cookies appear at that moment and Ellie grabs one. Mine says, "The lotus blooms in the rain-washed heart." I think I will take that personally.

68 Blooming Lotus

Ellie asked me not to take what has happened personally. Of course, it was personal. But she seems to be saying, No matter how it was intended, don't take it personally. That's very different. How another intends an action and how I receive it are not necessarily connected. I smile when I consider the implications of that statement. Ellie, who is so immersed in relationships, tells me not to be too influenced by others. They have certainly reacted to me but I'm not supposed to react to them. OK. That's requesting a nobleman's patience but I can be noble. Why not? If existence here is somewhat otherworldly, I can be the prince I've secretly known myself to be.

So, moving into my Prince Nick demeanor, I stand a little taller and walk a little straighter and I choose magnanimity as my style. I imagine a blooming lotus in my heart and that vision carries me. I can be a gentleman and a hero and a nobleman. And I don't have to react to my fellow citizens. Can I forgive them? I want to. The pain of Hildy's death and the assaults and having my car destroyed approach that uncrossable line, but why not forgive? Why respond with the same anger that was directed against me? Why fuel this game?

The truth is I'm tired. I can't maintain this pace and the intrigue is no longer intriguing. If some folks like to haggle about the sewer, why not? That's as good an enterprise as any other to work on. We all need a focus for our energy.

Today I don't know the difference between right and wrong or good and bad as clearly as I always have. Especially after listening to Ellie who says not to take all this personally. It seemed clear to me that Chase was the enemy but Ellie urges caution about that, too. Why? And why was I so sure he was evil? Because he's not like me? Because I envy him? Because I need someone to be evil so I can feel safe that I'm not?

But I've seen that I am. And that Lauren and Maddy and

Ellie are, too. And that's OK. I can forgive them. I certainly understand how each made the decisions she did. And because I understand and forgive them, I can forgive myself, too. That's taking a little longer but I know I must. If I want to let go of my past, which I absolutely do, I must let go of all of it and bless it and release it entirely. I can't afford guilt and I can't afford anger with anyone else or with myself. I will grow into Prince Nick because I can't survive if I don't.

69 Stillness

The next week I am calm as I go about my self-assigned duties. I walk every morning and evening, the ends of the day pressing toward the middle with the loss of daylight. I rake leaves and sweep the porch. My neighbors burn fires in their fireplaces and pale gray smoke twirls skyward. I love this time of year.

Each of the last 30 autumns, well rested from the long summer, I embarked on a new academic year. Hope wafted in the brittle air as leaves crunched underfoot. Hope, not only for the students, but for me — that this year will be better than any year before, that maybe this year I will recognize an as-yet-undiscovered talent, that I will connect with a student who accepts my guidance and appreciates my skill, that I will find someone who ingests my words and weaves my direction into her stories. I've wanted to mentor a writing student more than I've wanted to write myself. I'm a teacher at heart. The art of teaching passes human wisdom to another generation who will refine it and polish it according to their insights. And then duly pass it along. I was always proud to participate in that honorable tradition.

Not teaching this fall, I miss my interactions with the students, especially the freshmen, so eager and enthusiastic and idealistic with every reason to expect life to unfold benignly before them. The seniors already show signs of stress as they anticipate leaving their habitual haunts and venturing into an often unwelcoming job market. I'm glad I don't teach job preparation. I prefer to think I teach life preparation. But now that is "taught." Teaching was good to me and for me. I miss it.

However, today's challenges await. I downshifted severely after Hildy's death and my days slowed. Truly, her death is a tragedy. My blinders hid my truth from me. I didn't want to know myself below my neck. And Hildy represented all about me that wasn't intellectual. Yes, it was unfair and illegal that someone broke into my house and destroyed my home. But, the reality I now see clearly is that it couldn't have been avoided. My blinders created this desecration. I am responsible for Hildy's death even though an unknown villain wielded the knife. Only now, having lived in Los Osos, can I truly know that. It isn't logical and I can't convince anyone.

I feel Rosemary's arms around me. She whispers, "I understand, Nick. Hildy and I loved you but you weren't ready. Now you are. We still love you. We'll be with you."

Having backed off from the drama and pulled into myself, I'm thinking differently. I need time alone to remember myself. And what I've remembered these last weeks is how idealistic I, too, was when I was young, very young. In junior high I memorized passages from Don Quixote and imagined myself in armor. I admired Robin Hood's daring and conviction and envisioned myself befuddling armies of oppressors. There was a time before I was afraid, when I hadn't closed myself off, when my heart was still intact and I dreamed. I believed that life was a wonderful adventure. I was a poet in my soul.

I'm remembering my soul these days. It's still here and it's honorable. Believing in honor at this point in life after all I've seen and experienced is more valuable than the days when I didn't know life and only hoped that fairness exists. Honor isn't simple and it isn't innocent and it definitely isn't nice. Honor is complicated and not clear-cut and, I hesitate to say it, inefficient. I've so prized efficiency that the Los Osos climate of "wait and see" irritated me. But now I appreciate the wisdom in waiting. Honor waits when waiting is the apparent course. After all the activity these last months, waiting sounds good.

I choose stillness.

70 The Impending Changes

And I practice stillness. By myself, before dawn, in my warm bed. By myself, after dusk, in my shadowy living room. With others around me, at Cad's or the grocery store. I'm with myself when I go out in the world. I trust my heart's knowing. And that's a statement I never thought I'd make!

After all the thinking and running around and busyness and organization and analysis, I'm back to what I was born with — my heart. I haven't ever trusted my heart. That's why I needed to think so much and live in the rarified air of the intellect. I hoped I could insulate myself from life's messiness but now I long to immerse myself in that messiness. I want complicated friendships, replete with feelings and conflicts and unknown futures. I crave quiet times with another human when we simply share what it is to be alive for the moment we're together.

I respect the sacredness of humans being human. Sometimes I marvel as I watch a mom picking out fruit for her kids in the grocery basket who clutch their sippy cups and whine. I'm fascinated by the older couple holding each other as they shuffle down the sidewalk, not daring to look around, each leaning on the other, willing themselves to remain upright. I watch the teenager with his head phones, body jerking, eyes closed, mind who-knows-where, enjoying his own daydream. These scenes are photographs of a second of a human life that has a past and a future. What a miracle that is.

I'm fascinated by all the persons who have thoughts and hopes and fears just as real as mine. All this incredible humanity swelling through the streets. I sit on the bench in front of Cad's just admiring humans in the act of being human and Donny walks by. He spies me at the same time I see him and without a word he sits down next to me.

"Good to see you, my friend," I say, not wanting to scare him with too much enthusiasm.

"Yeah," he grunts but I can tell he's doing OK. He looks at the cars, passing and parked, not looking at me. That's fine. I'm sincerely happy to see him, so just sitting here is enough for now.

"What have you been up to?" I ask, hoping to initiate a conversation, at least as much of a conversation as Donny can manage.

"Remember when my Dad was here?" He doesn't wait for or seem to expect a reply. "Well, he said there are some changes coming and that I should be ready."

"Really?" He grabbed my attention with that statement. "So, are you ready?" I tease him.

"Yes," he replies seriously. "I've packed most of my stuff and now I'm just waiting."

"How do you know what you're waiting for?"

"I'll know. My Dad says there will be a time when I need to move quickly but for now just lay low. Lay low. That's what my Dad says. Lay low."

"So, Donny, tell me what you do when you lay low."

"Me and the guys, we smoke some, we play cards, we take apart your old car, and we lay low. We lay low."

His stoner friends. That would be the only group in town which would accept Donny and they, no doubt, love him for his connections.

"So, Donny, your friends… are they treating you right? Are they staying out of trouble so they won't create trouble for you?"

"They're OK. They just like to get high. I hang with them and we laugh and then they leave and I walk back home to Granma Maddy's. She don't want them around her house." He stares down the street as though he's identified a walker. I don't want to lose his attention.

"But, Donny, don't your friends ever take you to their houses? Don't they invite you over? Don't they offer to drive you around? Friends help each other. How do your friends help you?"

"The guys, they're OK. Mostly they just want to get high. We don't do nothin' else."

"Why, Donny, I am surprised. Such a fine fellow as yourself and your friends don't want to show you how much they appreciate you? I could have sworn they'd take you to dinner. Why, by letting them smoke your Dad's weed you're giving them the biggest gift they could want and, on top of everything, as though unlimited highs weren't enough, your Dad has seen to it that they will never be prosecuted! How fine a deal is that! Those guys, your friends, should be grateful to you from the bottoms of their zoned out hearts." I hope he's considering my words as we sit silently. I must be careful. A few more minutes pass and he stands, announcing,

"Well, I gotta go."

"It's been great seeing you, Donny. I'll be here same time tomorrow if you happen to amble by." He leaves without an acknowledgment. He's the ace up my sleeve but I think I can parlay this hand into a pair of aces if I don't hurry.

71 His Friends, My Foes

I sit on the same bench at the same time the next day hoping that Donny will stroll by. Did he understand my invitation? Will he show? If he doesn't, what will I do? I wait for over an hour, trying to look pensive. As I'm considering leaving, Donny finally strolls by and sits beside me.

"Great to see you, Donny." He nods but doesn't look at me. I could find this trait annoying but I assume it reflects the mental illness which tortures him. I want him to talk to me. "So, Donny, are you staying busy? Do you and your friends have any business meetings planned this week?"

He doesn't look at me. "Just the regular."

I was teasing him but now I'm attentive. "What's the regular?" "Just the regular meeting Friday at the library."

He's dropped a bombshell but I can't react, displaying the excitement I feel growing in my chest.

"Do you meet with Carolyn at the library?" That's an obvious inquiry which shouldn't arouse doubt. "You meet with Carolyn every Friday at the library?"

Another grunt which I assume is assent. I want to be very careful. I joke with him, "So, you have a business schedule? I didn't know that. Are you a big businessman in these parts, Donny?" I smile to put him at ease but I am not comfortable.

"No, not really." He looks down the street.

"Oh, I bet you're just being modest. A fine well-connected fellow like you? I've seen how everybody here knows you and likes you. I'd think it would be no problem to run a successful business. I know you have the genes for it." I smile but I don't know if he sees my face. He's fascinated by something on the curb.

"Yeah, I know some things about business. But it's just a small business. And very secret. I don't tell no one about it."

"Well, I certainly don't want you to give away any secrets but I have the feeling you really are much more important around here than you let on."

"It's just a small operation so the guys and me can make a few bucks. And, of course, Carolyn. She's the big boss."

Carolyn? Carolyn is in business with these stoners?

"Now, Donny, you're confusing me. Is it your business or hers or are you partners?"

Donny squirms in his seat and looks around as though he expects someone to walk by. Too many questions. I have to back off.

"The guys and me we have a small business, not a big business. My Dad said he don't want no one selling his crop and he was serious. He let us know that he's making medicine and that the purpose of his crop is strictly for medicine. And he pays me and the guys to guard his crop. But when he's not around the guys take a little and sell it."

"Does your Dad know?"

"Nope, he don't know, but when he's not around Carolyn is in charge. She knows the guys and she knows that they are happy with just a little extra. So, she lets us sell just a little bit each week. And, of course, we split the profits with her. She calls it the cost of doing business. That's why we see her every Friday."

"Donny, do I understand that you and your friends guard the crop but that you also take a bit and sell it on your own and it's just between you and Carolyn and your father doesn't know?"

"Yep, that's pretty much it. It ain't no big deal really. He's got lots left and he don't miss what we take. He told us we can smoke as much as we want, that's part of our pay, so he don't know how much that is. No big deal."

"So, Donny, you and your friends smoke every day?"

"If we want. That's our job to keep an eye on the crop."

"And Carolyn knows all about this?"

"Dad said she is his general and that we are the lieutenants and that we report to her. So, we do. She's OK."

"So, where do you sell it?" That could be tricky indeed and could open up another scenario altogether. Even if Les sanctions the growing of marijuana, he can't let dealing pass unnoticed.

"Oh, Carolyn takes care of that, too. See, she knows the

guards at the prison up the road and they know people who want the dope and can pay for it and they'll never talk."

"So, it never gets to the street and no one free ever smokes it but you and your friends. What a good deal you've got going for yourself, Donny." Fridays must be the exchange day when they deliver the dope to be sold to Carolyn and she pays them. All this business going on in the community library.

Suddenly, Donny looks self-conscious. Is it because he's talked more with me today than he ever has? He fidgets, looks around, makes guttural noises, then abruptly stands. I speak before he gets away.

"Donny, I appreciate our talk today very much and you can trust that I will tell no one anything you've said. Your business is safe with me. I want to support you and I'll do anything I can to help you. Just let me know."

"It ain't you. It's the guys. They hate you and they don't want me talking to you. Now I've done it. Now they'll be looking for me. I gotta go."

"OK, Donny. If you don't want to be seen in public with me, I understand. You know where I live and you're welcome to come over anytime."

He turns his back and hurries away, head down. I sit back and consider the puzzle pieces he has just handed me. His stoner friends have no connection with Chase except guarding his fields. From what I infer they are unstable and explosive independent operators. He said they hate me. They think I threaten their operation; all they are interested in is the dope and a little cash. Now I realize that they are the thugs who destroyed my car and threw the rock in my window and placed my cap in the grave. Did they murder Deb? I need more info before I can go that far.

But now I know that I'm dealing with at least two entities, maybe more. These low-level miscreants are personally dangerous and scary but their interests are local and relatively small. They want weed to smoke and to deal and they will react violently if they feel threatened. Since Carolyn's in on it and they go to the library weekly, I can guess they wrote the threatening literary contest entry, too. Could they?

Did Carolyn?

Chase, on the other hand, is larger than life. I don't know why I say that because his initial performance at Maddy's was awkward. In the end he took control of that evening and completely shifted the tone of this whole imbroglio. He transformed himself into a public service savior who is loved and appreciated and honored. How did he do that? I was there and I heard the words and I've lived here since then. His armor truly shines in this town. And, yet, no one knows him. He is an elusive, mysterious, intriguing figure who seemingly exists above the earth but is somehow essentially connected to this town where he spends little time.

Another entity may be Carolyn. Is she playing both sides for her own benefit? What's her interest? Surely the few dollars from dealing wouldn't be adequate incentive for her to risk involvement in this scheme. What is it she wants? I gather that she knows Chase better than most folks. That's why she's been cold to me. To protect him or to protect herself?

Chase seems too good to be true. He's a nobleman saving this town by pursuing an altruistic experiment which will advance medical knowledge immensely. I'm skeptical.

72 Vengeance

Late the next afternoon I'm reading the paper and drinking tea when I hear a knock on my door. I open it to find Donny's two friends. They look neither happy nor calm. I don't feel safe.

What would Chase do? Take control of the situation smoothly and guilelessly. "Why, welcome, all my friends," and I'm out of the house with the door closed behind me before they can move.

"Gentlemen, let's walk, shall we? It's the time of evening for a brisk stroll." I turn my back to them and walk to the gate which they reach one second after I do. One second is all I need, however, and I stand just outside the gate in the dusty street. Dealing with dopers isn't much of a challenge. I wish there were walkers around but at this time of year when evenings are cold and dark early, the street is deserted. I raise my voice and stride into the middle of the dirt path that is our street. Thus far, they have not spoken and I wonder what it is they really want. Before I can turn and ask them, I receive a blow to the back of my head.

Not again, I think, as my knees buckle and I lose consciousness.

73 In the Bright Room

What day is it and where am I? I awaken in a bright room with a curtained window. The railing of the hospital bed answers one question. I look to the other side of the room and see Ellie sleeping on a cot. She snores softly. I close my eyes and try to remember how I got here. My head hurts and I am stiff everywhere. How long have I lain here? My stomach growls like a bear emerging from hibernation. I try to pull myself up but fall back hard against the pillow, thus amplifying the pounding in my head. With this little commotion, Ellie stirs and opens her eyes.

"Greetings," I offer in what I hope is a bright and genial tone.

"How are you feeling?" Her eyes search my face.

"Great. I'm just great. Except for the pounding in my head and the stiffness in every inch of my body. I don't know what day it is or where I am or how long I've been here, but, other than those details, I couldn't be better. And, dear Cousin, how are you?" "Well, I don't come unglued to get a phone call about you anymore. I thought you were past this, but it's OK. However, you have entered new territory with this latest adventure."

"What are you talking about? What's happened? The last I remember I was in the street in front of my house."

"That was Saturday. Your neighbors saw the incident — two men knocking you out — and called an ambulance. Les came on board and now the men are in jail."

"That was some fast work."

"Yeah, your neighbors were on the ball. They gave a perfect description to Les who knew the folks they described and knew where to pick them up. They were carted off within the hour."

Now Les is involved. My "inquiry" has suddenly become public and official. "And when they picked up the two guys, Donny was with them, bruised and bleeding. Les interrupted their mauling of Donny and he was taken to the emergency room." "Is he OK?" Have I endangered another person?

"He was released after he was stitched and bandaged. He'll be fine but he's shaken up. Maddy's keeping an eye on him, as much as she can."

It's hard to think clearly but I wonder if Donny's injuries will lead to a response from Chase. This is exploding and ensnaring a lot of people. It's no longer just my little escapade. I know I have to concentrate and reconsider this whole scenario but I can't with the incessant booms in my head.

A nurse, not in white but in a green cardigan and tan slacks, enters the room. After checking my vital signs she brings me a painkiller which offers me relief first and then knocks me out again.

74 For the Gods

Within the day I'm released to Ellie's guest bedroom. Lovely as it is with windows on three sides of the room overlooking a backyard sprouting cacti, this room has been associated with pain and debilitation for me. Lying here, I no longer feel powerful or clear or, really, hopeful. I just am. I'm here and I have no thoughts and no insights and no guiding vision. I'm OK with that. I only want to rest. As much as I sleep, I don't awaken refreshed. It's not a problem because I don't have the energy to make it a problem.

I just go along.

Cripes, I have become one of them.

But that doesn't bother me, either. Nothing gets to me. If I could manage it, I'd be concerned that I have lost so many essential brain cells that I'm not myself but I can't think about that now. I can only lie here and watch the curtains flutter in the breeze and the intermittent rays of sunlight dance on the bed. That's enough for me for today. No drive and no ambition and not one thought about the future. Maybe all that will come back tomorrow. I can't worry about it.

And so the hours and a night and a day pass and Ellie cooks and we talk and I sleep and life goes on without me and I trust that that is just fine. I trust. I drift off to dreamland again. When I awaken I hear hushed voices in the living room. I wonder who's there but I'm not curious enough to make myself heard. I'm in and out of alertness for the next hour until I must rouse myself to get to the bathroom. Passing by the corner of the living room, I notice several figures sitting on the couches and chairs but I don't stop long enough to greet anyone.

On my return trip, however, they are ready for me and they insist that I join them. Maddy sits next to Donny who has a bandage over his left eyebrow and a black eye. In the chair is Carolyn. Ellie hovers in the background. I'm glad to see my friends but everyone looks intensely somber. Carolyn stands and addresses us all as though she is the meeting convener. We watch her.

"Now that we are all together," she opens… and that phrase strikes me funny because I, for one, know that I'm not "all together." But she continues, "So much has happened recently and more is in the works." She hesitates. "We've tried to keep Les out of our business for years and he has gladly obliged but now with the recent violence he has been forced to act. Poor Donny has been hurt and we are here because of Nick." Everyone looks at me but no one speaks.

"And word of our latest mishap has traveled… actually, much farther than I would have guessed possible." She hesitates and looks at the floor, standing on one leg then the other. "We are now in a position we can't rectify easily. We've stretched the limits with Chase's experiments and we could only do so because Les turned his head." A useful phrase, I thought, although neither descriptive nor accurate. "You have heard Chase tell of the immense value his experiments may offer medical knowledge." I remember that Carolyn wasn't at Maddy's. Had someone told her what he had said? I don't think it was common knowledge before that evening. "But, now the situation has shifted and we're dealing with some different challenges."

"Donny looks pretty beat up to me. Is that one of the new challenges?" I ask and I'm surprised by the directness in my tone. "Donny took a… beating the other day and that was unfortunate." Is she trying to skirt the issue?

"From the appearance of his face I'd say it was more than 'unfortunate,'" I add. "Hey, Donny, how does your face feel? And how do you feel? Are you feeling safe these days?" I want to draw him in if I can.

"I'm OK, I guess…" and his words drift off.

"Did your good friends and business partners do this to you, Donny?" I ask.

"Yeah." He lowers his voice and his head.

"What kind of friends do that?" I practically shout, grateful that my head no longer aches. Maddy puts her arm on Donny's back. He doesn't look at any of us.

"Oh, yes, Carolyn, aren't they your business partners, too?"

I want to hear her take responsibility for this.

But she is clever. "There has been involvement from persons who are no longer available, so that problem has been solved and we can move on…"

"Wait, wait, wait, wait," I demand. "Things are not normal here and this is part of that weirdness. I, for one, am not ready to move on. I can't slide through another violent episode and say, 'Oh, well.' I have experienced so much since I've moved here. I've tried to adjust and I've said I will adapt and I've been thrown around, literally, but today I want some answers. And I think the answers lie in this room." I look slowly at everyone here. "So, now is the time. Today is the day we speak the truth." I want to take the control out of Carolyn's very adept hands and I want to direct the discussion.

"Of course," she begins, but I will not be intimidated. I interrupt her interrupting.

"Carolyn, you apparently have an agenda today and I want to hear it but I want to hear what is behind it first. I want to know exactly what your business dealings with Chase are. I want to know how long you and he have been in business. I want to know what you are getting out of all this! You wield much more power than a community librarian here. What's the game? Are you manipulating everyone in town including Chase?"

Ellie comes closer. "I haven't known any of this, Carolyn. Is what Nick says true?" She stands two feet from Carolyn with her hands on her hips awaiting an answer. But Carolyn says nothing.

Maddy pipes up. "Give us the score, Carolyn. I declare that as of today the Los Osos community game is over. All the cards go on the table, face up. No one leaves until we all agree. Now we are equals. So, spill it, Carolyn. What have you not said?"

Maddy holds a certain weight in the community as an old timer and as one who knows the history. Since she's been sober these last weeks, she's regarded with the deference accorded a respected elder. Thus, her words cannot and will not be dismissed. Carolyn realizes this. She moves from side to side and sits on a footstool. She looks tired. For the first time since I've known her, she doesn't respond easily and forcefully. In fact, she doesn't speak. Her head is in her hands so I can't discern her feelings or thoughts from her facial expression at this moment.

Donny speaks. "My Dad says that promises are serious business. He says that once you promise, you can't change your mind and you can't forget your promise. He says that when you owe another man, you pay with your life." Carolyn's head rests in her hands. Ellie kneels next to her. "Tell us the truth, Carolyn. We're your friends and we'll help you."

Carolyn lurches out of her seat and yells, "Stop it! All of you, stop it! You don't know what you're doing and what you're saying and what the consequences will be. This isn't a little storybook vignette with a happy ending guaranteed for everyone. You don't understand what's going on here!"

"Exactly!" I say. "I haven't understood since I've lived here but I truly want to. Will you please explain it to us?"

Everyone in the room inhales simultaneously and looks to Carolyn to speak. She turns her back to us and lowers her head. She clasps her hands and turns around slowly.

"All right, this is against my better judgment, and I think all of you will regret this day when you look back on it, but I can see that now you need some facts. Learning these facts will endow you with a lifetime responsibility which I think you may come to rue. But you are giving me no choice so I can't shield you from whatever happens next." She exhales and then we all do.

"Maybe you remember the stories, Maddy, that in the 1700s before this county had a population of 300 there were natives who migrated to the coast in the spring and the fall to pray. Part of their ritual was sacrifice — wild animals and humans. The story tells that any humans sacrificed volunteered to give their lives to the Great Grandfather Spirit to ensure prosperity for their tribes. It was considered an exalted act and only one young person a year was accepted to fill this honored position for the tribe. It was believed that good fortune would rain upon the family of the one sacrificed." I have not heard this history and from the fidgeting in the room I suspect that no one else has, either.

"As could be expected in any human endeavor, there developed a rivalry for the role of 'sacred offering.' The young person sacrificed was required to possess perfect health and character. They were models of virtue for their community and strove all year to live a life considered worthy of sacrifice."

Carolyn continues, "So, in this culture which valued moral purity and ethical behavior, there also grew a strain of fierce competition. It was thought that the one chosen for sacrifice returned in the next life as a ruler or wealthy priest. So, while a young person might cut short this lifetime, the next one was guaranteed to be prosperous not only for him but for all his relatives. Thus, it wasn't unusual for parents to urge a small child to live in preparation to be sacrificed. There was no greater honor that could befall a family."

Carolyn looks around to assess the impact of her words. Maddy nods. Donny plays with his fingers. Ellie seems engrossed.

"Vicious competition for this honor ensued. Since girls or boys could be chosen, a rivalry between the genders to sabotage each other evolved. Some young people sought to seduce likely contenders to render them unqualified to be chosen. The cousin, for instance, of a hopeful young woman might support her relative by sleeping with boys who also wanted the honor. If she succeeded, she nullified their candidacy.

"Promiscuity gave you power if you had already relinquished the goal of being the one chosen. Smoking hallucinogenic plants also gave you power. Supposedly, some unusually strong herbs grew here. If the candidate smoked the herbs and survived the ensuing psychotic break and could return to talk about the dreams and visions he had been given, that was a sign of power. From what I've read, not all who smoked returned intact.

"I read about one death that was thought to have roots in this competition. Numerous stories exist of mutilation. If you could cut off a rival's body part, you were assured that he could not be chosen since he was no longer a perfect physical specimen.

"On the one hand there was a great push to live an exemplary life. On the other was a similarly strong inclination to underhandedly influence the outcome in favor of your chosen candidate. The identified saints-in-training focused on developing their spiritual power while everyone else, or so it seemed when I read the stories, engaged in deception, cruelty, and betrayal. These two opposite motivations existed simultaneously in this county for generations.

"The coastal land was considered holy and not to be inhabited so only two times a year humans walked here. The rest of the year they lived inland a few miles. These ancestors boasted that they spoke with the gods. They portrayed themselves as intermediaries, not as limited as humans and not as omniscient as gods, but with characteristics of each group. And during the year they carried on with their commerce and their deal making with the assumption that they were blessed and protected by the gods who knew all they were doing and condoned it. Thus, developed an attitude of self-assuredness that whatever they did, because they did it, was acceptable and, probably, wise.

"Now we can easily appreciate the flaws in this thinking but in their closed and isolated society it was taken for granted that those who lived here, in Great Grandfather's Yard, were special, were chosen, were to be granted extra consideration. Clearly, some hubris and parochialism developed here, also.

"Because no ingress or egress occurred regularly for generations, the values and judgments existing here maintained without question. The county developed more like an island than a part of California or the United States. Because of geography and population, our citizenry grew very slowly without the influences the world accepted as natural.

"At some point in the history of our county everyone acknowledged that we are special. We didn't question that, we just knew it to be true and, even today, we know it. If we consider how little most of us venture out of the county, it's as though something is implanted in us that deletes curiosity about what we don't know. That trait contributed to survival when young men were required to keep the society flourishing. These days it leads to an insularity that is evident in our distrust of strangers and a curious lack of interest about the larger world.

"I sense a certain otherworldliness about the commitment of some of our folks to live a rigorously moral life. And where does that come from? Not from organized religion. That is the same everywhere in the world. The unique vision that is ours, and I truly believe this, comes from that 'knowing' that we are linked to the gods. Now, I can't explain this but those of you who have lived here will intuitively grasp what I mean."

I can see Ellie and Maddy and Donny nod their heads. I wonder if they appreciate that Carolyn can put into words what they have known "in their bones" since they have lived here. She is less of a native, having lived in the "real world" before moving here and so she can think and observe what those who live here take for granted. She doesn't wear the blinders that seem to be installed at birth on natives. And she doesn't reflexively identify with their way of thinking. She can see it and understand it with some detachment while still experiencing it. She hasn't been here 15 years so she is still well grounded in what I call consensual reality. But she is an intellectual so she notices the characteristics and tendencies and patterns of this area. She has known the folks and been a part of the community. She is both an observer and a community member. I admit that I am relieved to hear my suspicions confirmed in a structured reasonable framework. But she is not finished.

"Who we are today is very much built on who lived here before us. The land we tread is sacred, I agree with the natives, and holds that sacred mystery today. But I've noticed that today we don't know what to make of it or what to do with it so sometimes we're taken with our own arrogance and we think we can get away with what is patently unacceptable. I think Donny has been the victim of that arrogance." We all look at him and he nods. Suddenly, this makes sense to him and he has apparently lost his shame.

"And you've noticed the promiscuity that exists in certain

pockets but is generally condemned, certainly not appreciated as it was originally. What fit in the past has been perverted and misunderstood so that now we are confused and lack the moral grounding that anchored our ancestors so strongly. They were guided in every action. Every deed had meaning. They felt their connection.

"That's what we've lost. We don't feel connected to the gods or to anything eternal. We don't have standards that are meaningful. We all do the same things we've always done but we don't know why. And if anyone differs, we criticize and condemn but, again, we don't know why. We're operating without a rudder. And that was the exact quality which made our county so special — the powerful connection we had with the gods. That is what is valuable and so precious about this area. A sense of the ineffable is still here but we don't know how to frame that in modern terms. We're squandering the beautiful gift we've been given and we don't see it." She sighs and shakes her head. Her body slumps slightly. She looks at the ground and then slides into a chair as though she has exhausted her words and been exhausted by them.

I certainly didn't expect any talk about gods from Carolyn. She is The Intellectual in town. Is this what happens to intellectuals in this county?

75 Looking Beyond

My first hour awake and alert in a few days and I'm presented with tales of competition, deception, moral striving, and gods. I want to return to dream land so I retreat to my room. After the front door closes behind the last guest, Ellie presents herself and wants to talk. She's energized by the meeting.

"Doesn't this all make sense now?" she asks. Her eyes sparkle. "Of course, we had to be dealing with something overwhelmingly powerful and long-standing that has saturated this area. I always knew something was going on here."

"What do we really know? Carolyn tells us stories that may or may not be true but the facts are the same — Donny was beaten and hurt, Chase is growing acres of enhanced marijuana completely untouched by law enforcement, Carolyn may or may not be supplying weed to prison guards, Lauren has been unseen for weeks, my car was destroyed, my dog killed, and I'm recuperating at your house yet another time. Can you make sense of all this?"

"There is an explanation for all that's gone on and is going on. I don't know if Carolyn's is the understanding that fits best but I'll consider it. But there may be more."

I sigh and remember when life was intelligible, logic was reliable, my mind was a valuable tool, and problems could be solved. Now there are no problems, just situations, and logic is irrelevant. Why do I even have a mind? It only confuses me.

Ellie and I sup and chat and watch TV and soon enough I'm snoozing again. I dream of geese flying through the clouds. Above the clouds the air is clear and the geese talk among themselves.

76 The Mystery of the Growing Fields

I awaken to a day that is cold beyond crisp. With the chronic high humidity, the air carries microscopic icicles which pierce my cheeks. I'm bundled except for a few square inches of skin which absorb enough cold to chill my body. Pennsylvania this is not, however, I didn't expect biting wind from the California coast. Emerging from Ellie's car, we can see our breath. The glass door to the library is locked and the closed sign pulled down but Ellie knocks loudly, two, three, four times until Carolyn appears. Ellie pushes her way in, loudly commenting on the weather as if to excuse her rude entry.

"Ellie, Nick, good morning," Carolyn begins formally. "We're not open now but if you want to come back this..." Her words trail off as she watches Ellie bound past the checkout counter and into her office. I hear voices. I follow Carolyn who quickly follows Ellie's steps.

Over Carolyn's head I see lights and bodies. It's warm in here. Ellie is speaking with... I can't see his face... Chase. Now we are all in the office. Lauren is seated in the back against the wall, Donny is sleeping on the old sofa, Maddy sits in her wheelchair between the sofa and the round table. Only Ellie and Chase speak; the rest of us watch and wait. I nod at Lauren who doesn't respond. I sit in a chair at the table.

Ellie speaks insistently to Chase. "This mystery about your growing fields and your employees and the intermittent violence is way out of control. You know we love you, Chase, but you're ripping us off. You are destroying the heart of Los Osos with your manipulations and your secrecy." She says this with compassion and gentleness as she touches his arm. But her resolve is unswerving.

Whenever Carolyn tries to speak, Ellie shushes her with her

other hand. Ellie knows what she wants and focuses on her target. I recognize this strategy. It's her realtor-wrapping-up-a- sale mode. She's not going to let anyone else in this conversation although Carolyn is the only one who tries to speak. Ellie has established her dominance.

Chase is not intimidated. He looks tired, older than that night at Maddy's a few weeks ago, and a bit distressed. But his voice is clear and strong.

"This is it," he begins. "The time has come, much faster than I thought possible. We've received an offer from Merck to take our research to the next level through their laboratories and I signed the contract last night. They want to come in soon, not wait for more testing. Next week you'll notice some changes — a few signs, a few fences, and some security officers. Phase One, my work, is over. So, essentially, I'm out of the picture as of now."

"Wait a minute, Chase," Ellie replies. "You can't just walk away and leave us with the fallout."

"The fallout will be millions of dollars for this area, hundreds of jobs, prominence in bio-tech engineering for the next decade. You should be thanking me." Is he disgusted with this small town wrangling?

"You're planning on exiting this town completely? And what about your son and your crops?" Ellie asks.

"Donny comes with me. Maddy is welcome to come," and he looks at his mother-in-law, "but she wants to stay. And I'll find new jobs for my employees."

"Your employees are drug addicts and ne'er-do-wells."

"Carolyn has already placed them in a rehab center when they're released from jail."

Ellie turns to Carolyn. "And have you been selling drugs to the prison guards?" Chase's head jerks. His eyes lock with Carolyn's and they laugh.

"Of course not. But I'm glad you heard that story. We've assuaged the employees with that tale to keep them from initiating any entrepreneurial activity on their own. If I could keep them satisfied by thinking they were getting away with something, then we could be safer." Carolyn smiles.

Ellie focuses again. "Safer to do what? Do you expect us to

believe this fairy story about Merck and millions and reducing suffering? You've been growing illegal drugs! Does that mean anything to you? Are you completely above the law?" Apparently, she is reading my thoughts.

"Wait a minute. You sell real estate and tell potential clients this is a special, blessed area. Well, we agree with you." As Carolyn speaks she walks over to Chase and puts her arm through his. "You don't know how special this area is. There is magic here and we've found a way to harvest it in physical form that can be manufactured and distributed and sold worldwide. Not only is that magic, it's a triumph that has taken years of work and research and negotiation. Chase has carried what is blessed about our little area to a higher level and found a way to share it with everyone. We should appreciate his hard work and insightful business sense. We should thank him!"

She moves to kiss him on the cheek but he turns his head and kisses her on the mouth. A long slow kiss. These two are a couple! From the looks in the room only Ellie and I are surprised.

Now Carolyn relaxes and laughs and sits at the table. "OK, everybody, sit down. This will be our last meeting. We've been working on this project for more than a decade. We could see it would have life-changing results for everyone but we needed to keep it quiet while we were negotiating with Merck. We were close to concluding our deal when Nick moved to town and stirred up the locals."

I pipe in, "That's why you were always so cold to me, isn't it, Carolyn? And why the diversionary history lesson, huh?"

"I couldn't take a chance that you would quash all the progress we had made when we were so near completion. I owe you an apology, Nick, for the attacks, but you could have ruined everything for us." "What about Deb's death? Did you murder her just to protect your project?"

"I regret that she died but no, we didn't murder Deb. Some of the guys accosted her but her death was unrelated to that incident. She would have died from an embolism, whether in the hospital or not. Her time was marked. We didn't cut her life short."

"That's a little too slick for me," I interject. "You have no feelings about your friend and neighbor?"

"Of course, we have feelings about her but our project will save millions of lives and introduce a painkiller the world has not known. If it were up to me, I'd have Deb back with us. But it isn't and we can't do anything about it and it's time to move on."

I find this reasoning off-putting but Ellie is speaking to Carolyn. "You seem to believe that the results of your eventual contribution to the world justify anything you choose to do. When did you become so callous?"

"You may call it callous but we call it prescient and inspired and, really, magnanimous. I don't know why you aren't grateful to us!"

Now it's "we" and "us." Of course, she would be interested in the influence Chase commands. She's not small town material. But is she pulling the strings? She is smarter than he is, I gather, and she certainly takes over group situations and directs them as she wants. I'm not ready to let her get away with this now, though.

I turn to Chase, "So, you have quite a high rolling life, I gather." I try to be folksy and sway this to a male bonding situation. "I've seen pictures of you with gorgeous women and politicians and business moguls. That life must be exciting compared to little Los Osos."

He is smarter than I thought. "This is home and will always be home. My roots are here and my loyalty is to this community. I'm giving you the biggest contribution I can."

I continue. "Why is dope grown here better than dope grown elsewhere?" He sits straighter and his eyes gleam. "The minerals in the soil here are different from anywhere else in the world. So, when we plant seeds here from plants in Asia, they develop in a way which hasn't been matched. But we know that it's a matter of time before someone else comes up with another discovery. That's why we had to accelerate our research."

Carolyn looks uncomfortable. "We must be going," she says to Chase and then to the rest of us.

Ellie jumps in immediately, "No, not so fast. This

community has been disrupted for months. In fact, you, maybe you both, have changed us forever. The Los Osos we have lived in no longer exists and it never will again. We've loved this area and, unilaterally, you shifted everything. You've chosen what you wanted and you made it happen and you don't seem to acknowledge the impact that has had and will have on the rest of us. The soul of our town has been destroyed!" Ellie's eyes narrow.

Chase stutters a few words but Carolyn stands and loudly says, "That's nonsense. This will be a finer community than it ever has been. You will always have the history which is what makes this place sacred. You'll always have the location, separate from major urban areas, which ensures that development will be gradual. And now, in addition, you'll have more than adequate income to complete the sewer, the curbs, the streets and anything else you want. But for now, we must depart. Come on, Chase, let's go." Obediently, he stands and rouses Donny and the three of them leave the building. The rest of us don't speak for two minutes. I, for one, can't believe what I've just heard.

Ellie breaks the silence with a laugh. "Of course, Carolyn finds a way to get herself out of our town. She'll live the way she wants and do what she wants and push Chase when she needs a change. He needs her direction and she needs his connections. And they can rationalize that they haven't really hurt anyone because of the medical miracles that loom. They can even feel good about themselves for propelling us into the 21st century."

Lauren hasn't spoken before this but now she rises. "Don't be so quick to condemn, any of you. They have provided us with services and benefits. They were respected and valued until Nick came on the scene. Then they got spooked and moved too quickly and got sloppy. But what they've done is done and we stand to benefit greatly." She looks at Ellie, "Time passes and things change and whether we like it or not, we change. And there is always loss with change but there are gifts, too.

"The money is minor. We've all been through so much since Nick drove into town and the status quo was overturned. We talk about how much we love this area and what we have here but we threw it over pretty quickly, didn't we, when we had the chance. I know I perverted my gifts and acted out shamelessly. I wasn't thinking. And we all did that. We didn't recognize the power that's here if we open to it.

"The gifts that we've been given by living here are wonderful and special and, really, extraordinary... but they're not ours to hold onto. We can use them and grow. We can develop in new ways. We can open up. But, see, we didn't do that until Nick came. We were content to hold onto what had existed for decades and we glorified something we didn't understand. Since Nick's been here we've all had our eyes opened. We've been through experiences we've never imagined and we've grown."

She looks at Ellie. "I know you have, Ellie. You're more relaxed and trusting and open. And Maddy, hasn't your life changed? You don't drink! Isn't that marvelous?" And she hugs Maddy's shoulders. Maddy touches her eyes with a tissue before she speaks.

"Calm down, Lauren, you're about to float away." Maddy looks around, assuring herself that she has everyone's attention. "Some things will change and some things will look the same. Most of us will forget all this by next month. But some of us have some decisions to make."

77 The Call

I wake to a vibrant sunrise, streaks of orange and pink painting the sky. Stretching my arms, I shuffle into the kitchen to make coffee. I'm calm as I settle into the over-stuffed sofa to sip the warm drink and breathe the comforting aroma. The phone's ring pierces my tranquility. Who calls at this hour? I don't recognize the number. Hesitantly, Iofferaweak Hello.

"Is this Nick?"

"Yes. Who's calling?"

"Marco. I'm from Mexican Law Enforcement. Nick, do not disclose the fact of this call or the information I share with you to anyone."

My heart jerks and lurches in my chest. I'm not ready for whatever this is. I think to myself, "Why is a Mexican Law Enforcement officer calling me?" "Are you alone?" he asks.

"I am," I reply.

"Do not record this conversation. This is official government business. I prefer to speak with you in person but that is not possible. The situation is urgent."

I try to sound calm, but desperation packs my chest. Can I trust him? My head tells me that he sounds legitimate, but my heart hesitates.

"I've been following you and your investigation of Chase Slate," Marco continues.

Marco then discloses that Chase is illegally exporting marijuana from our seemingly idyllic town. The news hits me with gale force. As Marco details the evidence that he has uncovered shock, sadness and despair engulf me. How could Chase who seems so invested in our town's future be choreographing such egregiously unlawful activities?

Questions flood my mind as Marco speaks and the implications of this revelation sink in. The truth I thought I had discovered is now overshadowed by a darker reality. Los Osos, with all its layers and complexities, has yet another dimension -- one I had not fathomed. The skies outside darken. Once filled with vibrant hues, they now mirror the storm brewing within me. My trust in my perceptions has been shattered. I'm throw noff balance.

I set the phone down, my coffee now cold. The taste of bitter realization lingers on my tongue. In Los Osos, secrets nestle beneath secrets that nestle beneath more secrets. A dark underbelly of illegal activities thrives here. The weight of this revelation settles heavily on my shoulders.

The visions Chase and Carolyn had painted for our town's future were purely fabrications. They successfully created a fantasy world that everyone accepted. I realize that I also was tempted to succumb to its allure. Why not? This town is plagued with sewer issues that impeded its growth. This has been a point of contention for more than a decade. Residents have argued and proposed unrealistic solutions and taken sides. We seriously thought that solving the sewer dispute would eradicate our problems. I see now it was only a distraction. A very effective distraction that successfully obfuscated the underground dynamics they wanted no one to see.

But Marco has shined a bright light into these distorting shadows. Now we must see the truth.

"I knew it," I said to myself. Everything flashed through my eyes. I won't walk away from this crime. I know that I must be involved in correcting this evil state of affairs. A state of affairs that no one else understands. Again, I'm in this alone.

Another set of memories flashes back in my mind. As a professor, I saw injustices happening in the university but I didn't speak. I feared that I would lose my colleagues' respect and that I would engage the administrators' ire.

Rosemary told me, "Stand up for what is right." But I did not. Her voice still reverberates in the back of my head. When she left me, I lost my integrity, also. Without realizing it, I have mourned that loss ever since without fully grasping the significance of the hole in my heart.

Now I cannot escape my challenge. The end is near. The question is when and how I get there. I truly don't know.

78 Shattered Glasses

I pick up my phone, trembling with a mix of anticipation and apprehension. The call I am about to make will forever alter the course of our lives in Los Osos. I dial Ellie's number first. She answers after two rings.

"Nick, what's up?" exuberantly she asks.

The news spills out of my mouth, the words tumbling over each other as I relay the revelations of Marco's call. Silence on her end is followed by a gasp.

"What should we do, Nick?" Ellie's voice quivers. "I'm scared. Our lives, our safety...everything feels so uncertain now."

"I'm calling Maddy to inform her of this. Join us in a conference call." I dial Maddy's number and eagerly she joins us.

Maddy's anger travels through the phone line. "It's about time Chase pays his dues! He has ripped us off unconscionably for years. He takes what he wants and disappears. Well, I've had enough. Let's burn his ass!"

This is the Maddy I respect. A calmness settles over me with a strong sense of purpose. I continue, "This is a challenge that has been placed before us, and I believe it's an opportunity for us to make a difference, to protect Los Osos."

I pause for a long moment. I am at war with a Mexican drug cartel - a powerful scenario. The extent of this work is larger than I am. I am a retired professor who came to an unknown town with one goal in mind - settling down until my sunset years. I don't have any resources to protect myself, and this is totally not how I expected things to turn out.

At the same time, I know that this is my challenge to accept. This is exactly what I must do. "Think about it," I say to Maddy and Ellie. We have the chance to expose the truth and to make a difference. This is bigger than just the three us. It's about the thousands, even millions, of lives that will be affected by the dismantling of Chase's operation."

Slowly Ellie speaks. A mix of uncertainty and newfound determination powers her words. "You're right, Nick. We can't let fear paralyze us. Los Osos has always come together in times of need, and it's now our responsibility to protect each other, to stand united against this darkness."

Maddie's voice chimes in, her tone resolute. "It's time to do what is right. And the right thing to do now is to safeguard this town's future."

"I will operate discreetly," I say. "I will follow Marco's orders. But I have to move to another house today. There are eyes and ears everywhere."

As we end the call, I slip into thought. A surge of hope courses through me, propelling me forward. For the first time in a long while, I feel the urge to pray, to seek guidance and strength for the challenging road ahead.

I pray not only for our own safety but for the courage to face the storm that brews. With renewed purpose and a flicker of hope, I take a deep breath. I'm ready to pack my bags and leave.

Suddenly, I hear my window glass break and shatter. Again?

A stone wrapped in paper lies in the shattered glass.

Louder than ever, my heart pounds in my chest.

79 The Green Light

"Déjà vu," I mutter to myself. Am I dreaming?

I bend to pick up the stone thrown through my window. I unwrap the paper and see the message written in blood: "I'm coming for you."

I stand here breathing heavily but I am not afraid. The weight of the situation settles upon me. The trust I place in Marco is a connection forged through shared purpose and a mutual understanding of the gravity of the situation. His thoughts mirror my own.

It seems to me that this man is a stronger version of myself, a version I could use right now. I have yet to unpack this persona within me. Looking back at what I've been through in the last few months, I realize that this side of me pounds on the backdoor to my mind, demanding to come out. This version of me has lain dormant for years. Now it is ready to serve its purpose.

Amidst these thoughts, a chuckle escapes my lips as I contemplate the irony of my life. Here I am, apparently placing my trust in someone I have only spoken to on the phone for a few minutes. But I know the truth of my existence is much grander so, of course, I leap into my next phase.

At that moment my phone rings. I answer the call and hear Marco's voice, calm and steady.

"Nick, the time has come, The Mexican government has coordinated with national law enforcement. The wheels are in motion. We have the green light."

A surge of excitement courses through me. This is it, the moment I have been anticipating.

Marco continues, "I have received your information. The evidence you gathered is strong, Nick. This is the proof we need to arrest Chase. We will move swiftly and strategically but you must remain hidden until we give you further instructions.

"We're going to corner him, but we need your help to nab him in Los Osos. When he goes to other locations, he's always surrounded by a bunch of security officers, but it's only in Los Osos that we can catch him with minimal security. Los Osos seems like the ideal spot to do it without much risk of retaliation. Recording him admitting to his lies will speed up the justice process."

As I absorb Marco's instructions, I understand the pivotal role I am to play in bringing down Chase. Days turn into nights as I immerse myself in the role of a regular Los Osos resident. I observe the comings and goings of the town, the nuances that conceal Chase's empire. Law enforcement officers discreetly position themselves.

As I go about my daily routine, my senses heighten. I am attuned to any indications of Chase's presence. Every interaction, every conversation, holds the potential for a vital clue. I meticulously document my findings. The weight of responsibility sits heavily on my shoulders, but I remain resolute.

Then, Marco calls. His voice carries a sense of urgency and excitement. "Nick, we have tracked Chase to a secluded location," he said. "This is our chance. We need you to confront him and to record his confession. We will be close and we will apprehend him."

Adrenaline courses through my veins. This is the moment I have anticipated. My heart pounds as I make my way to the designated location. The authorities, hidden in plain sight, prepare to descend upon Chase.

I approach the secluded spot, my steps measured and deliberate. With each passing moment, a mix of determination and nervous anticipation simmers in my blood. My heart pounds in my chest. And then I see him. I lock eyes with Chase. The man who has held Los Osos in his grip, who has profited from the pain of others, now stands before me.

"Chase!" I call as he walks toward his black bulletproof car with three of his bodyguards.

"Professor Sanders! It's nice to meet you again. How may I help you?"

"I have a question." I slip my hand unto my pocket and I click the recorder on.

"Merck…" I continue.

"Yes, what about Merck?" Chase interrupts. "Haven't I made myself clear? What's with all these interruptions, Nick? You are not a Los Osos resident to begin with. You are an outsider who came here and interrupted this peaceful town with your pathetic brainwashing! Leave us alone!" Chase exclaims.

"I can't just sit back and accept this injustice, Chase." My lips are trembling. I'm trying to calm myself as much as possible. My heart is racing, pounding so hard that it feels like it's about to burst out of my chest. The only way to ease this overwhelming feeling is to finally say what I've been wanting to say for days.

"Merck disagreed with your proposal five years ago. The profit-sharing was solely in your favor and Merck dismissed it. There was no project, Chase. Merck is not going to build a laboratory here. You lied."

A wide grin spreads across his face and he laughs. "You are brilliant, Nick," Chase exclaims. I am stunned by Chase's cool reaction to my words. How could this not bother him?

"Yes, Merck did disapprove of this project. But what you don't grasp is the extent of my plan. We are building vast farmlands both within the United States and beyond our borders. We have international buyers lined up, ready to invest in our vision. And you don't know that. Or…" he moves closer to me.

"…you want a piece of the pie, don't you?"

I step backward.

Chase continues, his voice dripping with confidence.

"You see, Nick, there's a bigger picture here. Los Osos is just the beginning. Our farmland project will revolutionize agriculture, providing sustainable solutions and feeding nations across the globe."

"Yes!" I shout. "Selling Los Osos' farmland to the Mexican drug cartels is a grand idea for providing sustainable solutions for yourself." I say resolutely, unbothered by the danger in front of me.

"Right, Chase?"

The bodyguards surrounding Chase exchange uneasy

glances, their guns still trained on me. But suddenly I hear the clicking sounds of a dozen rifles being cocked. Police officers emerge from the bushes. I freeze.

The bodyguards and Chase lock eyes. With commanding voices, the law enforcement officers shout, "Hands on the ground! Now!"

The bodyguards hesitate, their eyes darting between Chase and the armed police officers. Then, reluctantly, they slowly lower their weapons and step back. Police officers calmly move closer with guns locked on Chase and the bodyguards.

I see more officers emerging from the benches and the buildings nearby. This is the end, I think. Chase stares at me with anger as he and his bodyguards yield. He raises his arms and kneels to the ground in surrender. The law enforcement officers work swiftly, handcuffing Chase.

80 The Loose End

Three months have passed and I continue to work to restore a semblance of normalcy to my life. I hope today will be uneventful. I appreciate "boring" and I want more of it. So, I should have recognized the signal that introduces chaos into my life—the phone rings. Innocently I say Hello. I am greeted by a voice that shivers my spine—Chase's.

"Nick," Chase's voice oozes with a mix of controlled anger and menace. "I will hunt you down, and I will kill you."

My heart races, and my hands tremble. The phone falls to the floor. How has Chase managed to contact me? Isn't he in prison?

As I try to steady myself, the front door swings open and Ellie rushes in, tears streaming down her face.

"What has happened, Ellie?"

She chokes back her tears, struggling to speak. "Chase... he escaped," she utters.

I can feel my world tilt on its axis. The past is not past. I had thought I could move on but suddenly, rudely and without warning, I'm dragged backward. I can't escape the worst nightmare of my life.

But I have learned that I am strong. I don't know what I will do but I know that I will not be defeated. I had hoped that my challenges would end. Instead, they have evolved into a more complex reality.

Los Osos is a state of mind that I will carry with me everywhere I go. It strengthens my soul. I am ready. No matter what comes next, I am ready. And it seems that there is always something going on here.